KINGS GROVE OF ACADEMY

PSYCHOTIC

USA TODAY AND
INTERNATIONAL BESTSELLING AUTHOR

KATIE MAY

Copyright © 2022 by Katie May

Edited by Jennifer Jones of Bookends Editing
Cover by Jodie-Leigh Plowman of JODIEELOCKS Designs

PSYCHOTIC   KATIE MAY

*To those readers who like their fictional men
psychotic and obsessed with their girl.
I see you.*

FOREWORD

This is a dark contemporary reverse harem romance with strong language, sexual situations, and scenes of graphic violence. This particular book deals with issues readers might find triggering, such as self-harm, suicidal ideation, and mild sexual assault.

INTRODUCTION

Psychotic is the second book of a slow-burn, contemporary, academy romance. Despite the characters being in high school, I definitely do not consider this young adult. It contains strong language and sexual situations, as well as murder and violence. It's a reverse harem romance, meaning that our main character, Ellie, won't have to choose just one man to be with at the end of the series. If such material offends you, I recommend putting this book down.

Our female lead, Ellie, also starts off as innocent and naïve, though she does become stronger as the series progresses. I love writing about character growth, and this series has it more than any other. Badasses aren't born as badasses, and Ellie is no exception. However, I can promise that by the end of the series, you'll grow to love her as a character.

The men, on the other hand, are all hardened alphas and serial killers. Though there is no bullying from the guys whatsoever, you still might want to hit them across the head because of their decisions and secrets. Trust me. Their actions will come back to bite them in the ass, and they'll need to grovel and repent in order to regain Ellie's trust.

I hope you enjoy!

PROLOGUE

I glanced surreptitiously at the five of them out of the corner of my eye, praying that I wasn't being too obvious. The last thing I wanted to be was some creepy stalker chick.

They sat at their usual table in the center of the cafeteria, laughing and joking amongst themselves. It was almost as if the rest of the world didn't exist outside the five of them, as if they were in an impenetrable bubble we onlookers could only dream of popping.

I tried to ignore the prickles of energy running across my skin as I flipped the page in the book I was reading.

Landon, of course, sat at the head of the table, resembling a long-forgotten prince who had just reclaimed his kingdom. His light brown hair was pushed away from his artfully chiseled face, and his silver eyes shone like molten metal in the dim lighting, *accentuating the violet rings around each iris. As I watched, his lips twitched upward in a responding smile to whatever Dominic had just told him.*

Dominic's platinum blond hair curled around his ears in a way that drew attention to the prominent planes of his face—harsh cheekbones, strong, clean-shaven jawline, and emerald green eyes that always alternated between amusement and ire. Amusement whenever he was around his best friends. Ire when he was around me.

I could feel my heartbeat pick up speed as I slid my gaze from Dominic to Ryker. My dark prince was scowling down at his plate of untouched pasta. A gasp got lodged in my throat when he glanced up, and though his gaze wasn't directed at me, I still found myself drowning in those blue eyes. They resembled shards of ice, sharp enough to do irreparable damage if anyone were to look directly into them. Then again, everything about Ryker exuded lethality and danger.

Zane sat on the opposite side of Ryker, a shit-eating grin on his face as he told a story that involved a lot of hand gestures and head nods. With his bronze skin, messy, onyx hair, and broad shoulders, Zane was just as sexy as the other men, even at sixteen. But unlike the others who always looked half inclined to stab someone, he had a perpetual smirk pasted on his face as if he found the whole world and everyone in it amusing. Honestly, Zane reminded me of an overgrown puppy—though the one time I mentioned it to him, he shuddered and said, "Don't be cruel, princesa."

Finally, my eyes landed on Beckett, the newest

arrival to Grove Academy. He had transferred only a few months ago and already had half the school in a tailspin. Girls were desperate to get his attention, and guys wanted to be his best friend, but he seemed oblivious to them all. I couldn't articulate it with words, but I found myself grateful that he seemed…repulsed by the attention he received instead of enthusiastic. I had no idea why, but I refused to dissect it.

"I'm going to do it," a sly voice said determinedly from the table next to me. I glanced toward the woman who'd spoken before quickly focusing once more on the book.

Paulina, I thought her name was. Next to her, her stepbrother, Dane or Dune or something, scowled, his features twisting and his eyes hardening to granite.

"Gonna do what?" he grunted out, sounding irritated.

"Ask them out," Paulina said stiffly.

A few of the students at their table tittered.

"Good luck with that." A girl chortled. "I tried asking Landon out a few months ago, and he practically bit my head off."

Landon?

I felt the color drain from my cheeks at her words, and my heart stuttered a painful warning.

Ignore them, Ellie.

I tried to focus once more on my book, I honestly did, but Paulina's lilting laughter drew my attention kicking and screaming back to her.

"Oh please, Rebecca." She scoffed and tossed a strand of silvery hair over her shoulder. "You have no

boobs. If the guys are going to say yes to anyone, it isn't going to be you."

Rebecca's eyes flashed with hurt as the rest of the table broke into raucous laughter.

"Oh, fuck off, P," she snapped haughtily. "You know they'll say no to you as well. You don't have…" Her voice lowered to a whisper. "Glasses. And brown hair. And tiny boobs. And…well…you're not a meek, little mouse."

I quickly glanced back at my book just as I felt the full weight of all of their stares on my profile. Heat rose to my cheeks as I tried to comprehend their meaning. Surely they weren't implying what I thought they were implying, right?

The guys and I were friends—just friends. And I used that term loosely. They only seemed to want to hang out with me when it was convenient for them. They didn't seem to mind that I sat alone most days during lunch time, that I had no one to partner up with in my classes, that I never hung out with friends after school. They sometimes acted like I didn't exist, like they didn't even know me, despite the fact that I could constantly feel their gazes on my skin, filling me with a baking, pervasive heat.

But when we were alone—when no one else was watching—they would be doting and attentive, acting like no time had passed and we were all best friends. And to be honest? I let them. I needed the companionship and comfort only they provided me, even if I did feel like a turd on the sole of their designer shoes ninety-nine percent of the time. Did that make me a masochist? A sucker for pain and heartache?

"You don't have to do this," Dane gritted out, his jaw clenching tightly.

Paulina scowled and stood from the table, ignoring Dane and smiling coyly at Rebecca.

"Watch and learn, sweetheart," she cooed, rearranging her top so a considerable amount of cleavage was showing, including the strap of her bright pink bra. She smirked as Dane's scowl deepened before flouncing in the direction of the guys' table.

I swore I couldn't breathe when she reached where they were sitting and all five of them reluctantly turned in her direction. My hand clenched my book so tightly, the paper began to crinkle in my grip.

Why did romance books have to lie? Why did they make it sound like happily ever afters were plausible when the entire universe darn well knew they weren't?

Paulina's obnoxious laughter reverberated through the cafeteria as she twirled a piece of hair around her finger. She leaned forward far enough that if one of them wanted to, they could probably see down her shirt.

Instead, the five of them kept their attention firmly fixed on her face as they listened to whatever she said. Most of the time, the five of them were so different, so expressive, that I could see their varying personalities reflected through their smiles and eyes. Just then, though, they looked eerily similar, like they were one mind with five separate bodies. Matching scowls tugged at their lips as their eyes turned cold. Hard. Unforgiving.

When Paulina placed a dainty, manicured hand

on Landon's shoulder, I just about died...which was completely irrational. They weren't mine. We were just...friends, and fair-weather friends at that.

"Fuck off, Paulina," Dominic grumbled loud enough for the entire cafeteria to hear. He was kind of a dick like that.

Paulina gaped openly, volleying her gaze between the five of them as if she wasn't used to being turned down. Her hand automatically dropped back to her side as if she'd been burned.

Ryker snarled softly.

"Did he stutter?" he snapped out, folding his arm over his chest. He was wearing the Grove Academy uniform today, and it looked strange on his muscular frame. I was so used to seeing him in black and gray hoodies with the front unzipped to reveal his scarred chest that he looked almost too...covered.

Why did I like him with less clothes on?

Don't think about that, Ellie. Don't!

Paulina stiffened imperceptibly, her hands turning into talons by her sides.

"She'll never love you, you know," she hissed. "You're such assholes."

Zane smiled as if he had just received the best compliment ever. "Thank you!"

She'll never love you?

I replayed Paulina words, wondering what she meant by them. Was that a generalized threat, basically saying that no woman would ever love them the way they were? That no woman would want to be with them?

That wasn't true. At all.

Everyone *wanted to be with them.*

Including me, though I didn't dare focus on that traitorous thought.

As Paulina stomped away, trying to maintain what little dignity she had left, the guys glanced in my direction. I swallowed convulsively as I met each of their gazes, one after the other. The tension between us felt like a live wire. One wrong move and I'd be struck by electricity. My heart fluttered wildly before I lifted my hand and gave them a tiny wave. I swore all five of their lips curved upward and their eyes softened.

That fluttery feeling evaporated like smoke when the bell rang overhead, signaling the end of lunch, and the five of them immediately looked away...almost as if the entire exchange had never happened. As if their eyes hadn't been piercing my very soul, flaying it open and allowing it to weep blood.

I quickly gathered up my book and shoved it into my backpack just as heat seeped into my back from a familiar body behind me. I froze, my breath hitching, but didn't turn around as a golden hand grabbed my tray of food and removed it from the table.

I finished placing everything inside of my backpack, slung it over my shoulders, and spun around just in time to see Landon throw my tray away for me. He walked out of the cafeteria with the other four guys surrounding him, not one of them sparing me a glance as the heavy cafeteria doors slammed shut behind them.

I tried to ignore the tingle of disappointment that prickled the skin on the back of my neck. I tried to tell myself it didn't matter that they were ignoring me.

The six of us...

We were broken. I knew it, they knew it, and the world knew it. Our pasts had been tarnished with loss, heartache, and pain, but somehow, we had found each other in the dissonant chaos. We were each an individual thread on a beautiful tapestry that was uniquely us. Nobody else could fit.

But maybe we were also the stitch capable of closing each other's wounds. The bandage that could stop the flow of blood.

Maybe, just maybe, we were what we needed to heal.

CHAPTER 1

Zane

I've always believed that every type of blood has a different, distinct smell. Some are reminiscent of pennies—copper and stale air combined, almost as if you're chomping down on rusty metal. Others are sweet, while others still send a sour tang wafting through the air.

The blood currently staining my hands, face, and body has the distinct scent of musk. Maybe it's from Dane's cologne, maybe it's his natural scent, maybe it's my own sweat, but it contaminates the air in a sickly cloud.

Á la cunt, bottled by none other than *moi*.

The guys don't usually allow me to fall this far down the hole—the hole tainted by bloodlust and madness, by darkness and sin, by animalistic cravings and ravenous hunger—but we're not thinking rationally. *I'm* not thinking rationally. So…I fell, tumbling head over feet into an abyss of oblivion and darkness that cuts at my skin and fucking soul like garden shears. I can try to crawl my way out of this madness, but there's no guarantee that the Zane who emerges on the other side will be the same man who fell in.

This new one…

He's broken. His nails have been ripped off from clinging onto the rock face for too damn long. His body is now gaunt, his hair disheveled. His eyes hold a crazed glint that he's kept hidden for years and years and years, all in a futile attempt to appear sane.

Ellie's gone.

The love of my fucking existence, my light, is gone.

The Paragons of Prosperity have her.

That last thought plays on a loop in my head, an ominous soundtrack that accompanies the skittering of my pulse and the sloshing of blood in my ears. Cymbals clashing together. Drums being pounded on. Organs screeching their tenor tune. All of them begin to blur together in my head until I can't even hear myself think.

Fear and anger collide, leaving nothing behind but a flaming, smoking wreckage like two cars meeting head on.

Because with Ellie gone, there's no reason for my sanity not to ditch this joint too.

Bye-bye, sanity. It was nice knowing you, you smug, annoying bastard. Have fun…wherever the fuck you go when you're not here. I think you need a nice, long vacation for putting up with my shit for so long. Maybe enjoy a cocktail on a beach while stroking your dick and planting flowers or whatever sane people do.

I'm dimly aware of Landon shaking me, attempting to garner my attention, but I can't pull my gaze away from Dane's distorted face. His eyes are wide in death, his features slack, but no one can miss the fear sketched onto his face. The anguish. The agony.

I made him suffer before I killed him.

I made him drink his own goddamn blood, and it's still not enough. We're no closer to finding Ellie now than we were forty-five minutes ago.

"We're not going to get to her in time," I whisper, wanting desperately to stick my knife into another warm body. Any body. Male. Female. It doesn't matter. Nothing matters if I don't get my sweet Ellie back.

They say that obsession is a poison that runs through your veins, a poison that you need to bleed out in order to survive. But I never believed that nonsense. My feelings for Ellie have made me stronger, brighter, faster than the average man. There's no denying I'm obsessed to the point of being clinically insane—that has never been a question—but I'm only obsessed because I love her so goddamn much that it drives me crazy. Even picturing a world without her in it sends me spiraling over a ravine, nothing but craggy rocks and churning water down below. But I'll willingly throw myself over that cliff edge and allow the waters of hell to carry my soul away if it means being with her.

"Snap the fuck out of it!" Landon bellows in my ear, but I'm too far gone to respond to him.

A memory bombards me, and I willingly sink into it with a sigh of contentment.

I'd always been a scrawny kid. A life of malnourishment and neglect would do that to someone.

A heavy exhale left my lips as I peered into the kitchen cabinet, rifling through the meager contents my parents left behind when they decided to travel to Spain for five months.

Our farmhouse was grand—over five levels of elegantly-furnished bedrooms, two dining rooms, and even a game room—but they couldn't be bothered to keep food in the goddamn cupboards for their eleven-year-old son.

With a heavy sigh, I grabbed one of the last granola bars I could find and hurried outside. Bloated, gray storm clouds hung low in the dark sky, the threat of rain imminent.

Shit.

I glanced at my bike in dismay, but there was nothing I could do at the moment. Maybe if I would've thought ahead, I could've called Landon or Dom and had their parents pick me up...

But no. I didn't want to bother them, and I sure as shit didn't want them asking questions.

My backpack hit the center of my back as I swung my leg over the bike and settled myself on the uncomfortable, bony black seat. I was in desperate need of a new bike, but I suspected I would get one for Christmas. After all, that was one of the things my parents excelled at—making sure they looked good in front of their rich, pompous friends. Why else would they splurge and purchase all the toys money could buy around the holidays?

But having them home meant having my mother around...

I sometimes believed my dad had good in him. At least, I believed he loved me in his own way. I half suspected he flew my mother out of the country all the damn time to keep her away from me. We both knew what would happen if she were home.

I could already hear her cruel taunts and insults echoing through my mind.

Crazy.

Deranged.

Psychotic.

Hear them enough times, you'd begin to believe they were true.

Phantom pains ran down my back like fire as I remembered the feel of the belt buckle the last time she was home. The scars on my skin had healed somewhat—at least, they weren't nearly as noticeable as they had been before—but the marks marring my soul, on the other hand...

I doubted they would ever heal properly.

I began peddling the bike the long distance to Oak Grove Preparatory Academy. It sat a few miles away from Grove Academy, the high school, and was blanketed by thick trees on either side. Some of the trees looked to be growing inside of the school, if that were even possible, reaching through the windows and popping out of the ceiling in an unique architectural design that I personally found atrocious and tacky.

By the time I arrived, wind was whipping at my face and rain splattered my cheeks. My dark hair stuck to my scalp, and I was sure my backpack was completely drenched.

I hurried inside ten minutes late.

The secretary lifted an eyebrow when I hurried past her, but I simply grinned and gave her a finger gun salute. I knew she wouldn't call my parents, though, mainly because she knew they didn't like to be bothered. The last secretary who called to complain about me was fired the very next day.

I ducked into the classroom just as Mr. Leaper finished the morning roll call.

I'd never liked Mr. Leaper, with his beady brown eyes, ash-blond hair, and hideous bulbous nose. He always stared down that big ass nose of his with an air of superiority that annoyed the shit out of me. He thought he was better than me, than us, and he never failed to remind us of that.

"You're late, Mr. Lorenzo," he said stiffly, his oily mustache seeming to twist with his lips.

"Maybe you're early," I countered immediately as I moved toward my seat in the back of the room. Landon and Dominic gave me concerned looks, but I waved away their questions as I threw myself into the wooden seat. They'd been my best friends since my family first arrived here, never once making fun of me because of my broken English. And it was because they were such good friends that I had to keep the truth about my parents a secret from them—I didn't want their pity or judgment. Not that I thought they would judge me, per se, but they both had amazing parents who worshiped the ground they walked on.

My stomach picked that time to let out an

embarrassingly loud gurgle. I frowned, staring down at myself, as one of the pricks next to me began to laugh. My teeth bared instinctively as I envisioned ripping out the asshole's throat, but a soft hand on my biceps stopped me.

I turned to see a cute, elfin-faced girl staring up at me with wide, innocent eyes fluttering behind her glasses.

Ellie.

My heart, as it always did when I was in her presence, began to pick up speed. I couldn't even admit to my friends how big of a crush I had on her. She was just so…cute.

Without a word, she handed me a tiny bag and then folded her hands on top of her desk as if she didn't have a care in the world. I glanced from her to the bag and then back to her again, one of my brows quirked. When she didn't turn to look at me, I slowly unzipped the bag and stared at the contents inside.

Lunch.

A sandwich, a carton of milk, a handful of grapes, a Tupperware of carrots, and a chocolate brownie.

My mouth began to water, but instead of giving into my baser impulses, I simply shut the case, zipped it back up, and put it on her desk.

A furrow manifested between Ellie's brows, but she didn't comment.

The rest of the morning was uneventful, and by the time lunch came around, I was hungry enough to eat my own foot.

"Hey!" Ellie tapped my shoulder in the hallway

until I was forced to turn and face her. She placed her hands on her hips and cocked one out to the side. For a moment, she simply stared at me, not saying anything else. My eyes searched her face as my teeth nibbled on my dry lower lip. After a long moment, she heaved out a breath and grabbed my arm, her tiny hand barely able to fit around my biceps even at that age. She was just so damn tiny. "Come on!"

I glanced helplessly in the direction of the cafeteria where I knew Landon and Dominic to be before following after her. But I would never pass up on the opportunity to hang out with Ellie. She was by far the cutest girl in my class. Dom and Landon would be so jealous I got to spend time with her.

She continued walking until we were in a quiet section of the hallway, away from the bustling cafeteria and classrooms full of students. Without preamble, she sat on the floor and patted the spot next to her.

"Whatcha up to, princesa?" The nickname flowed off my tongue before I could stop it, but if I thought she would be upset or embarrassed, I was mistaken. She simply grinned and patted the seat next to her once more.

Seeing no other alternative, and refusing to leave her when she obviously wanted my company, I sat down next to her and crossed my legs.

She didn't say anything else as she once again grabbed her lunch box out of her backpack and opened it up. I watched her with confusion and a tiny bit of trepidation as she ripped the sandwich in half and handed one slice to me. I opened my mouth in protest, but she shut me up with a firm look.

"No arguing," she warned as she began the painstaking task of separating everything in half. The carrots. The grapes. Hell, even the fucking brownie.

Somehow, she knew.

She knew that I was starving but was too proud to confess it out loud.

She knew I would be too embarrassed to take even a bite of her food in front of my friends.

She knew I would never willingly eat all of her lunch if she didn't have something to eat as well.

She knew.

That was the first of many days we went to that exact spot and shared a lunch.

And for the first time in years, I wasn't going home from school with a rumbling, gnawing pit for a stomach.

Ellie took care of me back then, and I'll be damned if I don't do the same now.

She's out there somewhere, alone and probably terrified but alive. I refuse to believe anything else. Any story that ends with her death is not one I want to read or even consider. Nope. I'm just gonna slam that book shut, throw it in a fire, and watch it burn, burn, burn. I'll be the best damn book arsonist that ever existed, and every fucking story that ends with her death will become nothing but charred ashes, the flames eating away their pages until not a single word is readable.

Burn. Burn. Burn.

"Zane!" Landon growls, getting in my face.

I blink at him, attempting to clear the lingering rage threatening to wrap around my mind like rusty chains. I need to remain coherent if I'm going to get my girl back.

"Let's fuck POP up," I tell him darkly.

I'm coming for you, princesa. *And anyone who gets in my way is going to pay the ultimate price—their death.*

Chapter 2

Ellie

There was a period after my parents died that I went through life in a daze. It was like sleepwalking…but it wasn't. Not truly. I was fully conscious and aware of everything around me, even as a tinny, almost mechanical voice in my head screamed at me that I didn't deserve to be happy when my parents were six feet in the ground. That voice remained incessant for the first year or two after their deaths as I lost myself to the grief and pain.

No, maybe that's the wrong word. Perhaps a better description would be to say I *surrendered* myself to the grief and pain.

It's reminiscent of going to the beach and wading into murky, turbulent ocean water. It licks at your knees, the cold slashing at your skin, but you continue moving farther until the water is up to your neck. And then you close your eyes, hold your breath, and dunk under, allowing the waves to carry you farther and farther away from shore. There's no relief, no escape, as your lungs begin to burn and dark spots materialize in your vision. Only then do you breach the surface, gasping for breath and panting. As you make your way back toward the beach, the sand suddenly feels too hot and prickly on your skin and you want nothing more than to dive back into the refreshing water and drown.

It feels as if your body is on *fire*, as if there's magma crawling through your internal organs, popping, crackling, and hissing in your bloodstream. Erratic spurts of heat well up, searing your throat, until smoke perfumes the air and strangles you like a coil of thick rope.

All of these thoughts run through my mind now as I stare at Blair's dead body.

Dead.

Because *he* killed her.

The Divine One—the malicious and psychotic leader of the Paragons of Prosperity.

And if he gets the chance, he's going to kill me as well.

His words from before tumble around in my head like ragweed in a ghost town.

Sacrifice.

Human sacrifice.

Bile burns my throat, licking at the sensitive skin like acid, as The Divine One—the T is capitalized, at least in my own mind, as if it's his full name, not just a title—turns his masked face in my direction. It's a beautiful mask, truly, with ostentatious gemstones lining a frame of solid gold. It offsets the red cloak that cascades around his figure like rivulets of blood. Of course, I don't know for certain that The Divine One is a man—the cloak obscures any and all curves from view and his voice is modified—but something about the way he walks leads me to believe that it's a male beneath the mask and robe.

"Come, dear Ellie," The Divine One says, wrapping a gloved hand around my shaking arm and pulling me forward.

"What are you going to do to me?" I demand, grateful that my voice doesn't tremble and betray my fear. I glance in both directions as The Divine One physically forces me out of the room and down the hall of the cave, but I don't see anything I can use as a weapon. And I sure as hell don't think I'll be able to fight him off when he has a gun in his free hand currently aimed at my temple.

The cave we're in is dark, lit only by torches scattered in intermittent intervals throughout the hall. Craggy rocks rest on top of each other, held together by clumps of dried mud and clay. The flooring itself is nothing but compacted dirt, though it feels almost sludgy beneath my shoes as if it has rained recently and water somehow found its way inside.

How the heck do I get out of here?

Terror like I've never felt—more potent than when I was dropped into a cornfield and forced to find my way home, more intense than when I was in an escape room with only an hour to save Dominic's life—strangles my airways, making breathing virtually impossible.

Blair's dead, her throat cut by the man herding me along.

And I'm going to be dead very soon if I don't find a way out of this.

My eyes continue to scan my surroundings as The Divine One stops at a room at the end of the hall, though calling it a room is too generous of a term. There's no door that I can see. Instead, the stones arch upward to create a makeshift entry into a small, nondescript closet. A single white robe rests on a rickety table directly in front of me, looking eerily like the angel costume I currently have on. One of POP's members stands opposite it, his arms crossed over his chest. No, wait. *Her* arms. When she moves like that, I can make out the distinct outline of breasts beneath the cascading robe.

"Get her ready." The Divine One's mechanical voice floats through the air as he shoves me forward. "She needs to be dressed for the ceremony."

"Don't do this," I beg, but The Divine One is already moving away in a blur of red. Before I can follow after him—and hopefully escape with my life intact—the female POP member blocks my entrance, her arms full of the white cloak.

"Strip," she instructs. Unlike The Divine One, she doesn't mask her voice. It's definitely female, though I'm positive I've never heard it before.

A surge of defiance I haven't felt in years courses through me. It steels my spine, straightens my shoulders, and notches up my chin.

"Strip," she repeats, a note of irritation in her melodic voice.

Grasping at whatever courage I can find, I bite out, "Make me."

With a hiss, she storms toward me, grabs the straps of my costume, and rips it down the center. I stand perfectly still, not fighting back, as the gown pools around my waist, baring my breasts to the cool air. She moves to pull the dress down my thighs, and with her head lowered like that, I see an opportunity.

I don't think, don't give myself a chance to second guess myself. My movements are simply instinctual, my fight or flight response kicking in and pounding through me like a distant army thundering down a mountain.

I attack.

With a cry I can't quite contain, I lift my knee up as fast as I can to catch her in the face. She squeaks in alarm as her hood flies back, her hand instinctively coming up to rub at her mask, but I don't waste time. Grabbing a fistful of her bright orange hair, I ram her face into the nearest wall and listen to the satisfying crunch of the mask cracking.

Run, Ellie. You need to run. You need to get out of here now.

"You little bitch!" she screams as she spins around. During the struggle, her mask has become askew, revealing a freckled face and crazed, emerald-colored eyes. I don't know her name, but I recognize her as a student in the year below me.

A student?!

That revelation settles in my stomach like a heavy rock as she charges at me like a bull, forcing us both to the ground.

"Stop it!" I cry as we grapple. I've never been in a physical altercation before—never even considered fighting another human being—but my body seems to know what I need to do before my brain can catch up.

All I know with unwavering certainty is that if I stop fighting, if I give in, then I will die.

"You don't understand anything!" she hollers, a little bit of spit forming at the edge of her mouth. "You need to do this, you dumb slut, or we're all going to suffer!"

And then it happens.

One second, she's on top of me, and the next, I've thrown her to the ground with an audible crack. I immediately stumble to my knees, my heart racing like mad, and prepare myself for the next attack. When it doesn't come, I lower my gaze to the girl, taking stock of the pool of blood now forming around her orange, vibrant hair.

Oh god.

Vomit crawls up my throat as my eyes meet hers—sightless. Vacant.

Dead.

She's dead.

I—

Oh god.

She's not dead. She's not. *She can't be.*

I shakily crawl toward her motionless body, resting two fingers against the pulse on her throat. Nothing. Not even a faint *thump-thump-thump*. Her blood seems to contour the dirt floor like sticky algae, a painting of red slashes and jagged lines.

Before I can stop myself, I twist my body and throw up in the corner of the room. Tears and snot run down my face, and no matter what I do or how I attempt to justify what just happened, I can't seem to calm down.

I just…

I just killed her.

A student.

Oh god.

Oh god.

Hysteria batters against my skull like a sledgehammer as I fall onto my butt and pull my knees up to my chest, hugging them tightly.

I didn't mean…

I didn't think…

I didn't want anyone to *die*.

I vomit again, and again, and again. I convulse until I fear I have nothing left inside of me, nothing left to give. I'd planned to…I don't know…knock her out like they do in movies. I didn't expect her to hit her head on the side of the table and die. No. No. No. I didn't want that. I didn't…

There are some people in the world who might be desensitized to death but that's not me. That'll *never* be me.

Still crying, my body racked by desperate sobs, I grab at the robe she had tried to force on me and quickly slip it on, desperate to cover my nude body.

Dead.

Dead.

Dead.

Blair's dead.

This unnamed female is dead.

Who was she? How did she get tangled up in all of this? Was she like me, someone plucked out of bed at night and forced to partake in POP's malicious games? Does she have a family? Siblings? A boyfriend? A girlfriend? Friends?

"You can't think about her right now," I whisper to myself, though I know her face will haunt me for days and years to come. I don't think I'll ever be free of her spirit haunting me.

But I need to get out of here.

I need to escape.

Walking hurts. To be completely honest, everything hurts—my body, my mind, my soul, my heart. Tears continue to stream down my cheeks as I force myself to take one step forward. And then another. And then another. I swallow down the gritty taste of sand that has clogged my throat.

I've never considered myself a crier before. When my parents died, I cried once at their funeral and then retreated into an icy fortress to wait out my grief. The last few months, however, I feel as if I've been crying more than ever before. There's an emptiness inside of me, a place in my chest that once housed a brilliant ball of light and joy. But that light has dimmed, tainted by monsters the world can't even begin to comprehend, and that joy has turned bitter and angry.

I'm so, so angry.

At The Divine One.

At POP.

At everyone in this entire freaking world.

I just want—no, I *need* all of this to be over.

Is that too much to ask?

I've just reached the open doorway when a figure

steps in front of me, forcing me to stumble back a few steps. My legs are so weak, so wobbly, that I fall onto my ass with a cry of pain. Blood—the girl's blood—sticks to my legs like syrup as horror and anger battle for dominance inside of me, a clashing of swords and shields.

"Oh, Ellie." The Divine One tsks his tongue as his gaze lands first on me and then the dead girl directly beside me.

My voice is surprisingly steady when I ask, "Are you going to kill me now?"

And I think I'll welcome death, if only to escape all of these feelings, all of these emotions, that send sticky goop through my bloodstream. The fine hairs along my arms turn to spikes as I stare into the face of death disguised in gemstones and gold.

The Divine One surprises me by throwing back his head and laughing. It's the strangest thing to hear through his mechanical, robotic voice—almost as if thousands of voices have been superimposed over each other to create an eerie, deadly symphony.

"You, my dear, are going to live." The Divine One extends a hand, but if he expects me to take it, he's solely mistaken. If I could, I would cut it straight from his body. Anger and hatred boil to life inside of me, simmering like water on a stove. They tangle with the anguish already present to create a toxic mixture I can't escape, one liable to explode at any second.

"Don't touch me." My voice is nothing but a whisper, but The Divine One hears it. I have the distinct impression he's smiling beneath his golden mask as he drops his hand back to his side.

"You're impure now, my sweet Ellie," he says, not moving an inch now that I've rebuffed his attempt at helping me to my feet. "I always knew there was a darkness inside of you."

"What the fuck—?"

"Congratulations, my dear child." The Divine One crouches down until his golden face is mere inches from my own. I have the sudden, irresistible urge to reach forward and tear it off, unveiling the man beneath it. Would he be another student? A professor? Someone else entirely?

One of my guy friends?

The latter thought has my throat closing up, even as my fingers begin to twitch by my sides. Before I can put my plan into action, he settles back on his heels, just out of my reach.

"Congratulations?" I repeat dumbly, using the back of my hand to wipe away some of the stray tears. Horror fills me when I find my hand bloody—and now, that blood has been transferred to my face.

No. No. No. No—

"You have completed round four of the Culling," he announces, gracefully rising to his feet and once more extending a hand. "I always knew you were too dark, too broken, to be my chosen one."

Without waiting for me to respond—to even wrap my head around his ominous words that pierce me like a hoard of angry bees—he grabs my arm and hoists me to my feet.

"Come," he says. "You need to change into your ceremonial robe. The sacrifice is about to begin."

Chapter 3

Ellie

A deep pain embeds itself in my soul, lingering, spreading through my body like a malignant tumor determined to plunder my mind and soul, destroying me from the inside out. Even knowing that the orange-haired girl wanted to kill me for some sort of fucked up sacrifice doesn't dull the sharp edges of guilt and pain that her death caused me.

But I don't get a chance to grieve or scream or one of the thousand things I want to do—because now it's my turn to die.

The Divine One's confusing words echo through my skull, rattling around in my brain like loose change, as I'm marched to another room, this one significantly smaller than the first. It has barely enough space to fit the tiny side table flush against the wall.

On the table, a mask and black robe rest—the same mask and robe I noted the other members of POP wearing.

"What is this?" I whisper, refusing to budge a single step. If The Divine One is deterred by my defiant nature, he doesn't show it. He simply shoulders past me and hands me the thick cloak and mask.

"Put these on," he instructs as I gape at him openly. When I continue to stand there, at a loss for words, he moves his arm upward, his sleeve falling away to unveil the gun in his hand—the gun pointed at my heart. "Put these on," he repeats.

With my dress destroyed, the last thing I want to do is take off the white robe and strip naked in front of him. But refusing isn't an option.

My breath hitching, I give The Divine One my back, trying to ignore the prickles of fear that race up and down my spine, and peel off the white robe. As quick as I can, I throw on the black one and rearrange it until everything is covered. I forgo the mask, leaving it on the table in a futile act of defiance, but The Divine One simply laughs jovially.

With sure hands, he grabs ahold of my chin, his fingers pinching my skin hard enough to elicit a gasp from my lips, and shoves the mask over my face, securing it behind my ears. I instantly feel as if I can't breathe, as if there's a rope tightening around my throat.

No.

"Good girl," The Divine One says, once again grabbing my upper arm and dragging me back into the hallway. My heart thrashes, twisting into a pretzel, as I'm frogmarched to yet another room.

Fear bleeds into shock and a little bit of awe when I take in the sleek, modern room I now find myself in. If the rest of the complex could be described as a series of caves and tunnels, this particular area has been plucked straight from a home design magazine. Compacted dirt turns into stark white tiles, polished so meticulously I can see my reflection in the surface. A self-serve bar rests against the far wall, and directly in front of it is a black leather couch.

At first, I don't think the couch is facing anything particularly special, but when I take a closer look, I see that it's a…window. At least, I think it's a window, though I can't decipher what's on the other side—all I see is darkness.

The Divine One makes a beeline toward the bar and pours himself a glass of bourbon. He doesn't offer me one—not that I would accept it if he did—and I half wonder if he's going to take off his mask to drink it. Instead, he simply sets the drink on the side table and reclines back on the leather couch, staring at the window intently. Maybe it's a television screen? But what would he be watching?

"Why am I here?" I croak out, once again searching for an exit, an escape. I debate fighting The Divine One, but with the gun in his hand, hanging lazily between a few fingers, I know it'll be a losing battle. But if he tries to attack me, tries to kill me, I'll fight with every breath I have.

I don't think I'm ready to die quite yet, and that realization chases away the last of the chill permeating my body.

"We're not the bad guys, my dear Ellie," The Divine One muses, keeping his gaze locked on the screen.

I hesitantly glance over my shoulder, through the door we've come from, but find it shut. Probably locked, knowing the sadistic bastard resting indolently in front of me.

No, escape isn't an option. Fighting isn't an option either. Which means…

Which means for now, I need to go along with whatever this is. Be a good little prisoner and make him believe I'm docile.

"You killed Blair," I whisper, pain tightening my lungs until it feels as if I'll never be able to breathe properly again. Blair had been one of my first female friends and the girlfriend of Piper, my roommate. To know that she's dead…

"And you killed Patricia," The Divine One counters.

I instantly freeze, every muscle in my body turning rigid. "Was that her name?" Those words are a breath of air, a gasp that's laced with pain and heartache. I know if I were to close my eyes, I would see her face and the blood surrounding her head like a demented halo. So. Much. Blood.

The Divine One ignores my question as he shifts on the couch, smoothing his gloved hands over his burgundy red robe.

"The Paragons of Prosperity have only ever looked after this town and the people in it," The Divine One continues.

"By forcing students to complete your fucked up trials?" Incredulity bleeds into my tone as I take a step closer. My hands ball into fists by my sides. "By killing them?"

I still remember hearing about the death of Ali, a participant of the Culling. Somehow, POP was able to stage her death to make it look like a suicide. I have no idea how they did it—who they paid off—but her parents will never know the truth about their daughter's death. Unless they were in on it…

"It started many, many years ago," The Divine One states, finally tilting his masked head to stare at me. "With Melody Ladouceur."

"Melody Ladouceur?" I parrot, my eyebrows touching my hairline. "The founders' daughter?" We studied her in my Town History class. Apparently, she was murdered, but no one could figure out who killed her. Overcome with grief, her parents moved to the town of Oak Grove to start over—hence the beginning of our quaint little town.

"She wasn't killed outside of Oak Grove, as the history books would make you believe. She was murdered *in* the town. Right here, to be precise." The Divine One rises in one fluid movement and walks toward the dark window, resting his gloved hand against the dark surface. "Believe it or not, her death *was* an accident. She got into a fight with her mother, and in a fit of rage, her mother threw her down the staircase. Melody broke her neck and died instantly."

"That's not an accident." Cold dread slithers down my arms, encasing both my hands in ice. "That sounds like a horrible mother with anger issues."

The Divine One tenses almost imperceptibly, his fingers flexing against the screen before straightening back out.

"Sometimes people need to do what they have to

do for the greater good—even if that means hurting family. Hurting blood."

I shake my head, but I can tell there's no use arguing. He's set in his convictions, and there'll be no changing his mind.

"So what does Melody have to do…?" I trail off, allowing him to fill in the blanks. I try to ignore the prickle itching over the back of my neck, the sound of warning bells going off in my head.

"When she died, her parents encountered a…change of luck," The Divine One tells me, and I can tell he's choosing his words carefully. Because he doesn't want to frighten me? No, that doesn't make any sense. Because he wants me to understand? "You see, before Melody's death, they'd lost their fortune and were on their way to bankruptcy. But when she died, they experienced wealth like never before. Geoff Ladouceur was voted to become the town's mayor. Selene Ladouceur started a profitable business after she discovered she was the heir of a very wealthy man." The Divine One clasps his hands behind his back, his spine ramrod straight almost as if his body is being held up by a metal rod. "They wrote it off as being merely a coincidence…until they discovered the history of the land they found themselves living on."

"What the fuck are you rambling about?" I demand, incredulous. He's talking crazy—absolute fucking crazy.

"The people in the town worshiped a goddess— a very powerful, very benevolent goddess. Cassia. She announced her presence with white daffodils—"

"You sound insane," I interrupt, placing both

hands in the air and taking an automatic step backward as if I can somehow fend off the crazy he's spewing. I'm all for people believing in different religions—or no religion at all—but he sounds utterly delusional.

"Maybe I am." He shrugs his shoulders as if he doesn't care either way, as if the topic of his sanity is irrelevant to him. "But all we know for certain is that the year following Melody's death, white daffodils appeared on her grave, a sign of Cassia's presence."

"Wait...*what*?" I squint my eyes as a new, horrifying thought suddenly occurs to me—he really *is* insane. Certifiably insane. Like, the type of insane that should see him in a hospital under lock and key.

I know where his story is going, and it fills me with unspeakable dread and horror.

"So they told their friends what they suspected," The Divine One continues. "And their friends decided to test out their theory." He pauses, allowing that unsettling revelation to sink in, to percolate in my stomach like a tub of acid, to erode my skin, before continuing. "There was a young village girl—Maggie. She worked at the local saloon—"

"No," I breathe in horror, understanding slamming into me like a wrecking ball.

"She was sweet. Wouldn't hurt a fly. A virgin. Pure." He speaks matter-of-factly, as if listing off attributes needed to apply for college or something similarly mundane. "That night, the group of them kidnapped her, went to the Ladouceur's mansion, and put a knife inside her chest."

I stumble back a step, unable to hear this, unable to wrap my head around his nonchalant words.

Darkness seeps into my vision, a curtain being drawn shut, and bile burns my throat.

"The very next day, one of the families struck gold. Another found a wealthy suitor for their daughter. A third had his invention bought by the US government. They realized that Cassia had looked out for them, but only because they appeased her with blood."

A tremor works its way through my body. I feel cold, empty, bereft. Dark splotches erupt across my vision, and I need to grip the wall for support. I swear my legs have turned into nothing but noodles, shaking erratically with every second that passes.

"And this sacrifice you keep mentioning…" I allow my words to taper off, to drift away like ashes on the breeze.

The Divine One spreads his arms out in either direction, as if encompassing the room at large. "We do it for the town."

"For the…?" A hysterical laugh bubbles out of me at the sheer absurdity of it all. "You're insane."

"The Paragons of Prosperity have allowed this town to prosper." There's a sharp edge to The Divine One's voice, noticeable even with the mechanical interface. "Our members do what needs to be done for the good of the town. For the good of everyone. Cassia has looked out for us for years and years and years. Just as long as we please her."

I take another step back until I'm flush against the wall, shaking my head from side to side. "You're insane." Those are the only two words I can think to use. He can't truly believe this crap, can he?

The Divine One doesn't reply. Instead, he simply types in a code on a keypad I hadn't noticed before until the black screen flickers out of existence, revealing a scene plucked straight out of a horror movie.

It appears to be the inside of another cave, a sliver of moonlight piercing a crack found high up above. But that's not what holds my attention—no, the figures cloaked in black do. I count at least fifty of them, if not more, all standing around a stone slab located in the center of the rocky, barren room. White daffodils decorate the perimeter of the room and the altar directly in the center.

I push away from the wall immediately, cold dread eclipsing the fear I felt moments before.

"What are you doing?" I demand shakily. When The Divine One doesn't answer, I scream, "What are you doing?!"

"What needs to be done," he answers in his cold, impassive voice.

On the other side of the glass, the members part, revealing two more cloaked figures stalking forward. Each of them hold one of the arms of a young, trembling girl. Her terrified eyes flicker from face to face as tears stream down her cheeks, leaving streaks of mascara in their wake.

It takes me a moment to place where I recognize her from—Amanda Barron. A senior like me. I think I went to her birthday party a few years back. We don't talk anymore—we didn't really talk years ago either—but I would know her from anywhere. Same wheat-colored blonde hair. Same bright blue eyes. Same pouty pink lips.

"What the fuck are you doing?" I scream, rushing forward to pound my fist against the window. I rip my mask off and toss it to the side, my hood falling down seconds later.

"They can't hear or see you," The Divine One says with a dismissive wave of his hand.

"Stop this!" I turn toward him, prepared to fight with everything I have, but he simply lifts his gun lazily and rests it against my temple, the cold barrel permeating my skin like ice.

"Silence, my dear Ellie."

"Fuck you!"

All I can do is stare in horror as they forcibly push Amanda onto the table. She struggles, screaming for help though I'm unable to hear anything where I stand on the other side of the glass, but no one responds to her pleas as they wrap rope around both of her wrists and her ankles. Her white robe flares around her, oddly resembling the angel costume I wore to the Halloween carnival.

"That was going to be you," The Divine One tells me, and I startle. For some reason, I almost forgot he was there. If he didn't have his mask on, I would feel his rancid breath on my neck, his smell tunneling into my throat.

"What?" I shake. Oh god, I shake. Terror blankets the room, a thread of rage ready to be pulled from the intricate tapestry.

"If you were pure, my sweet Ellie, that would've been you," The Divine One explains with a slow shake of his head, almost as if he's upset that it's not me on that stone altar. Vomit churns in my stomach at the thought—but that's nothing compared to the horror of what I know is about to happen. "But Amanda is pure—something that's very, very rare in today's society. Just ask your precious boys. They know more about this than what they told you. They know *everything*. They're the monsters that made you this impure creature."

My boys?

They know about this?

But I don't focus on his words. He's trying to break me, to destroy me, and I can't allow it to work.

"Stop this!" I scream hysterically, pushing all thoughts of my guys to the back of my mind to be dissected at a later time. "You can stop this! Cassia isn't fucking real. She's nothing but a delusion from fucked up elitists who think—"

The slap sends my head snapping to the side, pain blossoming on my cheek from where he backhanded me. I'm sure there'll be a nasty bruise there.

"Silence, child!" he snaps.

I can't hear anything on the other side of the glass, but I know Amanda is screaming and crying, struggling to escape the bindings cutting into her skin. One of the cloaked figures steps toward her, a dagger in hand, and I think—this is it. I'm going to witness my third murder of the day.

But the POP member doesn't kill her. Not yet.

He simply uses the dagger to cut down the middle of her robe, pushing it aside to reveal her naked body. She begins crying harder, futilely trying to cover her nudity from their penetrating gazes, though the straps holding her captive refuse to give an inch.

Rage darkens my vision. "You fucking perverted piece of—"

Another slap sends me tumbling onto the ground, but I immediately stumble back to my feet to glare at the disgusting man before me.

"Stop this," I grit out, my eyes watering and my teeth chattering.

Once again, The Divine One ignores me, focusing on the POP member who lifts his dagger into the air. I don't know for sure the person's a he, but he seems to be bulkier than some of the others surrounding him.

For a moment, he doesn't do anything, simply standing there with the dagger held in the air. It takes me a moment to realize he's speaking, though I can't hear what he's saying on the other side of the glass.

But The Divine One does, and he whispers the words as if he has spoken them a thousand times before. He probably has. "Cassia, the great benevolent goddess, the healer of the land and mind, listen to our prayers. We are unworthy men and women, and we humble ourselves before you. We get on our knees as praying servants and ask that you bestow us with your blessing. Accept this sacrifice, for our bounties will be plentiful under your guidance."

He can't…?

He can't seriously believe this shit, can he?

My rib cage is suddenly too small to contain my heart. It plays a dangerous game of leapfrog, jumping up my throat and clogging my airways. I can barely see through the sheen of glossy tears obscuring my vision, cascading down my cheeks in heavy rivulets.

"Stop this," I beg, but it's a whisper. I bang a fist against the glass desperately, but once again, no one hears or sees it. Instead of dropping my arm back to my side, I leave it against the window, almost as if I can provide comfort to Amanda through that one gesture.

But I can't.

God help me, I can't.

"No…"

The POP member lowers the knife in a swooping arc until it embeds itself directly between her breasts—but he doesn't kill her. Instead, he makes a shallow cut, deep enough to bleed but not enough to kill. Someone steps forward to take the knife from him, and he removes his gloves as well, handing them to a third member. Seeing his bare hands reaffirms what I already suspected—he's definitely a male, and when I find out who he is, he'll be the first to die.

The morbid thought slips into my head unbidden, but once it's been thrown into the world, I find I can't take it back. I don't *want* to. Something dark and cold settles in my chest, an immovable weight, and expands outward in an unfamiliar chill.

All I can do is stare at those rough hands with hair on the knuckles and wrist. A birthmark rests just below his thumb, and I focus on that, only that, as he rubs his hands through the blood.

No…

Both of his hands move in tandem, traveling outward and upward. His fingers flick over her nipples, eliciting another muted cry of terror, before lowering down her stomach in perfectly straight lines. They connect below her bellybutton, directly above the splatter of blonde curls. He removes his hands from her skin only to dip them back into the blood—almost as if it's his own personal paint—and move them to her belly button. He creates a single circle around her navel with a line through it before stepping away.

He extends a hand, and one of POP's members hands him the blade.

"Don't do this!" I scream at The Divine One, but I know my words will fall on deaf ears. I want to scream, cry, punch someone, but I don't do any of those things as I retreat further into myself, surrendering to the ice cascading through my veins, the fortress of snow and coldness.

My heart…

My heart is in tatters.

The POP member says something else, but this time, The Divine One doesn't translate for me. He simply watches in rapt fascination, and I swear he's holding his breath, just as I do.

Though I suspect we're holding our breaths for very different reasons.

The man lifts his arm into the air as Amanda opens her mouth to scream and scream and scream—a scream I'm unable to hear. And then the knife is in her chest, directly where her heart should be, and her soundless screams are silenced like a flame deprived of oxygen.

The Divine One's voice echoes from directly behind me.

"We're going to do such great things, you and

me, my sweet Ellie."

Something touches my neck—as light as a feather and equally as soft—and pricks my skin.

Drugged.

I've been drugged.

Darkness encroaches the edges of my vision, eating away at it like flames on a piece of paper, and I tilt to the side. The last thing I see before unconsciousness claims me is The Divine One's masked face staring down at me.

And then…

Darkness.

Chapter 4

I first learned the truth about POP when I was a young boy. I don't recall how old I was, but I was mature enough to recognize the difference between right and wrong—and murdering an innocent female was definitely wrong.

Not that I'm against murder—that would be hypocritical of me, considering all that I've done—but I know to aim my rage where it deserves to be. The men and women sacrificing young women to a goddess who doesn't exist? Yeah, they deserve my wrath.

I was sitting in the lobby of town hall, my legs kicking against the seat in irritation and impatience, when I overheard the mayor of all people in a conversation with his wife. Her voice was muted and tinny on the other end of the phone line, but I heard his answers clear enough. They were arguing, though the mayor looked more distressed than angry, about their young sixteen-year-old daughter. I stumbled to my feet and moved even closer to the office door, praying my dad remained in his meeting across the hall for a few more minutes. Apparently, the mayor was going to do something that his wife didn't approve of, but he kept repeating that he didn't have a choice.

That night, I told Dominic what I overheard, and the two of us decided to follow Mr. Mayor. It was supposed to be a joke, a prank, but what we discovered…

We saw him grab his own daughter as she struggled and cried, throwing her into the bed of a pickup truck. A bunch of men and women wearing flowing robes drove her away. The very next day, her body was found dead on the side of the road. Hit and run, the police said, but we knew differently.

Of course, it took us years to figure out the truth about what happened to her.

But once we did, you can bet your ass that Mr. Mayor was the first man we killed.

It was actually what brought our friend group together, created inseparable bonds that cannot be severed—dismembering a body will do that to a person.

All of the information we gathered, all of the people we tortured and killed… None of that means anything now. Ellie is still missing, and the night is drawing to a close.

Emotion clogs my throat when I think about what could be happening to her, what might've already happened—

No, you can't think like that, Landon. She's alive. She has to be.

I hold on to that silver of hope with both hands, wrapping it around my fist and pulling it toward me, praying I can infuse myself with it. I don't even want to think about what will happen when that precious, diminutive nugget of hope fades.

There's a beast inside of me, a darkness and pain that spreads through my body like a malignant tumor. It ravages my body and mind, tarnishes my soul, and I can barely recognize the shell of a man who remains.

"He's not talking."

Dominic's harsh voice pulls me out of my thoughts, and I turn toward our newest prisoner with heavy contempt. A small grin slants up my lips, bloodthirsty and malicious, as the man begins to cry harder. His death is imminent, and he can no doubt taste it in the air.

Mr. Brighton has been our school's counselor for over two years. I don't remember the name of the school he transferred from, but he has only ever been kind to the students and staff—if you didn't count taking part in sacrificial rituals, of course.

We first discovered he was a member of POP after we found the trademark cloak and mask hidden in his office. We kept him alive for one reason and one reason alone—we might need him for information.

I'm so fucking grateful we didn't decide to kill him right then and there when we discovered the truth about his alliance.

"Please." Snot cascades down his chubby face as he shakes like a wet dog—a scared, pathetic, insufferable wet dog. His face is a mask of bruises and shallow cuts, though that's nothing compared to the rest of his naked body. He's missing two fingers on his right hand and three on his left. His large belly has a smiley face carved into it—compliments of Zane, of course. "I don't know where they are."

"You do," Ryker states simply, softly, a whisper in the wind. A phantom. He's been mostly silent during the course of this interrogation, allowing the other men to take control, but just now, he steps forward, slipping on a pair of plastic gloves.

Mr. Brighton's face pales.

"You all do," Beckett agrees with a malicious sneer. His haughty British accent makes those three words sound almost lyrical despite the anger coating them. "But you've been trained like good little pups to remain silent, haven't you?"

Mr. Brighton begins to cry harder.

That's one thing I have to give them credit for—they're good at holding out under torture. The room where they sacrifice the girls is sacred, at least in their demented minds, and no matter how many people we torture, they don't spill its location. We've checked almost every building in this entire godforsaken town and have still come up empty. Dominic believes that they must be sacrificing the girls in a different city and bringing their bodies back to Oak Grove.

I just think we're not looking hard enough.

"I honestly don't know." More snot and tears run down Mr. Brighton's bright red face. "They blindfold us—"

"I don't believe that's true, Fred," Ryker says gruffly, referring to him by his real name. Without preamble, he crouches down before the horrid man and grabs ahold of his cock, holding it out of the way with one hand so he can rest his blade against the man's ballsack.

My nose wrinkles automatically.

Jesus fucking Christ…

Zane licks his lips in excitement, as if he's actually getting off on the violence and bloodshed. Knowing the twisted bastard as well as I do, he probably is.

"You may not know where the sacrifice takes place," Ryker states softly, though his tone suggests he doesn't believe it in the slightest, "but you do know something." His knife presses against the man's balls, eliciting a whimper from his bloody lips. "I want to know what that something is."

"Please—"

In a single second, Ryker has one of the man's balls in his gloved hand, throwing it across the room. It just barely misses Beckett's face, and the posh Brit squeals like a girl and practically jumps a foot in the air.

"Are you bloody kidding me?" he mumbles, scrubbing at his arms with a scowl.

Ryker ignores him and focuses on a bleeding, sobbing, hysterical Mr. Fred Brighton.

"The only words I want coming out of your mouth are answers." Ryker's throaty voice sends a chill even down my spine, and I'm the one in charge of this group.

Well, as in charge as a man can be of other monsters. We all know only one person has the capacity to tame these feral beasts, only one person holds all of our leashes, and we have no idea where the fuck she is or if she's even still—

Deep breaths, Landon. Deep breaths.

Dread fills me like cement, but I force the sensation aside and take a step closer, crossing my arms over my chest.

"Are you going to talk, Fred?" I ask darkly.

Zane dances up behind our old school counselor, holding the severed ball in his hand.

When Fred doesn't speak, either lost to the pain or too damn stubborn to save his own life, Zane grabs the man's chin with his free hand, forces his mouth open, and shoves the—

I look away, my stomach tightening with revulsion.

I do what I need to do—we all do—but sometimes, it can be too much for me. I don't *want* to live my life in shadows and darkness. However, there are not a lot of locations where a monster as savage and demented as me can thrive. Maybe that's why I clasp on to Ellie as hard as I can—because she represents everything I want for myself.

Light. Happiness. Peace.

Yes…

Peace. Serenity. Tranquility. She encompasses all those terms, and then some. Being with her banishes some of the shadows that have made themselves at home in my eyes. I don't feel as beastly anymore when she's staring at me with awe and fascination, a look I never want to see dissipate from her gaze.

It's why we kept secrets from her, why we withheld the truth. If she knew the truth about what we are—serial killers, murderers, monsters—she would want nothing to do with us. At least, that's what I believed, and maybe a part of me still believes it. But now, that decision is coming back to bite all of us in the ass.

We might lose her forever because of the secrets we kept.

Fred screams and screams and screams, his voice becoming hoarser by the second until it's a simple rasp of sound, almost reminiscent of Ryker's broken voice. But he doesn't die—Ryker and Zane make sure of it.

It was surprisingly easy to grab Fred Brighton off of campus. We simply paid a visit to his office where he was masturbating over a porn video of a man in a schoolboy costume sucking the dick of another man, and kidnapped him, knocking him unconscious and throwing him over my shoulder. We took the forgotten forest trails until we reached the van Dominic stole— and one we'll have to get our contact to destroy at a later date.

Fred Brighton doesn't have any family or friends, no one who will notice he's missing. His father died years ago, and his mother has been diagnosed with dementia and currently lives in a group home that is paid for by his estranged sister. He has an ex-wife who left him when she discovered he was fucking a college-aged guy. And that college-aged guy left him after he discovered he was fucking a high school-aged one. Fred decided to transfer to Oak Grove Academy— who, for some reason, allowed him to work with more minors, further proving the corruption of the town and school—and the rest is history.

So far, he hadn't shown an interest in any of the students here, but we kept an eye on him anyway. The second he made a move, we would've made *our* move.

The ringing of my phone drowns out the agonized screams from Fred. I have no idea what the guys are doing, but by the sounds of it, it's immensely painful.

I step over one of Fred's fallen fingers and carefully move out of the barn, greedily dragging in lungful after lungful of cool fresh air.

Zane's barn and farmhouse are located in the middle of nowhere. Literally. In one direction, I can see miles and miles of cornstalks. In the other, trees. It's what makes this place the perfect location to not only conduct our murders but dispose of them as well.

What's the point of a meat grinding station if we don't use it on animals who actually deserve death?

Inside, Fred's screams turn silent, and I hear Dominic curse loudly. Apparently, Ryker and Zane had a little too much fun with their toy, and now there's another body we need to dispose of.

And we didn't even get goddamn information out of this fucker before he died.

Fuck!

My phone rings again, and I absently press the green button to answer it.

"Hello?"

"Landon?" Ellie's wobbly voice echoes through the phone as everything inside my body goes still. A breath I didn't realize I was holding releases like a rope around my neck, even as my stomach ties itself into a pretzel. Hearing her sweet, musical voice…

My heart feels sluggish and sticky, and I find myself falling forward, landing on my knees in the middle of the yard.

Ellie.

Oh god…

"Kitten?" I whisper, the one word being carried away in the breeze. Behind me, I can hear one of the machines being turned on as the guys get to work cutting up the body and putting it through the meat grinder. "Kitten, where are you?"

The full weight of this moment settles on my shoulders like a heavy winter coat.

She's alive, at least for now.

She called me.

But where the fuck is she?

Is she okay?

Why does she sound so fucking terrified?

I want to eradicate all of the terror from her tiny frame and replace it with peace, just as she does for me.

Even through the phone, I can sense the fear wafting off of her, providing a tiny tremor to her voice.

"Kitten," I repeat as I struggle to suck in lungfuls of air, "where are you?"

The second I find her, the second I hold her in my arms, I'm never going to let her go again.

Chapter 5

My hands are painted red in the blood of the man we just killed. The man we dismembered. The man we burned in a tub of acid before Landon raced into the room, his eyes wild and frantic, and told us Ellie had called.

Ellie…

Her sweet name sits on my tongue like the most decadent of candies—sweeter than chocolate and slathered in sin.

We move like men possessed into the beat-up truck Zane always keeps on his property and drive like mad back to the school. The Halloween Carnival is still in full swing as we pull into the parking lot, jump out of the truck, and then race toward the pond on the opposite end of campus.

More than a dozen students have snuck away to get a little post-carnival action. As we venture through the forest, raspy moans reach our ears, accompanied by the slap of flesh against flesh.

"Yes! Jason, yes!"

"Just like that!"

"Harder!"

"Be a good little slut and come for me."

The pungent stench of sex contaminates the air, and in front of me, Beckett snarls in disgust—no doubt thinking how unsanitary outdoor sex is. Not that he hasn't envisioned taking Ellie against a tree once or twice…

Ellie.

Her name settles like a stone in my chest as blinding panic burns away all coherent thinking. If something has happened to her, if she's hurt in any way…

I bite down on the growl that wants to escape. Sometimes, I truly believe I'm more beast than man, as if something had been altered inside of me at a young age to create such an insane, competitive, possessive bastard. I'm crazier than those damn romance heroes Ellie likes to read so much. I'm a maelstrom of violence, and everybody better steer clear of me until I'm able to calm the fuck down.

I'm so lost in my thoughts that I barely even notice the couple fucking against a tree directly in front of me, the guy pistoning in and out of the girl as he bites down on her nipple hard enough for her to scream. I simply use his hair as a makeshift knob, pushing him to the side as if he's a door and then stepping through, ignoring the slew of angry curses that follow.

Finally, we reach the pond Ellie told us to meet

her at, and all five of us break into a run.

I see her instantly, and relief washes through me in a sweeping torrent that knocks me off my feet. She's alive. Oh, thank fuck.

But that relief is eclipsed by anger and despair when I take in her sunken cheeks and hollow expression, the light I've always come to associate with Ellie noticeably absent from her eyes.

"Who did this to you?" Zane storms forward, his body thrumming with electrical energy. I half expect him to begin convulsing and seizing as more electricity cascades through him in white-hot heat.

Ellie sits near the edge of the pond, not seeming to care that the ground is wet from the sprinklers a few hours earlier. Her knees rest against her chest, and she wraps both her arms around them, holding them to her body. She's shaking just as badly as Zane, though I suspect it's for a very different reason. Goosebumps pebble across her body as she shakes, and shakes, and shakes.

Grateful that I changed out of my bloody clothes back at Zane's barn, I throw my sweatshirt over my head and attempt to maneuver it over her own. She jerks away immediately, her head snapping up and spearing me with an unreadable look, and the sweatshirt falls to the ground between us. The sight of it in the mud makes my heart feel sluggish and sticky. In all the years I've known her, she never once rejected my clothing—even when she stupidly believed that I hated her.

Landon crouches down beside her and lifts a hand like he's going to put it on the small of her back.

When she flinches yet again, those damn demons returning to her eyes and flaring outward, he drops it with a small frown.

To the outside observer, Landon would appear unaffected by her appearance, maybe even aloof. But as his best friend for years, I can see the miniscule changes in his veneer that he tries to keep hidden—the way his hand shakes by his side, the way he blinks away tears, the way he stares at Ellie with wide, terrified eyes.

He sees the shadows in her gaze as well. The monsters. The beasts.

And he's terrified that he can't defeat them for her.

"What happened, kitten?" he asks softly, his hand once again twitching by his side as if he has to physically restrain himself from reaching toward her and pulling her into his arms.

"What happened?" A bark of dry, humorless laughter escapes her. She brushes at a few wayward tears that cascade down her cheeks with the back of her hand. "What happened? You're asking me what happened…as if you don't already know." A hint of accusation seeps into her gaze and voice, strong enough to make me startle. In all the years I've known her, loved her, I've never heard such vitriol in her tone before, especially aimed at us.

Beckett offers her a sultry smirk, at odds with the storm waging a war in his multi-colored eyes. The chocolatey brown one is laced with sadness and pain, while the verdant green one flashes with unconcealed rage aimed at whoever put those shadows there. Still, he manages a smile as he saunters forward, his hand raised as if he intends to pull her to her feet.

"Ellie…"

"Don't touch me!" Her voice is shrill, practically a scream, as she jumps to her feet and takes a few steps backward, her heels digging into the water.

"Careful!" Landon barks, tension lining his shoulders. "You don't want to fall in—"

"Why?" She throws her head back in another spurt of dry laughter. "Because then you won't be able to use me as a *goddamn human sacrifice*?" Her voice rises to a scream as we all stare at her in shock. But whatever she sees on our faces is the only confirmation she needs. She takes another step backward until her foot lands inside the dirty water and begins to cry. "So you knew."

There's no use denying it. Now that she knows the truth, there's no way in hell I'm going to lie to her again, and I know the others feel the same way.

"It's not that simple," I begin, but she whirls around to glare at me, jabbing an accusing finger in my direction.

"Don't fucking lie to me!" Her voice carries in the wind, and Ryker—where he's crouched down behind us all—tenses. I know he's thinking about the couples fucking in the forest. If any of them were to wander down here and overhear this conversation…

"Ellie, love," Beckett placates, taking a tentative step closer. "Keep your voice down."

"Fuck you!" Pure hatred radiates from her gaze as she glares at him, and it has enough impact to have his feet faltering to a stop. Hurt flashes across his face, but if Ellie sees it or cares, she doesn't notice. "He told me time and time again that you guys knew about all of this, but I never believed—"

"We have nothing to do with the deaths!" Landon interrupts. When Ellie gives him a dubious look, he continues on hurriedly, "We've been trying to stop POP for years now. When you were first chosen—"

"So you knew about POP for years?" Incredulity laces her voice, along with a handful of hurt and betrayal. More tears cascade down her cheeks as she stares up at him, as if he took her heart in his hand and crushed it in one fatal movement.

Landon begins to shake even harder. "Ellie, it's not that simple—"

"Do you have any idea what I've been through?" she demands on a sob, falling to her knees in the pond. Water sloshes around her, soaking the hideous black cloak, but she doesn't seem to notice. I imagine the water is freezing, and I want nothing more than to pull her from its depths, wrap her in my clothes, and hold her in front of a fire until she's warm again. But considering the fact that she's more likely to punch me in the face than allow me to hold her...

"*Princesa.*" Zane materializes in front of her, his eyes beseeching hers to listen to us, to understand our reasoning, to trust that all we've ever done was try to protect her and this town. But especially her. Does anyone else see the manic glint in his eyes? The crack forming down the middle, seconds from destroying him completely?

And I realize then...

This slip of a girl—barely one hundred pounds soaking wet—has the capacity to ruin us all.

"Let's just get you inside and in warm clothes, and then we can—" Landon begins when Zane seems incapable of speech, simply gaping at Ellie, at a loss for words.

Ellie cuts him off with a penetrating glare. "I've seen people die."

"Ellie…"

"Blair's dead!" she screams, grabbing at strands of her brown hair. "And I-I-I killed someone."

Her shaky declaration drops between all six of us like an atomic bomb. It physically causes me to stagger back a few steps as I look at her once more, really look at her, and finally understand the cause of the demons clawing at her skin, making themselves at home in her eyes.

"I saw a girl get sacrificed on some sort of altar because this fucked up town believes that a goddess will answer their prayers." A bark of deranged laughter escapes her as more goosebumps erupt on her creamy skin—this time from the cold. "But there's no one up there. No one is answering any prayers." She squeezes her eyelids shut, and a single tear gets caught on one of her lashes. After a moment, she snaps her eyes open and freezes us in place with a frosty glare. "And you guys knew about all of this for years? You knew that I was selected for the Culling and allowed me—"

"We were trying to protect you," Ryker bites out angrily—but that anger isn't directed at her. No. That anger is aimed solely at himself for failing her.

"You made me think I was all alone!" she

screams back at him. "If I would've had an inkling of what was happening to me—"

"You would've been terrified," Landon interrupts. "And we didn't want to scare you more than you already were. And what if POP discovered you knew more than what you were supposed to? They would've killed you!"

"Don't you see?" Ellie shakily climbs back to her feet, the black cloak clinging to her legs from the water. I recognize the cloak as belonging to the members of POP. Is she one of them now? Obviously they didn't kill her, so that means... "All these secrets... Three girls are dead. One of them was my friend. And I..." She trails off, once again raking her fingers through her hair, and then screams out, "FUCK!"

"You kept the truth about your participation in the Culling from us," Beckett points out. "And you did that because you were trying to protect us."

I know immediately he said the wrong thing.

She spins to face him, her eyes wild and crazy—just as Landon's were when he barreled into the barn to announce that she called him—and laughs hysterically. We watch her warily, awaiting the inevitable snap, when she stops cackling immediately and glares. Just glares. Silence stretches between us all, as taut as a bow string, before she spits out, "That's not the same thing."

Beckett, always trying to be the peacemaker, lifts both hands up in the air and ventures another step closer. "I know it's not the same thing, love. But we all did what we thought was best to protect the people we care about. Don't you understand? We didn't tell you the truth about POP because we care about you. All we wanted to do was protect you."

"No." She shakes her head vehemently. "You didn't tell me the truth because you were being selfish." She spins to face Zane, who stares at her with a manic type of intensity and possessiveness in his dark gaze. "Whose blood did I find?"

Her question throws us all off guard. A chill races up my back as I regard her.

Landon recovers first, his words dragging her attention away from Zane and onto him. Which is good, considering Zane looks less than five seconds away from grabbing her, shoving her inside a bag, and dressing up as Santa Claus with her as the only present for the holiday season.

"What blood are you—?"

"The blood in Zane's barn," Ellie interrupts, that dangerous, slightly crazed glint materializing in her eyes once again.

My god.

POP broke her.

That one thought tunnels its way into my brain and nests there. It flickers through me like a flame over kerosene as my mouth pops open before immediately slamming shut. I can practically taste the animosity simmering beneath her skin, demanding an outlet she can't quite understand. She's unused to feeling such strong emotions, such intense waves of violence and fury, and I imagine she's terrified of it. Of herself.

I don't know what happened when she was gone, what POP and that fucker The Divine One did to her, but it's enough to send cracks spiraling down her body. I just pray that we're strong enough to hold her pieces together until she can take over and do it herself.

In the meantime, we'll find POP and make them pay for what they did to her—along with all of those other innocent girls.

Landon's silver eyes lower to his feet, but he doesn't make any excuses or justifications for our actions. Because to be honest? There aren't any. We fucked up, and now, we're paying the consequences.

"We did what we needed to do in order to protect you—" he begins helplessly, thinking back to the time we tortured Dane in Zane's barn a short while before Ellie stumbled inside and found his blood.

"My god," Ellie breathes in horror. "So you killed someone?" I can't quite read the expression in her tone, the lines tightening around her lips and eyes. Is she terrified of us? Disgusted? I think I'll lose my goddamn mind if I discover she is.

"Not then," Ryker pipes in, cluing her into the fact that we *did* at a later time. Just a few hours ago, actually.

She blinks at him, her expression going carefully blank, before shifting her gaze to Landon and Zane. Then me. And then finally, Beckett.

She doesn't speak, but I swear I hear screaming in my ears and blood sluicing in my head as I struggle to maintain the precarious grip I have on my sanity.

Finally, she speaks, her voice a breathy whisper I need to lean forward in order to hear. "You allowed me to be drugged, tied up, scared—"

"No," Zane whispers fiercely, shaking his head

from side to side as if he can somehow forget the accusations she hurls his way. *Our* way. As if by denying them enough times, it'll make her words any less true and heartbreaking.

"Three people are dead tonight—one of them by my own hand—and this all could've been avoided if *you fucking told me the truth*!" Tears rush down her cheeks, highlighted by the huge golden moon high up above. A full moon. Its reflection ripples on the water in silvery strands. "You say that you kept secrets from me because you cared about me—"

"We do," Landon interrupts, his voice breaking at her use of the past tense.

She continues like he hadn't said anything. "But if I know you guys as well as I think I do, you remained silent because you were afraid I'd discover…whatever the hell happened in that murder barn of yours." She waves a hand erratically in the air, almost as if she can brush away the words like a hoard of pesky flies. "The truth about everything you've done."

"We'll tell you everything we know," Landon pleads. "Just let us explain."

And then she stares at him, and her eyes are devoid of everything that makes Ellie *Ellie*—no love, no compassion, no joy. Just…darkness. Darkness and shadows that distort her features until they become something unrecognizable.

I watch the change happen. I can see the exact moment when she decides that we're nothing to her— lower on the totem pole than even POP in her mind.

We lied to her.

Broke her heart.

Betrayed her.

And these are sins we can't atone for.

She focuses on Landon with that deadened expression, and his lips pop open in surprise—no doubt, he can see the same thing I do on her face.

"I don't need you to explain." Her voice doesn't sound like Ellie's. It's cold and cynical and heavy in anger. "I don't need you to say anything to me ever again."

"Ellie, wait—"

"I'm done with you, Landon," she whispers before flitting her gaze across all of us. We can't move, can't breathe. It's like she stuck her hand into all of our hearts, ripped out the organs, and then threw them in the shimmery silver pond behind her. "I'm done with all of you." She takes a step away, pauses, and then glances at us over her shoulder. "Just stay the fuck away from me."

Then she's gone, disappearing into the dense thicket of trees.

And something inside of me…

It shatters.

CHAPTER 6

Ellie

I can't run away fast enough.

It feels as if there's something—or someone—chasing after me, screaming at me, demanding that I slow down. In my head, I can hear the pounding of footsteps on the asphalt as a shadowy figure looms over me, shrouding me in its malevolent presence. My heart races, thrashes, beats to a rhythm I can't hear—shallow bursts followed by elongated, irregular ones.

I feel sick to my stomach, and I half expect to look down and see my hands still covered in blood. But no. I washed all of the blood away in the pond before the guys arrived. Still, I can feel the sticky substance between my fingers, embedded beneath my nails, on my palms.

My entire body shaking, I make a beeline for the main academic building and toward the front entrance. It's unsurprisingly unlocked—the school believes they're untouchable and never leaves the main building locked at night—and I'm able to slip inside without any of the giggling students seeing me. Without preamble, I head toward the lost and found box and sift through the contents until I find what I'm looking for— a change of clothes. Or more specifically, an oversized sweatshirt.

I rip the black robe off of me with a sob as I throw the sweatshirt over my head. It dwarves my petite frame, coming all the way to my knees, but at least I won't have to search for shorts or pants with it on. The fabric smells vaguely of sweat, and I wrinkle my nose instinctively.

Being in this sweatshirt…

It reminds me of all the times Dominic would throw his own sweater over my head, the same way he tried to do tonight. Maybe I should've let him. Maybe I should've listened—

Those thoughts are swept away in a rainstorm of bitter anger and betrayal, cascading through the bars of the storm drain until they reach the disgusting sewer far below.

My best friends… They lied to me. Lied to me for fucking *years*. They allowed me to believe I was all alone in this fight against POP in order to…what? Protect me?

A hysterical snort escapes me as I bring my hands up to my face, dragging them down my cheeks.

There's so much I need to ask them—how do they know about POP? Are they involved somehow? Who was that person they…the person they killed?— but I can't be around them. I can't even look at them without seeing all over again the three women who died in a span of an hour.

All of this could've been avoided if they just told me the truth.

I want to burn the discarded robe, but I settle on tossing it into the dumpster on the way back to my dorm. It feels as if weights are tied around my ankles, dragging me into the cement with every step I take. I'm trudging through marshy water, and I know I'll inevitably go under and drown. There's no other option.

The door to the dorm building is propped open with a brick when I arrive, and the halls are uncharacteristically silent. No doubt, all of the students will be at the Halloween Carnival or indulging themselves in a late night afterparty. I don't even see the normal RA at her station in the lobby.

But that's good.

I don't know what I'd do if I were to see anyone right now. Fall apart? Scream? Cry?

Ice imprisons my heart with every step toward my dorm I take. Will it be horrible if I fall to my knees right here and now and cry my eyes out? Cry for Blair, and the girl I killed, and the woman who was sacrificed, and the men I thought I knew but lost?

When I hear hysterical sobbing and sniffling, I think it's the universe's way of answering my silent question. Maybe the noises are a product of my overactive imagination.

What I don't prepare for is entering my dorm and seeing Piper, Victoria, and Jane crowded together in the center of the room.

Piper's on her knees, big fat tears running down

her cheeks as gasping sobs escape her parted lips. Victoria kneels beside her, rubbing a hand up and down her back soothingly. Jane stands slightly off to the side, her arms crossed over her chest and her frizzy hair standing up in all directions as if she's run her hand through it one too many times.

I stop immediately. It's a wonder I'm able to speak, let alone articulately ask, "What happened?"

Piper turns a tear-stained face in my direction. Her cheeks are red and blotchy, and her eyes and nose both seem swollen.

"It-it's Blair," she stutters out, before breaking into heart-wrenching sobs once again.

I go still. Not even my heart is beating as I fall into a merciful pit of oblivion, where the monsters and shadows of the world can't get to me. It's an oasis of my own making, where I retreat to a tiny corner of my mind away from the horrors and atrocities plaguing this godforsaken world.

So I hear Piper, I do, but my brain can't quite understand the words leaving her lips. They trickle through my brain like water in a strainer as I blink at her wordlessly.

"She's dead!" she sobs, wailing hysterically. Victoria wraps her arms even tighter around Piper, attempting to calm our distraught friend.

"Dead," I repeat numbly. But honestly? All I can focus on is the way the curtain behind her head sways in the breeze. We must've accidentally left the window open, and now, that white curtain is rhythmically shifting back and forth, back and forth, back and forth—

"We only discovered it a few minutes ago when Blair's mother called Piper. It was a car accident," Jane tells me in a wobbly voice, pushing her glasses further up her nose with the pad of her thumb. "Apparently, she was heading to a party with Patricia Longly and Amanda Barron—"

Patricia Longly.

The woman I murdered.

The woman whose head ricocheted off the table.

And Amanda Barron, the woman who I witnessed get murdered.

Who was stripped naked and cut open and stabbed and—

I barely make it to the garbage can before I dry heave, retching again and again with nothing left inside of me to give.

"It's okay, Pip," Victoria soothes from behind me as I vomit again and again and again and again—

"We're with you. Always," Jane agrees.

Piper lost the woman she loved.

Victoria and Jane lost one of their best friends.

It should've been me.

The thought slips in unbidden, a sinister whisper that feels like every nightmare I've ever had rolled into one. But even as I think that, I can't deny the sincerity of that statement, the truth.

If that gun would've worked when Blair aimed it at me…

I dry-heave again as this toxic cocktail of pain, anger, and betrayal runs amok inside of me, ravishing my insides like a poison I accidentally ingested.

"I just want my mom," Piper cries from behind

me, and I hear the shuffle of movement, the scrap of clothing against clothing.

"Jane? Can you call Piper's mom?" Victoria, as always, begins shooting off orders in her strong French accent. But even with her attempt to be impassive and strong, I can hear the undercurrent of pain behind every word.

Oh god…

"I'll get Piper downstairs and into my car. El?" I reluctantly lift my head from the trash can to meet her gaze, her eyes shadowed with pain and sympathy. "Can you start packing up Piper's stuff? Just a few changes of clothes for now—"

"I just want to go home," Piper interrupts in a scream, twisting her face to bury it against Victoria's neck as she clings to her best friend desperately.

"I know, *ma chèrie*. I know," Victoria soothes, her words followed up by a string of French condolences I don't understand. Over Piper's head, she says to me, "Put Piper's stuff in my room, okay? I'll drop Piper off at home with Jane and then return here to grab her stuff." She sniffles, a single tear dripping down her cheek and betraying her anguish, before she clears her throat and steels her expression over. "Jane?"

"Coming." Jane hurries to wrap an arm around Piper's waist on the other side, and moving as one being, the three of them exit the dorm, allowing the door to shut silently behind them.

Leaving me alone.

So, so alone…

I don't immediately head toward Piper's room.

Instead, I enter my own bedroom and slam the door shut, twisting the lock on the off chance one of the guys will choose to pay me a visit despite my explicit order telling them not to.

Blair's dead.

Amanda's dead.

Patricia's dead.

And now…

Now I'm a part of the organization who killed them.

POP.

Paragons of Prosperity.

The Divine One.

Your fault. Your fault. Your fault.

Those two words are a drumline inside my head, an incessant pounding I can't escape. They explode inside of my skull like atomic bombs, absolutely obliterating everything in the process.

Boom. Boom. Boom.

I can't scream out loud—not with the fear that someone may hear me—but that doesn't stop me from grabbing my pillow off the bed, throwing my face inside of it, and screaming, screaming, screaming, the sound muted by the fabric.

But it's not enough.

Nothing will be enough.

With a roar, I swoop my hand over my desk, throwing the contents onto the floor. A music box I got as a present from Landon shatters with a deafening crash, and a grim smile carves up my lips.

Destruction. Pain.

I need more.

I grab at my ukulele and hit it against the wood of my dresser until the instrument is splintered and unusable, the strings sticking in all directions. I throw the useless instrument against the wall, watching as it slides to the floor with another crack. God, I love that crack, that shattering sound.

I kick and punch and destroy—all of my precious pillows I've been collecting since I was a child, all of my books, all of my instruments. They become nothing but feathers and ripped pages and broken wood and metal.

With another anguished cry, I throw my fist back and pound it into the wall. Pain blossoms across my knuckles, but it calls to some twisted part of me, a facet of my soul I can't name with words. I…I want to do it again.

So I do.

By the time I'm done, blood smears the tops of my knuckles, and the skin there is already shifting into a hideous shade of purple and gray. But god, that pain feels good. So damn good. It reminds me that I'm still breathing, still alive, when three other women are not.

My room has been utterly destroyed. If anyone were to see it, they would believe that a tornado has run through and ransacked the place, tipping dressers and beds over and destroying everything in its sight. Blood stains the wall—a macabre painting that somehow seems fitting, considering the demure atmosphere.

As quickly as the rage entered me, it dissipates like flakes of ash in the air. I drop to my knees in the rubble of the destruction and grab a blanket off the floor. It's torn in more than one place, but it'll do the job.

In the midst of a room in chaos—of a heart torn into five equal pieces—I throw the blanket over my tiny body, curl up on the wooden floor, and sleep.

Maybe once I wake up, I'll discover this has been nothing but a horrible, horrible nightmare.

Chapter 7

The weeks go by at a long and grueling pace. At least, I think it's been weeks since everything that went down with POP, but it might've been days. Months?

It's almost laughable how out of it I am—it almost reminds me of the months following my parents' death. I'd glided through life then too, never stopping to smell the metaphorical roses or to take a picture of the scenery.

It's easier this way, I've come to realize. If you allow yourself to slip into this perpetual daze, this unending cycle of wistful dreams and fantasies, then you can pretend that the real world doesn't exist, that there aren't monsters who take the form of humans. God, I almost wish actual monsters existed, with weaknesses of wooden stakes and silver crosses. I don't know how to defeat an army of human beasts, only fictional ones. And heaven only knows that true evil—insidious and unparalleled evil—comes from mankind.

A lot of times, that specific brand of evil is willfully ignorant, which makes it even more malicious. Take the Paragons of Prosperity, for example. They don't seem to believe that they're doing any harm. And if they *are* doing harm, their convoluted minds have twisted it into a form of necessary evil—this mentality that the good outweighs the bad. Self-preservation and self-interest outweigh everything else, creating an unintentional but just as sinister evil compared to those that walk into a room with evil plans.

In the weeks that have followed the Halloween Carnival, Piper has left the school. I still text her from time to time, but I can tell it pains her to be around us. We only remind her of Blair.

I miss her fiercely, but I'm grateful she's far, far away from this house of horrors.

I haven't spoken to the guys in just as long. Sometimes, I can feel their eyes on me, burning cattle brands that mar my skin. And though a part of me desperately wants to turn toward them, I resist. Whenever I see their faces, I think of the secrets they kept from me—the secrets that inevitably led to the death of three girls. I don't blame them anymore. I don't even think I'm mad at them.

I'm just…

Done.

That's the word I'm looking for.

I can't be friends with guys who kept such life-altering secrets from me under the guise of 'protecting me.' That excuse is bullshit, and we all know it. They still haven't confessed the truth about Zane's murder barn, but I'm not sure I'll even listen to them if they did. I just want nothing to do with them, this school, or POP.

But I can't escape.

I tried. Trust me, I tried. I went as far as to send my transcripts to an academy across the country. Less than an hour later, I received a note in my dorm embroiled with gold.

Don't even think about it.

Attached to the note was a picture of my brother, Fischer. And I knew then, without a shadow of doubt, that they'd hurt my brother, maybe even kill him, if I chose to leave.

Once you're a member of POP, there's no escaping.

I don't know what The Divine One expects of me—to join their ranks willingly? To accept their vision of the future? To believe in their fucked up religion? The mere thought is laughable.

What does he even want with me? Why is he so obsessed with making sure I'm a part of his little, fucked up club?

He makes me do things. Tests, if you will. Or trials.

I'll discover tiny slips of paper inside of my locker, in the front pocket of my backpack, on my desk in the morning, sometimes even in articles of clothing.

So far, the tasks haven't been anything too horrible or atrocious, but I find myself with more questions than answers as the days drag on.

Fail your next Calculus test.
Don't go into the cafeteria today.
Tell Rachel Blankly she's a skank.

Stupid, ridiculous, tedious, *childish* stuff that has nothing to do with Cassia or POP. I half wonder if The Divine One is testing me, wanting to see how far I'm willing to go in order to appease him, to keep my family safe. I picture him in the opulent room he brought me to before, drinking out of a tumbler and chuckling as he thinks about the hoops he's making me jump through like I'm some sort of show dog for his amusement.

I still remember the tears that manifested in Rachel's eyes when I called her a skank in a cold, dispassionate voice.

But I did it.

Just as I did every other mundane task he assigned me.

When I'm not ruining my life following The Divine One's orders or fumbling through classes—my grades dropping as steadily as my health, both mental and physical—I'm in the library or my room reading everything I can about the town, Melody, Cassia, and POP. So far, my search has proved to be futile, though I wasn't expecting much. There's a reason the Paragons of Prosperity have been a part of this town for more than a century, and it wasn't because they were careless. A group like this thrives on anonymity, making it impossible for me to gather any intel on the group or its members or even their strange religion.

The guys will follow me from room to room, though they'll always pretend that I'm not there—

granting me space, I presume, though I don't dare call them out on it. Sometimes, I'll find a granola bar or an apple inside of my backpack, as if one of them, probably Landon, is trying to remind me to eat. Other times, I'll find my homework assignments completed on my desk when I start to get overwhelmed by my class load.

I never accept their offerings, but a treacherous piece of my heart begins to pound like an army of giants stomping down a steep cliffside each and every time they attempt to prove to me that they care.

I'm lost in my thoughts when a hand grabs my shoulder, the touch painstakingly gentle, and spins me around to face him.

Beckett.

He looks exactly as I remember him…but nothing like I remember him.

His chocolate brown hair is tousled, something I've never seen before in my life. He's usually so careful about meticulously grooming it, allowing the curly strands to frame his arresting face. Just now, they tumble in front of his eyes in desperate need of a cut. His eyes are the same, though, an enticing combination of colors I can get lost in—one a dark brown, a few shades darker than his hair, and the other a vibrant green. Staring into his expressive gaze is the equivalent to traipsing through the forest, surrounded by keen pine needles and thick trunks.

Today, his academy uniform is covered in—god forbid—wrinkles. Even his undershirt is askew, the buttons improperly fastened to reveal a sliver of golden skin.

Violet crescent moons settle beneath his mismatched eyes as he gazes at me, lines of strain enveloping his handsome face.

"Beckett," I say softly, my heart breaking at seeing him so distraught.

"Ellie…" His voice is practically a moan of need as his gaze travels from my toes to my head. "You need to eat."

Out of everything I expect him to say…that isn't one of them.

I blink at him once, trying to tamper down the slightly hysterical laugh that threatens to bubble up.

In the hallway, students push past us in a rush to make it to their classes on time. It won't be long until the bell rings and the hallway clears out completely, leaving me alone with the arresting Brit.

I suddenly feel tired—so incredibly tired—and it's like my shoulders are unable to carry the weight of even my backpack. I just want to…

Heck, I don't even know anymore.

I want to do something, but what that something is remains just out of reach, flaky bits of debris that blow away in the wind and funnel up into the sky.

"You need to eat too," I tell Beckett numbly, noticing the way his cheeks seem to cave in on themselves.

A heavy knot takes up residence in my chest, crawling up my throat until I fear I'm going to choke on it at the knowledge that *I'm* the cause of his sunken appearance.

Beckett laughs humorlessly and reaches into his backpack, grabbing out two packets of fruit snacks.

"I'll eat mine, if you eat yours," he teases, waggling his eyebrows suggestively, that familiar, flirty light returning to his mismatched eyes.

I hesitate, staring intently at the proffered fruit snacks, before relenting with a sigh.

His multi-colored eyes seem to glow as I rip the package open, watching him do the same.

The bell rings overhead, but neither of us move from our spot in the middle of the hallway. He simply watches me with calculating eyes as I chew on a tiny blue gummy in the shape of a bus. Every time I put a gummy into my mouth, he does the same until our bags are empty.

When silence continues to stretch between us—as taught as guitar strings—Beckett blurts out, "I miss you."

"Beck…" A tiny collection of tears form in my eyes, but I blink to clear them away before he can see. I can tell I failed when he takes a step closer, his expression tender, and brushes at one of the traitorous little assholes wanting to drip down my cheek.

"You're one of my best friends, El," Beckett says in a soft voice, his eyes ensnaring my own. "And I know you're mad—"

"You don't know what I'm feeling right now, Beckett," I interrupt, trying to gather my courage before I can lose it completely. But I'm shaking, I'm shaking so hard, and speech feels impossible.

Beckett's eyes dim, the vibrancy turning dull and subdued. "I wanted to tell you the truth—"

"But you didn't," I say with a slow shake of my head. "None of you did. And then you had the nerve to lie to my face about your secrecy being for my own protection—"

"It was for your own protection." Beckett pauses, a contemplative expression flickering across his face, before he sighs heavily, his shoulders collapsing. "But…it wasn't *just* for your protection," he concedes. "We didn't want to lose you."

"Look…" I struggle to articulate the words ricocheting around in my brain, bouncing off the walls and settling on my tongue before dissipating into dust. "I don't think I'm mad anymore. I'm confused, yes, and hurt. But I can't… I can't do this anymore." My lower lip wobbles, and I squeeze my eyelids shut to hide the searing pain splayed across his face at my words. "I just… I can't."

"If you're trying to protect us…"

"I don't know what I'm doing!" I bite down on my lower lip hard enough to draw blood—it's something I've been doing a lot, I've noticed. Drawing blood. Relishing that sting of pain that reverberates through my body. It's addictive, that pain, and a heady sensation that's capable of eclipsing the fear and horror constantly plaguing my every thought. "But friends drift apart all the time—"

"Is that really what you thought we were?" Beckett's voice is incredulous. "Friends?" He steps closer, something I feel rather than see as his body heat permeates my system. Goosebumps ripple across my flesh, and all I want to do is open my eyes and fall into him. It'll be so easy…

"Maybe things will be different after Thanksgiving break," I tell him weakly.

His finger captures my bottom lip suddenly, ripping it away from my teeth. My eyes snap open to find his own narrowed on my abused, bloody flesh. Something dark crosses his handsome features as a frown tugs down his lips.

"You don't get to hurt yourself anymore," he tells me, an anger I've never heard before seeping into his honey tone. "I won't let you."

"Beckett—"

"No, Ellie." He shakes his head adamantly, his thumb brushing back and forth across my lip as a flare of heat burns a hole in my stomach. "We understand that you want—no, you *need* space. We'll give you that. And we'll continue giving you that space for as long as you need." He steps even closer, so close that the planes of his chest brush against my breasts and stomach, forcing me to tilt my head up to stare at him. My breath sharpens, parting from my lips in an exhale that resembles a moan, but he swallows the sound with his thumb. "But we're not letting you go. Do you understand that?"

"You can't just—" I begin.

"Is there a problem over here?" a voice booms, but Beckett doesn't move away from me, keeping his thumb on my lips and his eyes on mine.

It's me who shifts my gaze to peer over his broad shoulder, finding Mr. Moreau glaring at us as he stalks forward.

"No problem, mate," Beckett tells our AP European History teacher cheerfully. Finally, he releases my lips and spins around to face the professor.

"Ellie?" Mr. Moreau turns toward me with a

quirked brow. Am I mistaken, or is there jealousy in his gaze as he shifts it between me and Beckett?

I take an automatic step toward the professor—not wanting to get into trouble—but Beckett captures my hand and laces his fingers with my own. Mr. Moreau's eyes drop to where we touch, and his lips thin.

"No problem," I manage to choke out, subtly trying to free my hand from Beckett's. He simply tightens his grip.

"We were just getting to class," Beckett attempts to charm in his thick British accent. Before he can take a single step in the direction of our shared class, Mr. Moreau moves in front of him, his scowl deepening the lines on his face. It makes him appear older, harsher, angrier.

"Ellie." Though Mr. Moreau's words are addressed to me, he doesn't take his penetrating glare off Beckett. "Why don't you come back to my office and—"

"No bloody way," Beckett hisses, taking a step closer. He says something to Mr. Moreau, his voice too low for me to hear, and I swear our professor's face whitens. Stark terror floods his eyes before he carefully masks it.

"Get to class," Mr. Moreau says, stepping backward to dismiss us. He keeps his eyes on the ground, as if he finds his polished loafers particularly exciting. "Before I'm forced to give you detention."

"Perfect." Beckett flashes him a blindingly white smile before giving my hand a tug. "Come on, Ellie."

I allow him to lead me down the hall until we're

out of view of the teacher. Only then do I rip my hand free and spin around to stare at him, one of my brows touching my hairline.

"What the heck was that all about?" I demand, folding my arms over my chest.

His face tightens. "What do you mean?"

"What did you say to Mr. Moreau to get him to let us go like that?" I press.

"I…um…" He doesn't answer—something akin to shame flooding his face—and my anger explodes out of me like a dam rupturing. Maybe my anger has always been there, a constant presence that I've chosen to ignore, but that volcano of emotion has finally bubbled up like lava.

"Oh my god. Are you kidding me right now? More secrets?"

"I swear it's not like that," Beckett rushes to defend in desperation, his eyes frantic.

"You have got to be fucking kidding me!" I throw my hands up in the air and turn on my heel, prepared to stalk away from him, but his quiet voice reaches me.

"You swore."

"Huh?"

Those two words are confusing enough to have me pause in mid-step, though I don't turn around to face him.

"You didn't use to swear," Beckett says softly, his voice hitching. Why does it sound as if his heart is breaking?

But he has no right to have a broken heart—not when he's one of the causes of mine shattering into five irreparable pieces.

I don't speak at first. What can I possibly say? What words can I use to make him understand? My mind is a storm, and my body is the rubble that remains, a wasteland of destruction.

I settle on, "I also didn't use to be a murderer," before walking away.

And this time, I don't stop.

Chapter 8

I hate the motherfucking holidays. Always have and always will.

Some people associate Thanksgiving with family and friends, community and bliss, parties and camaraderie. Me? I think about the time I woke up to the smoke alarm beeping, the gray smoke itself thick and cloying, twisting around me like a spiral and infiltrating my airways. I raced down the stairs, my heart in my throat, to see my mother unconscious on the couch, a needle sticking out of her skinny arm.

That was the only Thanksgiving she was home for.

Even now, my phone burns a hole in my pocket when I think about the slew of angry text messages she has left me.

Dumb whore.
Fucking ass.
Cocksucker.

On and on her rampage goes, all because I refused to give her the few dollars I managed to collect over the past couple weeks. Apparently, robbing her only son blind and beating the shit out of him in an alley isn't enough to satiate her twisted needs. That's the thing about being an addict and junkie—you're always looking for your next fix, your next hookup, clinging eagerly to whatever high you can get, no matter how you get it or who you hurt in the process.

Maybe that's why I'm so goddamn addicted to Ellie—because addiction runs rampant through my blood.

An odd sense of loneliness bombards me as I tug my sweatshirt hood over my head, using its shading as coverage. It's cold today, a fine layer of snow canvasing the walkway, but I can't afford a winter coat. If one of the guys knew the truth, I have no doubt they would buy one for me, but I refuse to tell them. I don't need their goddamn pity. To be quite frank, I don't need *them*.

Besides, they're all away with their precious families, spending the holidays with people who love them. Landon and Dominic are with their doting parents, while Zane has traveled to Mexico to visit his grandparents. Even Beckett took a plane ride back to the UK for the weeklong break in order to see his mom and siblings again, though I know it's killing him to be away from Ellie for so long.

Either way, they all have a place to go, a family who wants to see them, and arms to fall into and hold them up.

Unlike me.

With nothing else to do, I find myself partaking in my favorite pastime activity—stalking Ellie. The heat of the building nearly suffocates me as I step through the glass doors.

It's twisted, God only knows how fucked up it truly is, but I won't rest until I know for sure that she's safe. After everything that went down with POP, we can't afford to leave her alone for even a second. She may hate us but that doesn't change what we feel for her.

She's our sun, our moon, our entire fucking world, and I'll protect her with every last breath my chest possesses.

A low growl slips from my lips at the unintentional way I transitioned into the plural proposition. She's not *ours*. She's *mine*. At least, I want her to be mine, but the truth is much more daunting and terrifying.

Wanting her as mine and actually making her mine are two completely different things. Right now, it's a dream I grasp desperately, praying it doesn't blow away in an unexpected gust of wind. Even I can admit that it's a futile dream, like wanting to pluck the stars from the sky and lasso the sun from the heavens, but it's the only one that keeps me going. It's the blood that pumps through my veins, the chemicals that make my brain light up like fireworks on the Fourth of July, the reason my damaged heart continues to beat. Believing in a future for us allows me to put one foot in front of the other, even when a tinny, mechanical voice in the back of my head screams at me to give up.

That voice, which sounds an awful lot like my

mother's, reminds me that I'm a failure. An unlovable, useless failure.

She'll never care about you.

She'll never love you.

She left you.

I press a fist against my forehead, as if I can somehow punch the words out of my brain, quiet their incessant babbling, but they remain there like goddamn toilet paper that won't quite flush.

What's even the point of dreams and wishes? Honestly, I don't understand them. It's not like you'll see me wishing on a goddamn star for my miserable life to end with a happily ever after. People like me, people doused in darkness and motivated by sin, don't have their wishes granted. Their dreams simply fade away, withering like paper in a fire, until there's nothing left but flaky ash that gets caught in the breeze.

But fuck, I want Ellie to love me more than I want to live in this world.

Currently, the object of my affection glances down at a slip of paper as she maneuvers the busy aisles of the grocery store. Almost the entire town has come to Frankie's Farmer's Mart to do some last minute Thanksgiving shopping, and my girl is no exception.

A tiny furrow erupts between her eyes as she glares at the empty shelf that is supposed to hold cranberry sauce—something she hates but her brother loves.

She murmurs something too low for me to hear, reaching into her coat pocket to grab out a pen and then brutally slashing 'cranberry sauce' off her list. I bite down a smile at her obvious irritation, loving more than anything the flash of color that dusts her cheeks whenever she's angry. But that smile nosedives like a plane missing a wing when she turns her profile to me and I see how skinny she has become in the few weeks since the Halloween carnival.

My heart thrashes, beating to a tune no one but she and I can hear, as I take in her sunken cheeks and pale complexion. I swear she has lost over thirty pounds in the span of weeks—and considering she didn't have those pounds to lose in the first place, I'm concerned for her overall health.

Fuck, why isn't she letting us protect her? Watch over her? Love her? Why does she think she needs to fight this battle alone?

Because you lied to her, Ryker, I tell myself in a snide voice. *You lied to her and broke her trust.*

But I did that to protect her! I protest adamantly, even as a little voice in the back of my head scoffs in response.

You just didn't want her to know the truth about what you are—a monster.

That single thought collapses in my stomach like a fifty pound rock being thrown over the edge of a cliff and landing in the water with a resounding thump, dislodging the tranquil water in the process.

Almost as if she can feel my eyes on her, Ellie's head snaps up and twists in my direction. Before she can see me, I stealthily move to the side and duck behind one of the shelves, pushing aside two boxes of cereal so I can still see her clearly. I watch as that tiny crease once again emerges between her brows before she shakes her head and focuses back on her list.

The need to go to her, love her, claim her is an incessantly nagging voice in the back of my head. It tunnels through all of my defenses until I'm stripped bare, naked and vulnerable and desperate for the woman he loves to notice him.

She's the air I breathe, and I need her to love me more than I need anything else. Me and only me. It may be selfish, but it's the truth.

I can't share her.

I won't.

But…

But I can't lose her either.

I'm pulled out of my morose thoughts by a tiny giggle carrying through the store, the musical sound as familiar to me as my own hand.

Ellie.

My eyes narrow when I see that she's no longer alone. No, *he's* with her, a charming grin on his face as she laughs at whatever asinine thing he's currently telling her.

Roy.

Fucking Roy.

The douchecanoe who had the nerve to take Ellie on a date…and then had the nerve to ask her out again. Most people in the school know to stay away from her. She's off limits to the male population. But Roy? He has more balls than I previously gave him credit for, because he's smiling at her without a single trace of fear in his expression.

Maybe word about her animosity toward us has spread around campus.

Maybe they know that she despises us.

Maybe all of the lowlifes of the school think they can finally worm their way into her perfect heart now that she has turned her back on us.

Fuck.

That.

Shit.

I inch a few steps closer, not even bothering to hide myself, as I listen to the asshole lay it on thick.

"I really like you, Ellie, and I think you can grow to like me too if you give me another chance." Roy offers her a timid smile, even as his eyes flare with unbridled heat as he carves a pathway down her body with his gaze.

My teeth bare instinctively, my hands balling into fists.

"You really want to try again?" Ellie asks softly, a note of disbelief in her tone as she quirks an eyebrow.

"I mean, yeah. You're…well…you're fucking awesome. Beautiful, smart, funny, kind. Only an idiot wouldn't want to be with you."

And only an idiot would dare to ask her out after he'd been warned explicitly not to speak to her again.

I'm still inching forward, so close I can inhale Ellie's flowery scent, and she stiffens abruptly, her back going ramrod straight as if she can suddenly sense my presence. Didn't I read somewhere that an animal always knows innately when a predator is at her back? That she can somehow sense the beast a second before he pounces?

I try to ignore the gritty taste of sand in my mouth as her eyes slide over her shoulder and land on me, her mouth thinning into a grim line. Abruptly, she turns back toward Roy, as if she's trying to pretend I don't exist.

As if goosebumps hadn't pebbled on her arms the second she knew I was near, belying the tension currently coursing through her body.

Her body still responds to me, even though her brain and heart rebels.

"I would love to go on another date with you, Roy," she tells him in a syrupy voice that has a growl slipping past my lips. A coldness settles in my heart, planted there by a snowstorm that refuses to relent, a whipping of wind and a flurry of showers. Even her smell tunneling into my throat can't dispel the anger that surges through me, especially when Roy's smile widens, turning smug and cocky.

"It's a date then," he tells her, his eyes flicking over to me. For a brief moment, stark terror splays itself across his face before he smooths his expression over, fear giving way to that smug superiority that has me grinding my teeth. He knows, just as well as I do, that I want to kill him. Does the dumb fuck have a death wish? "I'll text you."

"Yeah," Ellie agrees softly as Roy scurries away like his ass is on fire. His ass *will* be on fire if I have a say in things. It's not my favorite brand of torture, but it gets the job done. It's interesting how loud a man can scream when he has no skin left on his body—his vessel nothing but charred flesh with a broken, beaten soul inside of it.

Only when Roy's completely gone, disappearing into one of the nearby aisles, does Ellie turn toward me.

"Are you following me, Ryker?" she asks, not bothering to hide the suspicion in her voice.

My pulse skitters as I remain silent, simply staring at her through the hood of my sweatshirt. My throat itches, and I know that if I were to speak, the words would come out husky and scratchy, as if someone had taken sandpaper to my vocal cords.

My hands curl and then uncurl in and out of fists as I hold her stare, memorizing the shape of her face. Everything about Ellie is perfection—from the brown hair that cascades down her shoulders in loose curls, to the glasses perched on her nose, to the frown currently marring her pillowy pink lips.

Lips that I've imagined kissing more times than I care to admit.

Lips that Roy *might* kiss in her attempt to spite us.

A flare of insane jealousy erupts inside of me—kerosene added to a flame—as a tiny hiss escapes my parted lips.

"You can't go on a date with him," I manage to grit out, resisting the urge to grab her, drag her over my knee, and spank that perfect ass until it's red with my handprint.

"Why can't I, Ryker?" She gives me an indolent look, cocking her hip out to the side as if she has no fucks left to give. I can tell it's an act almost instantly—her eyes are guarded, her lips curled downward distrustfully.

Because you're mine.

Because I love you.

Because I can't stand the thought of anyone else

with you.

But those words don't leave my lips. For one, she'll think I'm crazy. For two, I have no right to feel such intense, possessive ownership over her when we're not together and we've never been together. For three…

Well…

I really, really don't want her to think I'm crazy.

She bites down on her lower lip for a moment, her hands absently rubbing at her arms, before she heaves out a breath and changes the subject.

"Do you have any plans for the holidays, Ryker?" she asks conversationally, her tone carefully neutral. That kills me more than the knowledge that she agreed to go on a date with motherfucking Roy. Usually, our conversations are natural—she's the only person I'm capable of having an honest-to-God conversation with. The words simply flow off my tongue, somehow able to form a semi-coherent and articulate sentence. And sometimes, we don't even need to speak to understand one another. The silence is laced with secrets and questions and answers and confessions that we'll never say out loud.

But that has changed.

Everything has changed.

I mutter something noncommittally, shoving my hands into my sweatshirt pocket and twisting the gray fabric.

"Well, okay then," she murmurs, dropping her gaze to the ground at my lack of response. I mentally curse myself for being such a dumbass when the words I've been looking for, the words I've been dying to say for months, pour out of me in a rush exhale.

"You don't want to go out with Roy," I say huskily.

She freezes, her body jolting as if she's been electrocuted, but doesn't peel her attention off the floor.

"Excuse me?"

"Because you know that there's more to our story than this." Desperation bleeds into my voice as I beg her to understand, to hear me, to allow my words to penetrate the preconceived notion she's constructed.

At first, I think my words have gotten through to her. And maybe they have, though it doesn't change the anger simmering beneath her impassive veneer. She told Beckett she wasn't angry at us anymore, but I don't think that's true. Maybe she believes it to be, but she's holding on to…something, something dark and tainted, that has ruined our relationship. Maybe that 'something' is fear that we'll lie to her again. Guilt over what happened to Blair and those other two women. Horror that we might've been able to prevent it if we consulted her about what we knew.

Either way, those toxic emotions have soured her opinion of us, and simple words—though true—won't be able to eradicate weeks of hurt and pain.

"I need to grab a turkey," she mumbles, spinning on her heel and hurrying in the opposite direction of me. She pauses, nearly running into the back of an old man attempting to grab a can of peas off the shelf, and whispers, "Ryker…"

I hold my breath, waiting to hear my verdict like a prisoner on death row, but she simply sighs and faces forward once more.

"Happy Thanksgiving, Ryker," she tells me softly, and then she's gliding away, taking with her the last shred of good in my life.

Chapter 9

Ellie

The pink-stained morning sky feels particularly taunting at this hour, its vibrant swatches of red and gold twisting together to create an illusion of something beautiful and ethereal. The sun barely crests the skeletal tree branches, and its light catches on the fluffy snow down below, causing it to shimmer like minute diamonds that wink in and out of existence.

It's a beautiful winter wonderland, but its beauty only serves to hide its sinister secrets. Does anyone think about the dead grass beneath the white blanket? The fallen, decaying leaves now frosted over? The animals struggling to find shelter as the world freezes around them?

Why do things have to die for change to be made? And why does the grim reaper have to be so beautiful?

Behind me, the Thanksgiving feast I spent hours painstakingly preparing sits cold and forgotten on the table. The smell of turkey permeates the air like a phantom as I drop my forehead against the cold glass and sigh.

The towering grandfather clock tick-tick-ticks away, the sound an accompaniment to the pounding of my heart. I can actually feel the beat of the clock, the music rushing through my veins. My fingers begin to tap against the windowsill automatically, adding to the beat, hearing music in its melancholic song—

"Shit. Shit. Shit. Ellie, I'm so damn sorry I'm late," a breathless voice exclaims from behind me. In the window, I can see Fischer's flustered face as he shrugs off his coat, dislodging inches of snow in the process from where it had fallen on his shoulders, and moves toward the table.

"Late would be an hour or two," I reply softly, lifting one finger to wipe at the condensation staining the glass. An eerie smiley face made out of sharp lines and jagged curves smirks back at me. "Not ten."

I finally turn to face my brother, my heart thrashing at the prospect of being face to face with him for the first time in months. For the first time since I started senior year at Grove Academy. For the first time since I was kidnapped by POP and taken into their ranks. For the first time since I…broke.

Can he see the changes in me?

Can he tell how broken I've become?

The part of me that has been screaming for weeks, clawing at the surface of water, desperate for air, wants to go to him. Have him wrap me in his arms. Hear him tell me that everything will be okay.

But I don't.

I simply stand there, my heart bleeding and my hands shaking.

I haven't seen my brother in *months,* and now that he's finally here, finally home for the holidays, I find I don't know what to say to him. The words get trapped in my throat the longer I stare at his painfully familiar—yet at the same time, unfamiliar—face.

The brother I once knew and loved would've never left me alone on Thanksgiving, reappearing at five in the morning on the following day.

I know that his job is important and that he's insanely busy, but I wish…

I don't even *know* what I wish for anymore.

Claws of depression sink into me, coiling around my heart like wispy shadows and shredding my very soul until it resembles confetti.

There are some days I wake up with a pep to my step and a perpetual smirk gracing my features. But there are other days when the darkness is too much for me to bear, too much for me to endure, and it smothers me, wrapping me up in its icy embrace. I go through the days like a machine, craving the comfort only my pillows and blankets can provide. Begging for an escape.

Right now, I want nothing more than to dive beneath the covers and sleep the rest of my life away, allowing my eyes to flutter open only when the pain has subsided. I can't… I can't *stand* these invisible, insidious monsters tearing apart my insides, crawling out of my stomach like some sort of gory horror movie creature and breaking apart every rib in the process.

The darkness hasn't been this bad since my

parents died, and I half wonder if I'll lose myself to it. To the darkness. To the pain. To the *agony* tearing at my seams.

"You can help yourself to the food. I'm not hungry anymore," I tell him, nodding toward the feast still spread out on the table. I sent the staff home early yesterday morning—on Thanksgiving—to enjoy the holidays with their own families, so it's just been me. Alone. In a house that feels too big and yet too suffocatingly small all at the same time.

My thoughts drift to Ryker when I saw him the other day at the grocery store.

Is he spending the holidays alone as well?

I know he has a mother, but he doesn't talk about her often. From what I gathered piecing together a few different conversations, they're estranged.

The thought of him experiencing the same crippling loneliness that I am has my throat closing up, but I sweep the debilitating emotion beneath the proverbial rug.

Thinking about Ryker—thinking about any of them, really—hurts too much. Their betrayal is still too raw, a wound that hasn't quite scabbed over. I don't know if it's still bleeding, but it's painful enough to leave me speechless.

"Ellie…" Fischer grabs for my wrist, his touch as light as a feather, and my eyes slide to his unwittingly.

He looks exactly as he did the last time I saw him—a proud and arresting man, with a shadow of a beard lining his jawline and brown hair that curls around his ears. His hazel eyes are more piercing than my own, capable of seeing straight past your defenses and whittling their way into your soul. A few scars distort the pale skin of his neck from an accident in college, but they're the only blemishes I can see.

Fischer has always represented everything I loved about this world—strength, loyalty, and compassion. He's been more than just a brother to me, but a parent as well, as unyielding and immovable as a mountain.

But even family can let you down.

"There was an issue at Eaglecrest that required my attention—" he begins as a heavy sigh leaves my lips.

Eaglecrest is the company my parents owned before they died. It's a shipping company, though what that entails remains a mystery to me. I have no intentions of taking over their business once I graduate high school, and Fischer knows this. He's already in talks with some buyers to take it off our hands—not that we need the money. Between our parents' life insurance, my brother's job as a state senator, and all of our family's investments, we're set for life.

"Let's just eat..." Fischer pleads, leading me toward the table and guiding me into my usual chair near the center. The two places at each head of the table—where my mom and dad used to sit—remain empty, as they always do when we eat together.

Fischer offers me a bright smile as he begins filling his plate with cold peas, corn, turkey, mash potatoes, and stuffing.

The hollowness in my chest, the hollowness that has been growing and expanding for over a month now until it's the size of a black hole, subsides a little bit, though it doesn't completely close over. It's almost as if that smile sewed together a few of the broken pieces inside of me.

Of course, that stitch is easily able to unravel when I think about the five guys who—

"Delicious!" Fischer's enthusiastic voice drags my attention back in his direction, where he has a spoonful of stuffing inside his mouth.

I raise an eyebrow dubiously. "It's cold. And hours old. And—"

"Delicious," he interrupts, a little bit of food drizzling down his chin.

I snort before I can help myself, and just like before, a little more of the darkness percolating in my soul dissipates. I'm with family, with someone who loves me unconditionally, and The Divine One can't get me here. He *won't*.

"This is who our town elected as state senator?" I cock an eyebrow as he feigns hurt, his mouth still full of half-chewed food.

"Hey. I won that election fair and square, meanie." He flicks a cold pea at my face, but I duck to the side before it can make contact with my nose. "And maybe I'll even be a United States senator…" He trails off, allowing the words to settle prominently in the air, stretching between us like a wire, as I gape at him.

"You don't mean…?"

"They think I have a good chance of winning," he tells me, an enigmatic light entering his hazel eyes as he leans across the table. "And by then, you'll be out of high school and an adult, and—"

"You'll feel comfortable leaving me," I finish for him, a heavy rock thumping in my stomach, my good mood from seconds before evaporating. I suddenly feel sick, and I'm immensely grateful I chose not to take a bite of the cold food. I bring a hand to my chest instinctively, as if that one gesture will somehow keep the contents of my stomach *inside* of my stomach.

Fischer's smile tightens and twists, turning into a severe frown at odds with the joy I saw only moments ago. A stab of guilt hits me at the thought that *I* put that pain in his expression. Me.

All you do is hurt people, Ellie. That's all you're good for.

"I'll never leave you, El," he tells me softly, reaching across the table to take my hand in his. His thumb lazily rubs back and forth over the top of my still slightly bruised knuckles as he holds my stare, once again ensnaring me in that intense, penetrating gaze of his. "You're my baby sister. If you feel uncomfortable with me running for office—"

"No." I shake my head adamantly, the keen blade of hope for a better future dulling the sharp edges of apprehension and the pain I feel over the prospect of losing my brother. He deserves this. He deserves the world, if I'm being honest. I refuse to hold him back from his potential. "This is your dream. I just…"

"You miss Mom and Dad, and you're afraid of people abandoning you," Fischer finishes, somehow able to articulately speak the words clunking around in my brain. I'm not even sure I would've come to the same conclusion if he hadn't spelled it out for me. But now that he said it…

It feels as if my heart is too small, too tattered, to hold any emotion that isn't tainted by malice and anger. Bitterness stomps down on my already beaten form.

How is it fair that my parents died, leaving us as orphans?

How is it fair that Fischer was forced to uproot his entire life to look after his kid sister?

How is it fair that The Divine One lives while my family's dead? While Blair's dead?

How is it *fucking* fair?

"I can see the shadows in your eyes," Fischer pipes in unexpectedly, his own gaze lowered beneath heavy lashes.

His innocent words pour acid in my stomach, and I squirm.

"I'm just tired," I tell him flippantly, a chill racing up my back.

Does he know?

Does he know about POP and The Divine One?

I dismiss that theory almost immediately but not because I believe it to be untrue.

If there were anyone in this town who would know the truth, it would be Fischer.

But if he knew and didn't tell me…

If he were a part of it…

I would never recover.

Still, I can't ignore the kernel of suspicion, of distrust, that finds a home inside of my chest. Almost immediately, that emotion is swept away in a tidal wave of bitterness and anger over the fact that life has been so goddamn cruel to make me suspicious of my own brother.

Is this a look into my future?

Distrusting everyone I come in contact with, wondering who has a black robe and white mask at home hidden in their closet? Who has the elusive red robe?

Fischer cocks his head to the side, his smile sad, before he graciously changes the subject.

"You're right. This food sucks. How about we order a pizza or something instead?"

I blow out a breath, relief exploding inside of me, and offer him a timid smile. "I really am tired though…"

"You haven't forgotten our Thanksgiving tradition, have you?" He places a mocking hand over his chest, aghast.

Once again, I raise my eyebrows dubiously. "Now? It's technically not even Thanksgiving anymore."

Fischer flashes me a wicked grin as he stands from the table, moves toward the hallway, and returns with a haphazardly wrapped present. He sets it on the table in front of me, and it doesn't take a genius to know that there'll be a pillow beneath the bright pink wrapping paper.

It's been our tradition for as long as I can remember—Fischer will give me one Christmas present to be opened after Thanksgiving dinner. Usually, that present is a pillow Fischer has collected throughout his travels.

A single tear slides down my cheek when I think about the dozens and dozens of pillows I destroyed back in my dorm room—just another thing I'll never get back. Just another thing I destroyed. Pain bombards me, hammering at my skull, but I accept the present with shaky hands and rip off the paper.

Another tear joins the first when I unveil the heart-shaped pillow with fluffy purple trimming splattering the sides.

"I… It's amazing. Thank you, Fischer." My voice breaks before I can stop it, because suddenly, it's too much. Everything is too much.

The pain.

The fear.

The guilt.

All of these emotions have been eating me alive for weeks, destroying my skin and soul like an army of ravenous maggots, but they explode out of me now.

Fischer doesn't demand an explanation as he moves around the table and wraps an arm around my shoulder, guiding my face into his chest. My hands curl into his dress shirt as I twist the material, tugging at it as if I'm afraid letting go will mean losing the man the shirt belongs to.

"What do you need, El?" he whispers, his voice just as broken as mine had been. His body trembles as he soothingly rubs a hand up and down my spine. "Tell me what you need."

For the pain to go away.

For the guilt to assuage.

But I don't say any of that, mainly because I know he can't help me with those issues. They're mine and mine alone, a pain that has unfurled in my chest like a sleeping tulip planted in the bed of a riverbank and now stretching toward the sun. There are some truths that must remain whispers in the wind, coveted secrets that you latch on to with all your might and never let go.

I don't know what I'm going to say until I say it, until the words leave my mouth on a breathy exhale. Until Fischer's arms tighten imperceptibly around me and his body stiffens.

"I want to take a self-defense class and learn to fight. I want…no, I *need* to be able to defend myself."

He doesn't ask me what happened, though I know his mind is conjuring up the worst possible scenarios. I want to put his mind at ease, but I don't know what to say. Offering an explanation, even a fake one, will only lead to questions, and I'm not strong enough to answer them.

Murder flares in his brown-green eyes when he finally pulls away, but he manages a sage nod.

"All right. Whatever you need to dispel the shadows in your eyes, Ellie."

I don't know if it'll help, but…

But it feels like a step in the right direction.

Chapter 10

Beckett

My teeth rattle as pain threatens to rip me apart.

Dad's cruel, domineering face overtakes my vision as he sneers at me, a tiny bit of spit forming at the corner of his mouth. He licks it away almost absently, that penetrating glare of his never leaving my face.

I remember a time not that long ago when that glare would've made me tremble and cower, made me throw my hands up into the air instinctively to shield my face. Now, I simply stare at him with my lips set into a grim line. Cold. Unyielding.

Prepared.

One of his hands holds my journal while the other balls into a tight fist. His gaze flickers to one of the pages that hangs open, revealing a sketch of a gorgeous dress with an off-the-shoulder neckline and flowing skirt, before leveling back on me.

"I didn't know I raised my son to be a goddamn fag," he hisses, his lips curling away from his teeth in revulsion. A second later, his fist connects with the side of my face, forcing me to the ground.

I take the abuse without a single cry of pain, though I'm sure my eyes emanate danger and vengeance. All I can think about is wrapping my hands around his thick throat and squeezing until the life bleeds from his eyes. Maybe once he's dead, my mom can go a day without having to douse her face in makeup to hide the myriad of black and blue bruises mottling her pasty complexion.

He needs to suffer, needs to pay, for all the pain he has caused our family.

Years ago, I would've been horrified by the direction of my thoughts, but my worldview has changed, becoming warped with shadows and darkness.

I no longer fear death and its implications.

Why should it scare me, when I've become the master of it?

I draw my attention back to my father, but he's no longer in front of me. Instead, he's across the room, his hands wrapped around someone else's throat, holding her against the wall.

"Mom!" I lurch forward, fear strangling my airways, but it isn't my mother dangling helplessly in my father's hold.

It's Ellie.

The world holds its breath as my rage teeters toward absolute insanity. It resembles a bulbous, hovering storm, seconds from unleashing its torrent on the world below.

No one is allowed to hurt Ellie.

No one.

The body that has once resembled my father's warps and distorts, shaggy brown hair giving way to a garnet red hood. His cruel face—with that perpetual scowl and malice-filled eyes—turns into a gold mask that obscures all of his features from view.

The Divine One.

"Ellie!" I roar, running forward as fast as I can, but it feels as if I'm on a treadmill, as if every step forward I take actually propels me backward. My heart thrashes in my chest, crawling up my throat, as I scream her name again and again.

I feel more like a beast than a man at that moment. The roaring fire in my veins reduces me to ash, narrowing my vision until Ellie's face is all I can see. I'm a hellion plucked from the fiery depths below with the sole purpose of protecting this waif of a girl with every fiber of my unworthy being.

The Divine One slowly twists his head to stare at me, but he's no longer wearing the mask. Instead, I find myself peering into mismatched brown and green eyes, a cunning smile splitting across the man's face.

My face.

With my hands wrapped around Ellie's throat, holding her suspended against the wall.

She claws at my wrists desperately, her skin turning an unnatural shade of blue, but the stranger wearing my face doesn't release her. He simply smiles at me, as if he's reveling in my pain and misery. The slash of red on his face where his lips are supposed to be resembles blood.

I dream of the grim reaper, and the face it wears is my own.

I wake with a gasp, nearly flinging my arm into the face of the woman sitting in the seat beside me. It takes me a moment to get my erratic heartbeat under control as my pulse thrashes, my hands turning damp with sweat.

Blinking the remnants of sleep from my eyes—and trying desperately to scrape away the mold infesting my brain from that nightmare—I glance out the window of the airplane. We seemed to have started our descent, the buildings and cars nothing but dust mites down below. Insignificant. Forgettable. But still, somehow, noticeable. I take comfort in the cerulean sky dotted with fluffy white clouds as I tamp down my mounting panic and horror.

What the bloody hell is wrong with me?

I bring my thumb to my mouth and nibble on the tip as my thoughts race back to my dream.

God, I can still see the terror in Ellie's eyes as that *monster* held her against the wall, choking the life out of her. I can still hear that horrible gurgling sound she made as she clawed at my hands.

A shiver works its way through my body before I can stop it.

Obviously, I understand the first part of the dream. My trip home had been…eventful, to put it mildly. Dad had been a bloody wanker—no surprise—

and felt the need to assert his superiority over someone he deems as *lesser*. When the abuse first started, years and years ago, I tried to plead with my father that I wasn't gay, that I just liked designing and drawing, but those pleas fell on deaf ears. Now, I don't even bother to defend myself, refusing to give the sadistic asshole the satisfaction of me begging for mercy. What's the point of feeding the fire of a homophobic bigot?

I scrub a hand through my brown hair—slightly longer than I usually wear it—before thinking about the second half of my dream.

The Divine One choking Ellie.

And then…me. Choking Ellie. Killing her.

An anvil pounds against my brain, and my lids feel like they're made of concrete. A splitting headache unfurls behind my eyes, and I absently rub at the skin with the palm of my hand in a futile attempt to alleviate some of the tension.

I know in my heart that I'd never hurt Ellie, so what did my dream mean? Is it simply guilt that I already hurt her mentally? Fear that my secrets will be the cause of her death?

That thought has a cold, persistent chill spreading through my body like a winter storm, and another shiver works its way through me.

If anything happens to Ellie…

You can't think like that, Beckett. You can't.

The rest of the flight is uneventful. Only an hour later, I find myself standing outside the airport with my luggage on the ground beside me and a duffel bag slung over my shoulder.

I glance helplessly at the phone, at Ellie's contact

name, as a ball of lead takes root in my stomach. Before everything went down with POP, she agreed to pick me up from the airport the day before Thanksgiving break ended. Obviously she has no intentions of doing that anymore, and a part of me understands why, but that knowledge doesn't dampen the unbridled pain that cuts through me like a javelin.

I debate calling the guys and asking for a ride, but I haven't talked to any of them since break started. We've been… Well…

To say our relationship is tumultuous is an understatement. We've barely talked to each other since that horrible night less than a month ago. Landon and Dominic have remained inseparable, but the rest of us have been shoved to the outskirts. Ryker has withdrawn from us all, building up walls around his heart and taking to the shadows for comfort. I texted him ten times over the break, but he didn't respond to a single one. And Zane…

I heave out a breath as I think about Zane the last time I saw him, when the jackass decided to 'prank' me by cutting the brakes of his own damn car. I'd asked him to drive me to the airport, and he thought it would be hilarious to almost kill us both.

He's losing his ever-loving shit, and there's nothing any of us can do about it.

I vow to myself that I'll start fixing our shredded bonds, stitching back together a friendship that's been years in the making, one forged from blood kand tears. These men are my brothers, my best friends, and the sooner they get that through their thick skulls, the happier we all will be. Maybe I can convince Zane to kidnap them with me so we can create matching friendship bracelets out of the skin of our enemies and then plan a murder together. Murder always makes them happy.

I scrub a hand across my mouth as I think.

Step one—get all five of us talking again.

Step two—once we're a coherent machine, we can work to win our girl back.

Step three—Get Ellie back.

Though maybe step one will work better if we can accomplish step three first…

I still remember the day I *officially* joined their group, the day my life changed irrevocably.

The day I killed someone.

The charcoal pencil moved rapidly over the journal page as I shaded in her eyes. The dark black color failed to encapsulate the vibrant blue-gray, but it was the best I could do under the circumstances. I nibbled on my lower lip, dragging it between my teeth, as I moved onto her flowing hair next.

Lately, all of my drawings had featured the tiny girl with guileless blue eyes, a cute button nose, and plush, kissable lips. But every picture I created felt…lacking.

How could I possibly draw eyes that smiled enigmatically? Lips that parted with laughter? Hair that glistened in the sun?

Everything I drew paled in comparison to the real thing.

I could admit that I've had a few crushes over the years, but that word seemed too tame, too insignificant, for what I felt for Ellie. I'd only been here three months, and already, she dominated every single thought I had. What I felt for her was utterly foreign and extremely terrifying. It was infinite yet infinitesimal, a loop that never ended. I could try to run from it, run from her, but within minutes, I'd end up exactly where I started.

Her face was indelibly tattooed on my eyelids, her voice ringing in my ears long after she'd left a room.

Even as I sat in the library on the opposite side of campus from her, I could feel her like a blade in my heart, twisting and tightening with each consecutive second.

But I couldn't have her.

My new friends wouldn't allow that.

That thought stabbed in my brain like a flaming blade as I tightened my grip on the pencil.

I may have become friends with Landon and his crew, but that didn't mean I was in. Truly in. There was still stuff they didn't involve me in, secrets they kept from me, events they didn't allow me to join in on. I tried to tell myself it didn't matter, that I didn't even really want to be at this school, but that was a bloody lie.

It mattered.

It mattered a fucking lot.

I wanted to join their group more than I wanted to goddamn breathe. If I were initiated into their merry little gang, then maybe they'd allow me to be with Ellie. To ask her out.

I almost snorted at how ridiculous that sounded.

No, they would never allow me to take her on a

date, and not just because they were all desperately and helplessly in love with her.

I blew out a heavy breath before slamming my notebook shut. It wasn't as if I could concentrate on my work a second longer anyway. My mind was too consumed by them. *By Mania and Ellie.*

"You're fucking sick," a voice jested on the other side of the bookshelf. Despite his negative words, I could hear the distinct lilt of amusement lacing his tone.

"That little tease has been leading me on for too damn long." The second voice was quieter than the first, almost as if he was making sure that their words remained between the two of them.

That piqued my interest.

What could they be talking about?

I'd be the first to admit that I thrived on gossip. At my old school, it was the only thing that kept me alive.

Did you hear? At lunch today, Francis Willis is going to beat the shit out of that Beckett freak.

Thanks, no thanks.

I always considered gossip a warning, a heads up, a way to get the fuck out of dodge, so to speak.

"You're not going to get away with this," the first man insisted, and I could've been mistaken, but I thought he almost sounded fearful. Hesitant, maybe?

My fingers tapped silently against the wooden table as I held my breath. If these fuckers were planning to do something, something malicious, then it was my job to report them.

Or stop them myself.

"She's always in the music room at this time of night," the second guy exclaimed with a laugh.

Music room?

Something dark and caustic filled my veins as those words dug into my neck like a garrote.

Was Ellie still in the music room? That was where I last saw her, a half hour earlier.

My rage built inside of me, the feeling reminiscent of pressing a flame to dry kindling. It felt as if my body had been doused in gasoline, and that tiny fire had turned into an inferno.

"Just keep watch," the dude hissed, their voices fading as they stepped away. "Make sure those fuckers don't see."

"Tyler..." the first man pleaded.

"Let's see how much the little princess likes it when I push up her skirt and ram my cock into her tight, little pussy."

The two of them laughed, their voices finally retreating as they exited the library, and for a long moment, I couldn't move. My hands felt frozen where they gripped the table, my legs numb.

And then anger shriveled my lungs until what little air they'd been able to hold left. The rage...

It was like nothing I'd ever felt before. I thought I felt true anger when I saw those random boys pick on Ellie and pull up her skirt a few months ago, but that paled in comparison to what roared through me now.

Because I knew those two guys were on their way to the music room, to Ellie, and were going to do something so unspeakable, I couldn't even think it without anger curling through my veins.

I left my backpack and journal behind and raced out of the library. I didn't stop running until the silhouettes of the two assholes came into view, slinking in the shadows of the main academic building.

"Maybe I'll let you have a turn with her," Tyler joked to his friend.

"I don't know if Ellie's really my type..." the second guy mused contemplatively. And then he fucking laughed. "But I'll never say no to some free pussy."

If there was any doubt that they were talking about my girl, it dissipated with their words.

Nobody was allowed to hurt Ellie. Fucking nobody.

Panic warred with fear inside my chest as I debated what to do. I could call the police, but there was no guarantee that they'd get here on time. Same with security and the headmaster. It was after hours, so I doubted there'd be any teachers around.

My stomach churned madly as the boys moved toward the front entrance of the main academic building, and I knew I was out of time. I couldn't let them hurt Ellie.

I raced across the lawn on silent feet, only stopping when I was directly behind the boys. My hand came up over Tyler's mouth as I pulled him kicking and screaming around the side of the building.

He was big...but I was bigger. Maybe not physically, but right then, it felt like I could move fucking mountains. My determination and anger gave me a strength I didn't know I possessed.

It took his companion a few seconds to realize

what was happening, but when he saw the two of us, he charged at me, his head lowered like a battering ram.

I cursed, releasing Tyler and jumping to the side as the asshole lunged at me. Tyler took my lapse of concentration to aim a punch at my stomach.

"You're fucking dead, asshole!" Tyler bellowed, spit flying from his mouth. "Cody, grab his arms."

The second man, Cody, apparently, reached for my wrists, but I jumped away before he could grab ahold of me.

Fuck!

Tyler roared with rage and charged at me again, but this time, I was ready for the fucker. He was horribly predictable—using his sheer size to bring me down instead of relying on agility or even his damn brain.

I stealthily stepped to the side and grabbed a fistful of his hair, slamming his face against the wall.

Cody threw himself at me, but I strategically released a groaning Tyler and threw a fist at Cody's face a split second before his body would've connected with mine. Before Cody could get his bearings, I focused my attention on Tyler and pounded his face against the brick wall a second time. Blood splattered, staining the brown in bright red barely visible in the moonlight, and it was fucking beautiful.

"Get the fuck out of here," I whispered, pressing my lips against Tyler's ear so he could hear how serious I was. "And don't you dare even think to look at Ellie again."

Tyler froze beneath me, and I heard Cody bark out a laugh where he attempted to straighten his bloody, broken nose.

"Is that what this is about? That little bitch?" Tyler snorted as rage darkened the edges of my vision like fire charring old paper. "Look, I'll let you have a turn with her if you want to—"

I didn't think.

Just reacted.

My hands wrapped around Tyler's neck, and I twisted it sharply to the side. His body fell to the ground, his head bent at an unnatural angle as his eyes stared sightlessly at the moon.

Motherfucker.

I got blood *on my favorite sweater.*

I glared at the offending stain as Cody began to curse. "Shit. Shit. Shit. What did you do? What did you do, you fucking psychopath?"

Oh…shit.

Rage coiled inside of me like a hungry beast, and my head snapped up, my eyes locking with Cody's. Fear distorted his features, and a twisted part of me reveled in it. He wanted to hurt Ellie. Rape her. And now, he was going to pay.

Cody turned on his heel and broke into a run, but I was faster. He struggled, attempting to buck me off, but I held on as tight as I could. If he ran, if he got help, then I'd go to prison. I'd be forced to leave this school, leave Ellie, all because I took out the fucking trash.

I placed my hand on Cody's mouth as he screamed, attempting to break free, and our bodies fell to the ground. We tussled in the wet grass, but fear made Cody's movements sloppy and weak. Soon, I found myself on top of him, my hands around his throat as I squeezed, squeezed, squeezed...

I tried to muster up an ounce of guilt, a sliver of remorse, but all I felt was relief. *These were bad, bad men, and I had a feeling that Ellie wasn't the first girl they targeted and probably wouldn't have been their last. People like them were sick. So fucking sick.*

Unbidden, my mind drifted to my father before I shoved the errant thought aside.

My hands were still around Cody's throat even though he had stopped moving, even though his eyes were wide and vacant, even though his face was an unnatural shade of white, his lips slightly parted on an exhale he couldn't release.

My fingers, still smudged with charcoal, itched with the need to draw him just like this. Dead. Scared. It was disturbingly beautiful.

But then the realization of what I did slammed into me like a wrecking ball, and I felt light-headed.

I killed him.

I'd just killed two men.

Oh god.

My life was over.

Panic burned away the rage as I stumbled to my feet, glancing desperately from body to body. What did I do? What could I do? Turn myself in? Hide the bodies?

Oh god.

My stomach spasmed, trying desperately to empty itself onto the floor, as I dug my phone out of my back pocket. I could feel my fingers shaking as they darted across the screen, dialing a number that I had memorized.

These men didn't know me that well—and for all I knew, they'd turn me in—but I was out of options. I needed my friends, my brothers.

It might've been the stupidest decision I'd ever made, but it was the only card left in the deck. I was out of options.

"Yes?" Landon's curt voice greeted me on the other end of the line as I shakily ran a hand through my tousled hair. My attention snagged on that damn blood stain on my sweater, and for some reason, that bothered me more than anything else that had happened tonight. Certainly more than the dead bodies on the ground.

I'm a sick, sick man.

"Landon." My voice was hoarse. Weak. Raspy. "I fucked up."

He was instantly on alert, and I could almost picture his molten silver eyes drilling a hole in my head. "What happened?" he demanded.

"I was in the library, and these two men...oh god...the things they were saying...the things they were going to do..."

"Beckett, breathe!" Landon growled, and I found myself obeying his demand instantly, inhaling deeply and exhaling immediately afterward. The acid in my stomach continued to sluice around as I worked to modulate my breathing.

"They were going to rape Ellie," I whispered, and the silence that descended was almost stifling. Every hair on the back of my neck spiked up.

"Were?" Landon growled, picking up on the past-tense, and I could hear the sound of him moving—

no doubt to check on Ellie.

"I...I killed them," I whispered, knowing it was fucked up. Knowing that he'd hate me. Knowing that I was going to spend the rest of my life behind bars.

This time, Landon's silence only lasted half a beat.

"Where the fuck are you?"

"Behind the academic building." My hands shook.

"Stay right the fuck there. We'll be there in three."

He hung up before I could respond.

I didn't know what I expected—for him to call the cops, for him to restrain me himself—but that wasn't what happened.

I learned how to dismember and destroy my first body that day.

Mania may had been born when I first arrived at school and joined their friend group, but it fucking flourished when the other four discovered I was just as sick and sadistic as them.

We were murderers, thieves, and liars...

But we were also hers.

I absently ponder how my thoughts have changed since Ellie sent us away all those weeks ago. Before Halloween, a tiny part of me secretly wanted Ellie to choose me and *only* me. I didn't want to share her with the other guys, despite knowing how they felt about her. I wanted her as my girlfriend, my confidante, my world. I'd hoped that the guys would move on once they saw how happy we were together.

But now, that has changed. I no longer covet

Ellie as only my own. Maybe I've always known that she doesn't belong to just one man. Hell, she doesn't belong to *any* man. *We* belong to *her*—and once I made that distinction in my head, the rest of the puzzle pieces fell into place.

A girl like her deserves to be worshiped and revered, and the best way to do that is to give her a goddamn harem.

Now comes the issue of convincing the others of that as well…

We all know how one another feels about her, but I don't think any of us—except for maybe Landon—planned ahead. I think we've all secretly assumed that she would choose one of us, and we were all secure in the knowledge that the one she would pick would be ourselves. But I know that will never work. The others are too in love with her, too obsessed with her, to allow any one man to have her to himself. And Ellie would never be able to choose only one of us, knowing how we felt about her. I see the way she is with Landon and Dominic, with Ryker, with Zane. She needs them just as fiercely as we need her, though I doubt she'll admit that even to herself, especially now.

Which means the only solution is for her to date all of us. At the same time.

I suspect Landon has come to the same conclusion as well, though I haven't asked him about it yet. What can I even say?

Hey, so, you know Ellie, right? The girl who hates us? The girl who sent us away? The girl we're all desperately in love with? Yeah, well, I think the only way we can all be happy is if we convince her to date all of us at the same time. Do you agree? We can work on a timeshare or a schedule. You can have her every Tuesday, and I'll take every Wednesday. Fridays will be a free-for-all.

He would probably deck me across the face.

And then I have to think about how Ellie would react to such an absurd idea. Would she be horrified? Aroused? Happy? Does she even think about us that way?

Don't even get me started on Ryker and his possessive, bullshit ways…

Ugh. So much to do in so little time.

First thing's first—I need to find a ride back to campus and reassemble the super squad. AKA, Mania. And before *that*, I need to change my clothes, because the sweater I'm wearing is covered in wrinkles from the plane and there's a tiny coffee stain in the upper right corner that refuses to come out.

I'm not being overdramatic when I say I'd rather sit on hot coals than wear something off the rack. And if that rack is in an airport? I shudder just thinking about it. I suppose a coffee-stained, wrinkly sweater is better than one displaying a huge airplane with the words 'There's no place like home…unless you're traveling.'

Okay, step one—get home.

Step two—change my clothes.

Step three—call the guys.

Maybe I can call a taxi now and—

Even as the thought forms, a black car pulls to a stop in front of me and the backseat window slides down.

My thoughts turn jammed, broken, repeating noncommittal words over and over again as I gape at the person staring back at me.

Ellie looks radiant this morning, her hair curled into perfect ringlets that cascade down her back like silk. Her glasses slide down her button nose, but she uses her pointer finger to push them back into place. She wears a cream-colored sweater that molds to her slim figure, and form-fitting blue jeans.

My heart trips over itself as I stand there, gaping like an imbecile.

Bloody hell, Beckett, say something!

"I…I didn't think you would come," I manage to stutter out, mentally cursing myself for having the articulation of a five-year-old boy. And to make it worse, I add, "Not that I'm against you coming. I like it when you come. You can come *all* the time if you want to. I can even help you come, if that's what you want. I mean, I'm good at giving rides. Errr…"

Smooth, Beck. Real smooth.

Ellie blows out a breath, disrupting a strand of wavy hair that has fallen into her face, and offers me a tiny smile, one that doesn't reach her eyes. "I promised, didn't I?"

My eyes travel over her, documenting and cataloging every minute change in her expression, each twitch of her jaw and slant of her lips.

God, I hate the sadness in her gaze.

My breath catches in my throat, my heartbeat thundering in a strange tango of anger and sorrow. Anger at The Divine One for putting that emotion in her eyes. Sorrow that I haven't been able to help her, to banish the shadows that haunt her.

Her eyes lift to mine, darkening with turmoil, before she smooths her expression over, adopting a feigned frown of indifference.

"Put your luggage in the trunk, please."

I do as she instructs before settling into the plush leather seat beside her. The driver—a man I've never met before—glances in the rearview mirror to ensure we're okay before slowly lifting the divider separating us from him. Soon, it's just the two of us.

I desperately want to break the silence, but I don't know what to say. Ellie almost reminds me of Ryker right now. Ryker is…fragile. Delicate. Like a butterfly. Like a stabby, damaged butterfly who hates himself.

Oh god. Does Ellie hate herself?

Does everyone hate themselves?

How do I get people to stop hating themselves?!

Ellie keeps her eyes locked on the window as we leave the airport, merging onto the highway in the direction of town. I survey her profile out of the corner of my eye, watching a muscle in her jaw feather, lines of strain sketching down her cheeks, poison spewing from her eyes behind those thick glasses.

She doesn't speak, and I don't dare to either. The silence is uncomfortable, an infestation of centipedes that crawl across my skin, but if Ellie feels the same way, she doesn't show it. She just continues glancing out the window, her expression impassive.

Finally, I can't take the silence anymore— deafening in its simplicity—and blurt out, "Did you have a good break?"

Dumbass questions for the win.

I mentally facepalm myself, especially when Ellie stiffens, only her eyes shifting to rest on my face before focusing once more out the window.

"It was…what I expected," she settles on at last, a note of despondency hitching the final word. God, even when she speaks, her voice sounds like music. She shifts on the seat to face me fully, a curl bouncing beside her cheek that she absently brushes away. I can't help but picture her in my most recent design— the dress my dad ripped up and threw away back at home. She would look fucking gorgeous in it, the material clutching at her chest before swooping outward— "How about you?"

Err.

What was the question again?

"Um…it was good," I manage to say, though I have no idea what we were even talking about. Our breaks? That sounds right.

She blinks, her tiny pink tongue snaking out to lick her upper lip, before she nods once and says, "That's good."

That's good?

That's good?!?

I try to adopt my usual flirty smile, but it feels strange on my lips, as if the muscles can't quite remember how to curve themselves upward.

"You really should visit, love," I begin, the nickname flowing from my lips before I can stop it. I wince but hurry on before she can comment. "You'd love it there. Ohh. I would definitely have to show you this cute boutique I found! It's a hidden gem. The designs…" I touch my fingers to my thumb and then bring my hand to my lips, blowing out a kiss. "Perfect. Some of the best stitching I've ever seen."

Ellie's smile begins to grow the longer I speak, a tiny twinkle manifesting in her eyes behind her glasses. It's the first genuine smile I've seen since I got into the car, and my heart gives a painful thump.

"That sounds amazing, Beck."

I practically preen under her praise like a damn peacock trying to show off my feathers.

Hoping to press my luck, I give her a salacious once-over, taking a great deal of joy in the blush that unfurls in her cheeks. It's only when I meet her gaze do I say, "You look beautiful today, Ellie."

I hold my breath, waiting for her response to my candid statement. Normally, I have more…*class* when it comes to her. Normally, I can hide my feelings behind a cocky grin and sugary words.

But fuck, I'm so goddamn tired of hiding, of pretending she doesn't dominate every spare thought that I have—not that I have a lot of spare ones to begin with. My world revolves around Ellie.

I know I've pushed her too far when her smile fades instantly, her eyes shuttering closed like blinds being drawn. A prickle itches over the back of my neck, reminiscent of a premonition, even before she says, "Thanks. I…um…have a date."

Yup.

I totally choke on my own spit as cold, eruptive wrath boils inside of me even as dread fills me like cement.

"You have a…?" Do I sound interested, as a

friend would? Or do I sound murderous, like a man in love would? I'll be the first to admit that I don't crave violence the same way the others do, but the thought of any man going on a date with Ellie has me seeing red. My stomach ties itself into a dozen tight knots even as I attempt to curb the baser impulse I have to bare my teeth and snarl like a cornered animal.

How is it possible that those four words pour acid in my stomach and make me feel like I'm dying?

I try to keep my voice carefully flippant, almost indifferent, when I say, "Oh?" My hands turn into claws, biting into the skin of my trousers. "Who is he?"

"Um…" She scratches absently at her wrist, her fingernails digging into her skin hard enough to draw blood. Are those… Are those scars I see marring her flesh? What the fuck? Before I can grab her wrist and demand answers, she drops her hands back to her lap, her sweater sleeve falling down and hiding her mottled skin from view. Even still, I can't stop the horror from engulfing me in an icy wave as insidious emotions claw at my insides.

I feel sick to my stomach, and I want nothing more than to confront her, to demand answers, but I know that will only push her further away. If I react to what I saw, she'll react as well, and I'm fucking terrified of what that reaction will be.

She wouldn't…?

She wouldn't try to kill…?

She wouldn't…?

My emotions turn into a huge ball that becomes stuck in my throat, making swallowing impossible.

"Roy," Ellie answers at last. I nearly forgot what

we were talking about, my focus transfixed on the scars I saw on her wrist. At least, I assume they were scars. Maybe they were just…paint splashes? Maybe she doodled on her wrists with a marker?

I can feel myself trembling, bursting with unparalleled energy, but I take deep breaths to keep the carefully leashed violence inside of me contained.

"Roy," I parrot briskly, my lips slanting downward.

Fucking Roy.

Micropenis Roy.

My hands itch to grab my phone and send a message to the other guys, telling them about this goddamn date.

But I don't.

I can't.

Because if Roy offers her even a sliver of happiness—a happiness we've been failing to provide for her—then who am I to take that away? I love her enough to want her to be happy, even if it isn't with me.

It kills me—it fucking destroys me from the inside out—but I know I need to remain silent.

You need to fix this, Beckett, a tiny voice whispers. All I want to do is tug Ellie into my lap, nestle her head beneath my chin, and inhale her floral scent. At one point, she would've welcomed my embrace, maybe even initiated contact. But too much has happened, and the ghosts haunting her expression are more prominent than ever.

Almost immediately, the list of goals I planned to accomplish change entirely. Sure, I still want to fix the bonds between me and Ellie, me and the guys, but a new one pops to the top of the list, overshadowing the others.

Step one—diminish the shadows in Ellie's eyes, no matter the sacrifices you need to make.

It's my goal, my duty, to make the girl I love smile again.

No matter the cost.

Chapter 11

Zane

What is a band without their lead singer? The Beatles without John Lennon? One Direction without motherfucking Harry Styles? They're Un-Direction.

We're Un-Direction.

Un-Directionfied.

A slightly deranged snort leaves my lips as I cross the busy street, not bothering to check for oncoming traffic. I dare a car to try and run me over. I fucking dare it. Those headlights? Yeah, I'd make them my bitches. Bitch righty and bitch lefty.

My hand shakes as I grab my phone out of my back pocket and stare intently at the app I downloaded a few weeks ago. As a prank, I decided to hack into Beckett's phone, so I'm able to see everything that he sees when I'm in the app. I planned to send duck pics to Ryker using Beckett's number, with the caption, "Wanna a beak of this?"

But then I decided that cutting the brakes of my car before I drove him to the airport would be even more fun.

However, that hasn't stopped me from snooping from time to time in order to see what my Brit friend has been up to. He mostly looks up clothes and shoes—if anyone is the Harry from Un-Direction, it's him, and not just because he has a silly accent—but he recently sent a text to Ellie that has made my blood run cold.

Have fun on your date.

That's it. Five simple words, but they've managed to electrocute me, skin me alive, and rip out my spinal cord all in the span of seconds.

Blistering, eruptive heat boils inside of me at the thought of someone taking my sweet *princesa* on a date.

It's Roy, isn't it? It's always some douchebag named Roy. Or Chad. Always fucking Chad.

Some wise woman named Kelly Clarkson told a story about a grown-up's Christmas list. A true grown-up's Christmas list? Weapons for murder, including, but not limited to, pointy knives, pointy swords, pointy throwing stars, pointy needles, and pointy orange construction cones. The construction cones are, of course, optional, but I find that they can do a lot of damage if utilized correctly.

My lips curl into a grim, malevolent smile as the taste of blood settles on my tongue. I want to lick my lips like a sadistic bastard, but that might look kind of creepy, considering I'm on a crowded street.

Oh, fuck it. I'm gonna do it anyway.

I begin licking my lips with a tiny smirk,

unintentionally meeting the gaze of a sixty-year-old woman with white hair and a wrinkled face. I don't immediately look away, so we continue to make awkward eye contact as her gaze sharpens, her mouth popping open in horror. After a moment, I bare my teeth at her, my lips peeling away in a snarl, and she gasps, quickening her pace and finally ripping her gaze away from mine.

For years, I was told by every psychiatrist and shrink that I was crazy. Psychotic. Deranged. I listened with an indolent front, nodding along like a good little puppy as they offered treatment plans and suggestions. Maybe that's why my mother hates me—because she knows the truth about me, the truth about my soul. She knows how fucked up I truly am.

I wonder what my shrink would say about my most recent obsession.

I file that under 'topics for future therapy sessions,' after I find a new therapist, of course. My last one had an…unfortunate accident after he got a little too handsy. He really should've watched where he was going when he crossed the street. You never know when a stolen semi-truck would mow a person down. Poor Mr. Jeffery.

Words settle on the tip of my tongue, words to a song that already exists. *"They see me rollin', in my semi-truck. I know Mr. Jeffery's gonna get down and dirty. Gonna get down and dirty. Gonna get down and dirty. Gonna get down and dirty."* Using the tune of "Ridin'" by Chamilionaire featuring Krayzie Bone, I continue weaving my song together, garnering a few looks from the people on the street.

Not that they know I'm singing about an actual murder, but more power to them. It must be nice living in a tiny bubble where the horrors of the real world can't touch you.

I don't know if my obsession with singing started because of Ellie or if there's always been music in my soul or whatever fucking cliché you want to say. Maybe I latched on to it because it was something that would bind us together—our shared love of music. She's the Beyoncé to my Kelly Rowland. The Jimmy Page to my Robert Plant. The Harry Styles to my Zayn Malik—because let's be real, no one can pull off a Zayn like another Zane. And now, with her gone, my life is meaningless. Even music doesn't hold the same appeal to me.

I reach the bowling alley Beckett looked up on his phone—no doubt the bowling alley Ellie is at with her Titty Twister. I refuse to say the D-word. The D-A-T-E word.

For a brief, brief moment, the world around me freezes, almost as if someone pressed the pause button on a remote. I no longer see the men and women in the parking lot as people, only as bodies. Blood adorns their faces as their hearts lay splattered on the asphalt before them. Wounds zigzag and crisscross across their faces as their sightless eyes stare back at me. For just a second, I'm surrounded by death and violence, and something inside of my soul sparks to life.

I squeeze my eyelids shut, pushing the macabre images to the back of my mind, and when I reopen them, everything is back to normal.

But the bloodlust saturating my heart and soul?

That's as persistent—and insistent—as always, a tiny voice that screams at me to give in to my primitive desires and hunt. Fight. Kill.

Instead of focusing on that, however, I think through some of the prank ideas that've been percolating through my head for weeks.

I wonder what Becket would do if I sprayed his nipples with cans of Lynx while he slept. Would they fall off like warts? I swear I read about that somewhere—

My heart catches in my throat when I finally enter the musty bowling alley, my eyes landing on Ellie immediately despite the crowd of people. I swear I'd be able to find her anywhere, even with thousands of people surrounding us. And Dicky Z, the name I gave my cock? He'll be able to point her out instantly like he's the arrow on a compass and she's north.

She's standing before a lane opposite the main entrance, near the arcade, holding a pink ball between both of her hands as she stares intently at the pins. As I watch, she bends her arm backward and then thrusts it forward again, the ball slipping free of her fingers…and immediately crashing into the gutter.

She squeals in alarm, spinning around to face Titty Twister who sits at a table, eating a slice of pizza. Grease drips down his chin as he wipes it away with the back of his hand like a fucking psychopath.

Roy.

Fucking Roy.

Just like in the parking lot, my vision sharpens into thin lines, until all I can see is the fucker's grinning face and messy brown hair. Blood drips from the empty sockets where his eyes once were, and bruises distort his face, turning his smirk into a grimace. His neck dramatically snaps to the side, revealing yellow-white bone, as he falls to the ground, dead.

I blink, and the vision is gone.

Roy's still alive.

Still breathing.

Still smiling at Ellie.

Still staring at her ass as she bends forward to throw the ball a second time—and I say throw, because she's definitely not bowling. She reminds me of an Olympic ax thrower trying to get the weapon as far down the lane as physically possible. It's insanely cute, and I can't stop myself from taking an automatic step forward.

For a brief moment, I imagine *I'm* the one on the date with Ellie and Roy is buried six feet under with a gravestone that reads, "Respect the Un-Direction."

No, Zane! You need to be smart about this.

Fortunately, I came prepared and now reach into my back pocket for my trusty baseball cap. I position it low over my face, hopefully obscuring my features from view, and sit at a table on the opposite end of the bowling alley.

Ellie, see me.

Don't see me.

Love me.

Don't love me.

Just look at me!

Don't look at me.

I don't know how long I sit there—watching Titty Twister flirt with my girl and hearing her awkward laughter in response to his stupid jokes—when a presence falls over my bent form. I glance up to see a woman staring down at me, her hip cocked to the side and her brow raised. I honestly can't tell you anything else about her—she's just another female in a sea of worthless nobodies—but I think she would be classified as pretty by human standards. Maybe even beautiful. By my standards? She's a piss-poor impersonation of Ellie.

"What's a handsome man like you doing all by yourself?" she purrs, bending forward to show me her cleavage. But while most men see cleavage, I see her heart—a good place to stab a person to ensure they die instantly.

"Go away," I mutter absently, trying to see past her toward my precious *princesa*. The bitch moves with my vision, and I notice more than a few nearby men eyeing her rack hungrily. Does she have good tits or something? Nah. Even without glancing at them for more than a second, I can tell they're way too big. Ellie's tits, on the other hand, are the perfect size to cup in both of my hands and squeeze—

"I see what this is about." The woman finally pulls away from me and steps to the side, her eyes following my line of vision to focus on Ellie as well. For some reason, I don't like her attention being on my girl. I don't like anyone's attention being on my girl except for mine. And maybe Landon's. Okay, Dominic's as well. And sometimes Beckett's. And Ryker, because he pulls off 'moody asshole with a heart of gold' so well. But that's it. I'm putting my foot down on five. "Is that your ex?" the woman questions curiously.

"No," I growl out instinctively, because an ex would imply that we're over. And Ellie and me? We're far from over. Like, if there was a rainbow, we would still be in Kansas singing depressing songs in black and white. Ain't no one going over that damn rainbow if I have anything to say about it.

"Does she know that?" the woman inquires, and I have to bite down on my growing irritation.

Fortunately for the annoying woman, I'm saved from responding by Ellie and Titty Twister taking off their bowling shoes and moving toward the counter to return them. As they step into my direct line of sight, I take note of Ellie's uncomfortable smile and the way her eyes constantly shift away from the douche.

She didn't enjoy her date with him.

At all.

Immense joy and relief bubble up inside of me, and I have to rein in the impulse to screech like a banshee at the top of my lungs and throw confetti into the air. I'm sure a bowling alley has a stash of confetti somewhere. Now, if I can find it…

"Hey, wait!" the woman exclaims as I slide out of the seat, prepared to follow Ellie and Titty Twister out of the bowling alley. "Can I get your number or something?"

I ignore her—because she seriously cannot get the hint—and duck outside a few seconds after Ellie and Titty Twister do. I keep my footsteps light, something I perfected over the years, as I scan the parking lot for them. My brows draw together when I don't immediately see them.

They couldn't have possibly taken off that quickly. I would've seen them enter their car or—

"Roy, don't."

Ellie's voice, laced with irritation and maybe even a trickle of fear, reaches my ears.

I begin to shake in the cold breeze, my thoughts warping until they're pictured in shades of gray. No color. No light. Just the monotony of dark gray that wraps around my mind like a rusty chain.

"Roy!" This time, her voice is higher, pitched with alarm, and I'm running around the corner before my brain can even catch up to what my body's doing.

Darkness pierces the numb barrier I erected around myself, inflaming my body with an incandescent rage. It bubbles through me, swirling in my stomach like molten lava, before erupting in a fatal surge of heat and violence.

Because the bastard has Ellie pressed against the wall, one of his hands on her hip while the other cups her breasts.

I don't think—just react.

He's on the ground in less than a second, and my fist is pounding into his face without a hint of mercy. I feel savage, unleashed, freed—the beast inside of me purrs in twisted delight, relishing the sting of pain reverberating through my busted knuckles. It's almost as if I can sense the man's pain, feel every cry as if it were my own, and I don't stop. I can't stop.

The darkness has warped my mind until only a beast remains.

"Zane!"

Blood.

So much blood.

It stains my knuckles, my hand, my wrist, my arm, my legs, my feet, my—

"Zane!"

Tiny hands grab at my shoulders, and I spin toward the intruder, my teeth bared, only to freeze when Ellie's wide eyes meet my own.

But I'm still not in control.

I'm not sure I ever truly was.

I'm off the asshole in seconds, spinning around to face Ellie fully. She stares back at me without a hint of fear in her fathomless blue-gray eyes, not a trace of worry or anxiety. She doesn't even glance at the bastard moaning and crying on the pavement behind the bowling alley; her attention is fixed on me with unnerving focus. The intensity is a dagger to the heart, twisting, clawing, *shredding* until I'm nothing but broken pieces at the feet of my queen.

I move forward until she's forced to back up, her body flush against the brick wall of the building. Her chest heaves, her eyes darkening with an indecipherable emotion, as she stares into the eyes of the beast. The eyes of a malicious, bloodthirsty monster.

I never wanted her to see me this way—imprisoned to the darkness inside of me, my movements puppeted by evil itself—but now that she has, I find that I can't look away. I want her to see me, see the *real* me, and not be scared. I want her to know that I'll protect her with all the monstrous energy roaming through my body, all of the darkness tainting and warping my soul.

"You shouldn't have gone on a date with him," I growl, ducking my head until my lips are a hair's breadth away from hers, until my breath ghosts her heart-shaped face. "Now, I'm gonna have to kill him."

"Zane…" I can't quite read her tone of voice. Is it a plea for the sick bastard's life? A moan of yearning? Or is that latter thought simply my wishful thinking?

"You don't want him," I continue, my eyes never leaving hers. I can feel the soft press of her tits against my chest, and I desperately want to pull her shirt up and see if her nipples are as hard as I imagine them to be.

"I don't want him," she repeats, seemingly in a daze. She swallows heavily, her tiny pink tongue snaking out to lick her bottom lip.

"I'm losing my goddamn mind, *princesa*." I press my forehead against hers, half expecting her to push me away, to tell me to leave her alone like she did a month ago. God, I still have nightmares over that night, my mind replaying that moment over and over again, an endless loop I can't escape. I've been beaten, whipped, tortured—everything you can possibly imagine—but having her send us away because of our lies and deceit was the worst thing that has ever happened to me. No other pain can compare. "I can't stand to know that you hate me."

"I…" She swallows a second time, and my eyes dip to the pale column of her throat, watching in rapt fascination. I wonder what she would do if I pressed my lips to the hollow of her skin, the stubble on my face brushing against her in delicious torment. I've had one kiss with her, but that won't be enough. It'll never be enough. Ellie's my drug of choice, and I'm so goddamn addicted to her it's making me insane.

"I don't want you to hate me anymore," I beg, unable to stop my desperation from leaking into my voice. Behind me, I hear Titty Twister begin to move, and I absently kick out until he falls back into silence.

Ellie doesn't break my gaze.

"I don't hate you," she whispers at last, one of her shaky hands coming up to curl around my cheek. Her eyelids flutter shut, something akin to pain flashing across her face, before she reopens them with a tiny moan that sends lightning straight to Dicky Z. "I can never hate you, Zane."

Her words soothe something inside of me, something frayed and burning, and I find myself leaning further against her palm like a kitten searching for pets from its owner. Every fiber of my being loves this woman in front of me, and to hear her say that she doesn't hate me, that there's still hope…

"I'll give you time," I whisper, tilting my head sideways to plant a tender kiss against the inside of her wrist. Her skin smells sweet, like flowers and cinnamon, and I can't stop myself from inhaling deeply. "But I'm not letting you go. I'll *never* let you go." I want to scream when I force myself to take a step away from her, to stop invading her space. All I want to do is gather her in my arms and pepper kisses across her face until she's mewling my name in a breathy voice.

Her eyes turn downcast, almost as if she feels my missing heat as keenly as I feel hers, before she flicks them toward a still groaning and crying Titty Twister.

"Don't kill him," she deadpans, though her eyes are carefully blank, as if she doesn't give a shit either way.

What the fuck happened with POP to make her like this?

I'm gonna kill them all, you mark my words.

The smile that carves itself into my face is colder than ice. It's rimmed with malicious intent and deadly promises.

"Maybe. Maybe not. I suppose we'll have to see." My smile turns genuine when I direct it at Ellie, because *she doesn't hate me.*

This might be the best goddamn day ever.

What would make it even better?

Murdering the fucker and then sticking my cock into Ellie's wet heat.

One day…

One day.

Chapter 12

Dominic

Landon: Dude, where are you? I'm at your house.

I precariously balance the phone on my knee as I tap out a reply, being extra mindful not to keep my attention on my phone for longer than a second at a time. Harvey has some strange rules about phones at the dinner table.

Dominic: At the asshole's house.

I turn off my phone before he can respond and glance up just in time to see my father glowering at me, his bushy brows drawn down low.

"What did I tell you about phones at the dinner table?" he rumbles, his hand clenching around the metal fork he holds. My idiotic half-brothers titter like damn morons as I roll my eyes heavenward.

"Sorry." I dig into the tasteless chicken with my

fork before he can come up with another reason to yell at me.

I fucking hate Harvey Rollins with every fiber of my being. My goddamn birth father. I don't remember my birth mother, Alisha, but I know enough about her to understand that addiction took her life. Harvey, on the other hand, has no fucking excuse for putting me up for adoption, except for the fact he's a piece of shit who wants what others have on his own terms.

It's not like he couldn't afford to take care of me. He lives in a fucking mansion, for Christ's sake, with an army of servants at his beck and call. He's a trust fund baby, as he likes to remind me time and time again, though that fortune will never go to me.

I have no idea how he was able to crack open the closed adoption record, but I suppose you're able to get away with a lot of shit when you're rich and powerful.

At first glance, one would think that Harvey Rollins is an unassuming man with a God-complex. He embodies a lethal superiority that makes me want to vomit, despite his small stature. He's slightly heavier than most men his age with platinum blond hair, the same shade as my own, and a trimmed beard. His vibrant green eyes appear almost beady and subdued, as if the muted light can't quite reach those glittery orbs.

Despite the fact I want nothing to do with Harvey and the new family he created, he forces me to go to his house every weekend for "family dinner." His words, not mine.

I used to grumble and complain about my frequent visits until Harvey made an absurd comment

154

about a woman named Cassia. Of course, he could've been referring to a completely different Cassia than the deranged 'goddess' POP members worship, but I don't know for sure. Until then, I remain watchful, my ear to the metaphorical ground.

Don't even get me started on Harvey's new wife—aka, life-sized Barbie. I swear the pervert has more plastic inside of her than the toy itself.

Dana Rollins is what you would get if you combined a nineteen-eighties Barbie doll with a Cabbage Patch Kid and then taped on a pair of basketball-sized balloons as breasts. Her stringy blonde hair—the strands so perfectly straight that they resemble spaghetti—cascades down her back, though if you look closely enough, you can see black near her roots. Her eyes are a little too blue to be natural, almost as if she placed vibrant contacts over her normally dull, gray eyes, and her lips are a little too pouty. Right now, she's staring at me with a hungry expression, and I have to hide my expression of derision.

On either side of her sit Tweedledum and Tweedledumber. Doyle and Dustin, my half-brothers. They're not biologically related to Dana or my birth mother, though. Apparently, they're the results of a one-night stand with a hooker in Vegas.

I wonder if my father would still stare at them with stars in his eyes if he knew they were fucking his wife. I made the unfortunate mistake of walking into the bathroom once to see Doyle fucking Dana on the ground while Dustin peed on her face.

No joke.

I still have nightmares to this day. And I may or

may not vomit whenever I recall the image. Look, I'll never kink shame or anything like that, and I'll be the first to admit that I have had plenty of dirty and taboo fantasies starring Ellie, but golden showers? With my stepmom? Hell to the no.

Fuck, I hate the weekends.

"So, Dominic…" Harvey begins conversationally as he cuts off a piece of chicken and uses his fork to point it at me. "How are your classes going?"

"He's probably failing because he's a dumbass," Doyle retorts with a sneer in my direction. Dustin chortles enthusiastically, reaching over Dana's head to give him a high five.

I pinch the bridge of my nose. "My god. How old are you guys? Five?"

They are who my father plans to give his prestigious family business to? I have no faith in the future of our world if Doyle and Dustin are its eventual leaders. They're twenty-two-year-olds with the mentalities of toddlers. Better them than me, I suppose. Fuck if I want to be my bio dad's little puppet longer than I have to.

Harvey's thick brows arrow downward as a frown paints itself on his face.

"Boys," he reprimands, the admonishment causing both of the twins to snap their heads in his direction. "Dominic's right. Behave."

I know immediately that Harvey said the wrong thing. Doyle's eyes turn to slits, spewing vitriol and hatred in my direction, while Dustin scowls at me. The twins absolutely hate it whenever the words

"Dominic" and "right" are used in the same sentence, especially if that sentence is said by our shared sperm donor.

But what can they do about it, really? Besides glower and ruffle their feathers in an attempt to look bigger and badder than everyone else in the room? They're too chicken-shit to talk back to Harvey, enduring his resentment in silence.

The rest of the dinner proves to be uneventful, and by the time the staff arrives to take our plates away, I want to get out of there. Fast.

"Dominic." Harvey stands, keeping his hands on the edge of the table as his eyes drill into my skull. I adopt a bored, almost indolent expression as I lift my eyes to meet his.

"Yes?"

"After dessert, can you meet me in my office? There are a few things I would like to discuss with you."

After dessert?

After goddamn dessert?!?

Dinners at my birth father's house are five course meals, with the final one being served hours after the fourth one. The last time I was forced to stay for dessert, I didn't get home until after midnight. I was forced to sit in the parlor—a fancy word for living room—and make awkward small talk with the staff and ward off my stepmother's wandering hands, all the while the twins stared on in jealousy.

Fuck my life.

No, seriously.

Fuck. My. Life.

My teeth grit together, a rebuttal settling on my tongue like melted chocolate, but I swallow the words down before they can escape. What can I say? I've always been a curious fucker, and my dad's words have struck a nerve in me. What could he possibly want? His office is his sanctuary—the equivalent of a man's toilet seat—and he has never let me step foot inside of it. Ever.

"Fine," I manage to say, pushing away from the table as well. "I'll be in the parlor."

Dad smiles, looking pleased with himself, and Doyle and Dustin glare even harder. If I gave a damn about their opinions of me—about the two of them in general—I might've been offended by the amount of animosity exuding from their smelly pores. But alas, I would rather listen to Homeless Bob down the street rambling about cursed turkey feet than the two of them.

Ignoring the glares burning a hole into my back—and the sultry caress of Dana's stare—I hurry into the pretentious parlor and plop down onto one of the sofas.

Harvey chose style over comfort with this room, and it shows. The couch is from the eighteen hundreds and is harder than a stack of bricks with a thin, floral covering overtop of it. A mahogany table rests opposite the sofa, constructed out of distressed wood and leaning precariously to one side. Still, the intricate trimming around the sides suggests that it has once been loved and well-used. A ten-foot-tall hearth takes up the entirety of the right wall, though I have no idea why one man would need that big of a fireplace. Is he burning bodies or some shit? All in all, the room is a mismatched, juxtaposed cube of historical furniture, modern appliances, and flashy decorations, almost as if it can't decide on one specific style.

I immediately take my phone out of my pocket and glance down at my still opened text chain with Landon. I type out a lengthy paragraph, prepared to bitch with him about how horrible this family is, when my thumb darts down to Ellie's name. Indecision flares within me, along with a healthy dose of need, as I stare at the picture I took of her.

Of course, she didn't realize that I had been snapping photos of her, but that's beside the point…

She's laughing at something one of the other fuckers in our group is saying, her head tilted backward and genuine mirth and cheer reflecting in her sparkling eyes. She looks radiant and ethereal, like the solar eclipse that you can't help but stare directly at, even knowing you'll go blind. My fingers trace her heart-shaped face as a painful lump manifests in my stomach.

Fuck, I miss her.

I miss her so goddamn much it brings me physical pain to even think about her.

What is she doing right now? Right this second?

For some reason, I picture her standing outside in the flurry of snow, her arms outstretched and her expression decidedly serene. But knowing Ellie as well as I do, she would've chosen to go outside without her motherfucking jacket.

In my fantasy, I picture taking off the suitcoat Dad always insists I wear to these farces we call family dinners. As I drape it over her delicate shoulders, she turns toward me with a soft smile. My cock hardens in my pants, because there's nothing I love more than seeing her in my clothes.

I can't explain it, and at this point, I don't even want to. I know it's fucking crazy—possessive, obsessive, and every other 'essive' I can think of—but it's my mission in life to see her in as many clothes of mine as I can.

The image changes, swept away by a fierce thunderstorm, and suddenly, I picture Ellie lazily walking around my bedroom in nothing but my T-shirt, her tan legs on display and her feet bare.

Before I can stop myself, before I can think better of it, I pull up Ellie's contact name and shoot her a text.

Dominic: We need to talk.

I barely breathe as I stare at the four words on the screen.

Fuck. Fuck. Fuck.

I desperately wish I can unsend them, because I don't know what the fuck I'll do if she rejects me. What if she doesn't respond? What if she responds and tells me to stay the fuck away from her?

Beckett mentioned in his last text that she's in a bad place, but what the fuck did he mean by that? How is she in a bad place?

I suddenly want to break into her house, sneak into her bedroom, and hold her in my embrace until she willingly gives up all her secrets.

The breath I haven't realized I've been holding

releases in a whooshing exhale as my phone pings, a new message appearing on the screen.

Ellie: That sounds ominous. You going to confess your undying love to me? *winky face*

I inhale sharply at her teasing reply, because honestly? She has no fucking idea. The idiotic girl seems to think I hate her.

But she's texting me back, so that means something, right? She's teasing me through text, so maybe she doesn't hate me. Maybe. Maybe. Maybe.

Dominic: You still mad?

Fuck, why did you send that, Dominic? Why!?! Never, *ever* ask a girl if she's mad. That's a recipe for her getting even madder.

For a second, Ellie doesn't reply, though I'm able to see through the read receipt that she saw my message. I hold my breath, my pulse skittering, when three dots appear on the screen, indicating that she's typing out a reply.

Ellie: I told Beckett that I'm not mad, and I meant it.

Dominic: Then why the fuck are you ignoring us?

Once again, Ellie doesn't respond right away, and I fear that my brash question scared her away. I'm always fucking doing it, as if my brain and mouth—or brain and hands, for that matter—don't have a goddamn filter or off-switch.

After a moment, a new message appears on the screen.

Ellie: I don't think this is about you guys anymore.

You don't think...? I read the text back five times, struggling to understand the words displayed and their elusive meaning. It feels as if my brain is made of pebbles and rocks, and those rocks have become dislodged, tumbling around in my skull like loose change.

Dominic: I don't understand what that means.

Ellie: I don't understand it either.

I bite down on my lip, debating what to say to her next, when she shoots me another text.

Ellie: What are you doing?

The innocent question has my heart beating faster, racing like a runaway stallion. My hands shake as I text out a response.

Dominic: At my birth dad's house for family dinner.

Ellie: Ew.

I smirk at her immediate response. I've complained to her more than once about how much I hate these fucking dinners, and my pulse skitters at the knowledge she listened and remembered.

Ellie: How has it been so far?

Besides my brothers glaring daggers at me, my father staring down his nose with a sickening superiority, and my stepmother batting her fake lashes whenever I glance up from my plate? Peachy.

But instead of saying any of that to her, I type out,

Dominic: Hell, as usual. But I'll survive. Enough about me. How has your break been so far? I miss you.

Before I send the message, I delete the last three words, not wanting to scare her away.

There's so much I want to ask her—about POP, The Divine One, the Culling, our relationship—but this feels safer. Our bond with Ellie is so precarious at the moment, so fragile, that I'm terrified of saying the wrong thing and destroying it irreparably.

Before Ellie can respond, the door to the parlor opens with a loud squeak, and I glance up, half-expecting it to be my father telling me to come to his office now.

It's not.

Dana stands in the doorway, wearing a bright red teddy and a translucent robe.

Oh, for fuck's sake…

"Sorry. I didn't see you there. I was just getting ready for bed," Dana purrs, stretching like a housecat.

I swear my eyes get stuck in my skull with how hard I roll them.

When I turn my attention back toward my phone, prepared to read Ellie's reply, Dana speaks up, a tinge of irritation in her voice at the fact that I'm ignoring her.

"I heard the chef is making chocolate cake for dessert. You love chocolate cake, don't you, Dommy?"

Dommy?

The fuck?!

Again, I ignore her, a tiny smile unfurling on my lips as I read Ellie's message.

Ellie: So did you know that Zane has a violent streak? Because I totally didn't. He's usually super cuddly around me!

Zane? Violent streak? I laugh out loud before I can stop myself.

That's the understatement of the fucking century.

Dominic: What the fuck happened for you to see his so-called violent streak?

"What's so funny?" Dana presses, and I feel the weight of her thigh against mine as she sits down beside me. My nose crinkles in disgust, and I not-so-subtly shift away from her, focusing on my phone.

Ellie: Bowling.

Dominic: Bowling? The fuck?

A tiny bit of jealousy unfurls inside of me at the thought of Zane and Ellie going bowling while the rest of us are stuck in the proverbial doghouse.

Ellie: Long story.

Dominic: Make it shorter and share the juicy details.

Ellie: Ohhhh. Do you wanna gossip with me, Dominic Black?

Dominic: We can paint each other's nails and do matching makeups.

Ellie: *laugh emoji* Matching makeups? LOL

Dominic: Isn't that a thing girls do at slumber parties?

Ellie: You want to have a slumber party with me?!

My thoughts drift to being in a room alone with Ellie at night.

Her gorgeous body spread out on the bed, her brown hair fanning around her angelic face…

Her perfect pink lips parted as she exhales my name…

My fingers sinking into her wet folds…

I can feel my cock jerk to life in my pants, hardening by the second.

Dominic: Don't tease me, baby girl.

I hold my breath, wondering if I took it too far with my blatant flirting. Though knowing Ellie, she probably doesn't realize that that's what I'm doing.

"It's getting kind of hot in here, don't you think?" Dana's annoyingly incessant voice draws my attention back to her with a growl of annoyance. She shrugs off the silky robe, leaving her in the skin-tight underwear.

I roll my eyes at the dumb bitch and focus back on my text messages.

Ellie: How am I teasing you?!? You know I love when you guys stay in my room with me!

Fuck, now I'm harder than a rock.

"Oh, you like what you see, don't you?" Dana purrs, her manicured hand gently grazing my thigh.

I shudder in revulsion, realizing that she has mistaken the cause of my boner.

Ew.

Ew.

Ewww.

Ellie articulated my thoughts perfectly.

Abruptly, Dana places her claw-like hands beneath my chin and forces my face in her direction. I give her a bland, uninterested look, debating the merits of snapping her fucking wrist for touching me without my permission.

With her free hand, she pulls down one of the straps of her teddy until her tit springs free. Her sharp nail circles the infected-looking, red nipple until she plucks it sharply.

"You like that, don't you, big boy?" she purrs as she does the same to her other strap, pulling it down and freeing her breast. Her eyes flicker to my cock, which is now as limp as a goddamn noodle. She slowly releases my chin, making sure I keep my attention on her, and then begins to play with her breasts with a grin that she probably thinks is sexy. "You like my big tits, don't you?" She presses them together as her fingers begin to twist her nipples. "You wanna suck them, don't you?"

I can't help it—I begin to laugh.

And then laugh even harder at the dumbfounded expression on her cunt face.

It's at the moment she makes the stupidest mistake of her miserable life—she reaches forward and touches my cock through my dress pants.

Before she can catch her bearings, I wrap a hand around her throat and push her against the couch. Her eyes flare wildly with excitement, before that excitement turns into a look of terror at whatever she sees on my face.

"You dumb whore," I spit out, tightening my hand around her windpipe as she finally seems to understand the predicament she's in. Her fingernails claw at my wrist, but I only tighten my grip. "Don't ever fucking touch me without my permission. Permission I'll never give you, by the way." I squeeze even tighter to reiterate my point, driving into her dumb fucking skull that *I'm not interested in her archaic cunt*. Perhaps the blonde hair dye fucked up her brain or some shit. I swear she has gotten more stupid with age. "I'll kill you without even batting an eye if you don't leave me the fuck alone." I release her throat with a grunt of distaste and jump to my feet.

"Fuck. You," Dana rasps out shakily, her hands coming up instinctively to rub at her throat.

"In your perverted dreams, you pedophile piece

of shit," I bark, already stomping out of the parlor and toward the front door.

I don't give a shit what my dad wanted to talk to me about. I need to get out of here before I make a mistake I'll regret.

Like murder every fucker in this godforsaken house.

Chapter 13

Ellie

When I was younger, maybe ten or eleven years old, I got picked on at summer camp by a girl named Marilyn. I don't remember what she used to tease me about, but I often retired to my cabin for long periods at a time, staring blankly at the wall and wishing I were somewhere else. *Anywhere* else. There was a gaping chasm in my chest where my heart should be, and that abyss only expanded as the days turned into weeks, the weeks turned into months, and the ridicule continued. I felt darkness encroach the edges of my vision as I struggled with all my might to hold on.

And then I received a letter in the mail from my mom, the paper perfectly folded and taped together with a heart sticker, and some of the pain coursing through me diminished.

My sweet Ellie, the letter read, the words now burned into my brain like a scalding iron rod. *I received your letter the other day, and to be honest, I'm worried about you. Some children can be very, very cruel, and their actions have nothing to do with you. I could easily tell you to ignore Marilyn, but I know it isn't that easy. If you want to come home, let me know, and I'll book you the first plane ticket I can find. But I wanted to address something first...*

You mentioned in your letter that you feel empty inside, numb almost, and you asked me if that was normal or if you were broken. I didn't have the words then, but I do now. Listen very closely, my beloved, and believe me when I say that there is nothing *wrong with you. You have a chemical imbalance inside of your brain that is creating unique obstacles and challenges you need to conquer. You are the strongest woman I know, my baby girl, and it's because you choose to keep fighting every day, even when you want to give up. You choose to get out of bed in the morning. That takes strength, immeasurable strength, and I'm so proud of you. I promise you, things will get better.*

All my love.

Mom

P.S. I plan to have a long, long *talk with the camp owner. If he allows bullies like Marilyn to attend, then I don't think this is a place I want to send my money and daughter.*

I stare at the familiar words now, my heart nipping at my heels like an angry hound. Pain blasts me from all directions as I hold the note lightly in my hand, careful not to create any new wrinkles. The sheet has turned yellow with time, the ink smeared, but it's one of the most precious possessions I own.

It's the last letter I received from my mom before she died.

There's nothing wrong with you…

A chemical imbalance inside of your brain…

I know there's a stigma about depression that's impossible to ignore. Some people seem to believe it's a switch you're able to flick on and off at the drop of a hat. Others believe it's the equivalent to being sad—but it's not.

I sit in the center of my bed, my legs crisscrossed, as my gaze flickers from the letter to the phone. I haven't heard back from Dominic since my last text, and another spark of pain explodes inside of me like errant fireworks being tipped over.

Talking to Dominic, joking with him, has made me feel more like myself than anything else these past few weeks.

I watched Zane beat the crap out of Roy, for Pete's sake, and didn't even bat an eye. While the old me would've been horrified by the display of violence, the new me didn't feel an ounce of regret or remorse. It's almost as if I can physically feel my heart hardening with every day that passes, the walls fortifying with layers of steel and cement. The thought terrifies me…and emboldens me.

But then both of those emotions are flushed away in a wave of self-loathing and bitterness.

It suddenly occurs to me that I'm completely alone.

I told the guys to stay away from me, and for the most part, they have. I haven't seen Piper since Blair died, and though Jane and Victoria still text me from time to time, I know that they're busy with their families and other friends. I'm just…someone to them. Not their best friend, but not someone they feel comfortable ignoring, either.

I'll never be anyone's first choice, and I know it's my own fault.

Fischer's gone, having driven back to the capital city last night, and our large mansion has never felt more deafening, even with the security team stomping around.

A knot cinches in my chest as horrible thoughts beat against my defenses, wearing holes and dents into a foundation I once believed to be impenetrable.

Useless.
Unloved.
Alone.
Murderer.
End it.
End it all.
End it.

A strangled sound escapes me—a combination between a sob and a howl of rage—as I throw my phone at my bedside lamp. It shatters to the floor, the noise almost musical, and I pause, half expecting some of my brother's men to come barging inside to check on me.

They don't.

The house remains silent.

I reach over the bed to grab my phone…and my fingers pause around a tiny shard of broken glass. I slowly pick it up and stare at the way the light reflects off its translucent surface.

It's…beautiful. Riveting, really. I find that I can't peel my eyes away as I twist it to and fro, watching the way it sparkles like a thousand diamonds. Almost absently, I press my thumb against the tip, cocking my head curiously to the side as a tiny bit of blood wells.

I press down harder, biting my lips to hide my grimace of pain as the red liquid drips downward, staining my pink sheets.

Something crashes downstairs, and I tense automatically, dropping the shard of glass back to the ground and slowly rising to my feet. Gradually, the pain running rampant through my body trickles away like water in a wrung-out sponge. In its place is a numbness that has my heart settling into a repetitive, almost comforting rhythm.

Keeping my eyes on the bedroom door, I crouch down and swipe up my phone. I can feel my lips arrow downward when I see the cracked phone screen. When I try to turn it on, the screen remains black.

But I don't panic.

No, there's not an ounce of terror in my body, not a smidgen of fear. I'm too numb for that. The pain that has been a constant in my life for weeks has turned into a dull ache, almost as if my body is trying to remember pain that my brain has forgotten.

What can these people do to me, when they already broke apart everything that I am?

I slowly slide open my bedside drawer and grab out a kitchen knife I stashed there when I first arrived home. It's wrong—God only knows how wrong it is— but I'm only able to sleep when the knife is beside me.

It's like I take comfort in the keen edge of the blade, the copper handle that fits perfectly in my palm.

Surprisingly, my hand doesn't shake as I hold the knife out in front of me.

No fear.

No anger.

Just…

Numbness.

And then, I wait.

It only takes a few minutes for my bedroom door to push open and for two robed figures to step inside. The one on the left stops when he sees me, his steps faltering, but the one on the right continues forward with sure, determined strides.

"The Divine One wishes to speak with you." The voice is feminine but gravelly, allowing me to believe that it belongs to an older woman. A teacher at my school, perhaps?

I keep my expression blank, the knife still raised protectively in front of me.

The woman, seemingly unperturbed by the sight of me with a weapon, continues forward until she's directly in front of me. Her gloved hand lifts until it's around my wrist, her touch painfully gentle, and it's only then that I realize she doesn't think I'll do it. She doesn't think I'll hurt her or anyone else, for that matter.

But she underestimates the monster inside of me. The monster they *made* when they destroyed me.

Keeping my expression bland, as to not give away my intentions, I wait until her attention is lowered, her masked gaze flicking to my other hand, before I plunge the knife downward.

Straight into her shoulder.

A sound of pained surprise leaves her lips, but I don't allow it to deter me. I simply shove her to the side and brutally wrench the knife back out of her shoulder, holding it once more in front of me.

The second POP member has paused, his hands raised placatingly into the air, as frost infiltrates my veins, freezing over my blood.

"Don't move," I hiss out, barely hearing anything over the rapid pounding of my heart. It reminds me of the baseline of one of the songs I've been working on, and lyrics begin to dance around in my head, each word more demented than the previous one.

Billie Eilish who?

The guy—at least I'm assuming it's a guy—doesn't say anything, but he also doesn't take a step toward me. He simply remains standing, his arms in the air, his masked face trained on me.

He doesn't spare his partner a second glance.

"Stay the fuck there!" I bellow, slowly backing up without taking my gaze off of him. He moves as I do, his feet pivoting to face me as I leave the room. I know the second I take my eyes off of him, the second I turn a corner in the hallway, he'll come after me.

Maybe I should've just stabbed him to save me the trouble.

The macabre thought slips in unbidden, burrowing beneath the numbness I erected around myself. A part of me is terrified for having such a thought, but the rest of me is just…done. So freaking done.

Two more members of POP materialize at the end of the hall, and I quickly veer right, running down the staircase.

Where the heck is my brother's security team?

How could they have let these people into my house?

Panic momentarily pierces the wall in my mind, and it's that emotion I latch on to, grasping with both hands and tugging with all my might, because it allows me to feel human again.

Panic. Fear. Guilt.

Those are normal emotions.

But this impassiveness? This numbness?

I'm nothing but a machine on autopilot, just as robotic as The Divine One's mechanical voice.

I pull open the glass slider and race outside, my breath escaping my lips in clouds of wispy air. Snow crackles beneath my bare feet, and I know I only have a few minutes before I succumb to hypothermia.

I'd been dressed for bed when POP infiltrated my house, and I'm wearing nothing but silky shorts and a thin cami, my feet bare.

Still, I don't stop running until I reach the garden near the back of the house. There's a gate that will lead me to the main road, and from there—

The thought cuts off as my eyes rest on the figure sitting on the stone bench in the garden, his golden face tilted upward like he's staring at the velvety black sky and twinkling stars, searching for constellations.

As if he can feel my presence, his face slides in my direction, the red robes rippling around his body like the blood staining my thumb and knife.

"Ellie. Have a seat." He pats the spot on the bench beside him as I glance fearfully in all directions. Everywhere I look, POP members stand at the ready, their features obscured by the heavy cloaks covering them from head to toe. Still, I hold my knife up protectively, daring one of them to come to me, to fight me.

"Why are you here?" I demand, but he ignores my question.

"I didn't know making you a murderer would give you such an insatiable taste for blood," The Divine One muses in his strange, mechanical voice.

His words have bile filling my stomach.

Murderer?

Taste for blood?

There's nothing wrong with you.

My mother's words play on a repeat in my head as I stare blankly at the monster behind all of this. Why won't he just leave me alone?

"You know," The Divine One begins in a tone that I could've sworn was nonchalant, "I used to sit in a garden just like this every night for years. Sometimes, my mother would join me." He absently rearranges the red fabric on his lap, his gaze moving toward a nearby tree. "You want to know what she told me?" I don't respond, but he doesn't wait for me to, continuing as if I gave him some form of acknowledgment. "She told me I was going to do great things in my life."

"And you decided to spit on her memory by becoming a psychopathic murderer?" I ask dryly, my voice barely above a whisper.

I swear The Divine One is smiling, though it's impossible for me to tell for certain with the mask in place. "My dear child, you're mistaken." He gracefully rises and takes a few steps toward me, stopping when I lift the knife threateningly. He nods toward the weapon, still dripping red with the blood of the unnamed female I stabbed, and says, "*You're* the one with the bloody knife."

I'm cold—so, so cold—but that's nothing compared to the frost that encompasses my heart at his words.

Every whip of wind against my face seems to scream at me, whispering promises and secrets that have a shiver rippling through my body.

"Why won't you just leave me alone?" My choked voice transitions into an anguished cry as a twig snaps behind me, forcing me to spin around and ensure no one is attempting to sneak up on me from behind. I quickly twist to face The Divine One before he can even think about moving a step closer. "You know I don't believe in this stupid stuff—you know that I'll never believe in it—so why won't you just leave me the fuck alone?"

The Divine One tilts his masked head to the side, the metallic gold catching in the flickering starlight.

He ignores my question, my plea, and instead says, "The Paragons of Prosperity have a task for you to complete."

A slightly hysterical laugh leaves my dry lips. God, I'm so cold, so numb, as if the snow battering me physically is a representation of the frost attacking me mentally at his words, honing in on me and sharpening into blades made of ice. All I want to do is fall to the ground and surrender to the blissful draw of unconsciousness, allowing slumber to dominate and defeat the panic warring against the numbness inside of me.

"Fuck you." I don't know where I get the burst of courage from, but the words tumble out before I can contain myself.

I brace myself for The Divine One's retaliation, but it never comes. He just continues as if I never spoke. "Have you heard of a man named Reece Whipers?"

"What? No." I shake my head, my confusion over the strange name momentarily eclipsing my need to answer his questions with insults.

I can feel myself tilting to the side as drowsiness grips my brain in a relentless embrace. Numb. So numb. I can't feel my feet, my legs, my arms, my fingers…

The knife slides from my hand and lands in the snow.

Still, The Divine One doesn't take a step closer, merely watching me with that golden mask.

"He's a United States senator and an…acquaintance of your brother. On December sixteenth, you will bring him to me."

"What?" His words don't make sense, rumbling around in my head with no definitive meaning. I blink at him wordlessly as another burst of heavy wind sends me careening to the side.

Suddenly, The Divine One is in my face, his hand around my neck, squeezing until a tiny whimper escapes me. This close, I can see every individual gemstone on his golden face, every intricate line that bleeds into the next. If I had the use of my hands, if I wasn't seconds from collapsing, I would knock that darn mask off his face and end this.

If I could grab my knife…

He tightens his grip around my throat as a cry of pain and fear escapes me.

"You will do what I say, my sweet Ellie, because the alternative is using your darling brother for what I have planned. So I'll let you choose…Reece Whipers or Fischer?" Maybe my brain is playing tricks on me, maybe I'm hallucinating because of the cold, but I swear the lips carved onto his metal face actually twitch into the beginnings of a malicious smile. It sends a cold chill skating down my spine that has nothing to do with the snow. "December sixteenth, Ellie. Remember that date."

Remember…

That…

Date…

And then, darkness consumes me.

CHAPTER 14

Ellie

My research shows me three things about Reece Whipers.

One, he's a senator, like The Divine One said, with only a few bills under his belt.

Two, he's younger, maybe in his early thirties, and is married to a pretty woman with pin-straight black hair and a severe expression.

And finally…he's squeaky clean. There's not a single scandal I could dig up on the elusive senator.

So why the heck is The Divine One after him? How does Reece relate to POP?

It doesn't make sense, but then again, nothing about any of this makes sense.

Obviously, The Divine One knows I'll never willingly work for his cult, so why does he keep pushing the issue? His…interest in me is beginning to border on obsessive, and that scares me more than anything else. Obsession leads to irrationality, and irrationality—especially from someone like The Divine One—can only lead to death.

And what do my guys have to do with all of this? Why is everyone so afraid of them? How are they able to remain untouchable? How did they discover the truth about POP in the first place?

Question after question begins to pile up inside of my head like the Leaning Tower of Pisa. Any second, the building's going to collapse in a sheet of smoke, debris, and wood, annihilating everyone in the immediate vicinity.

A tiny part of me—the same part that has been internally screaming for days now, demanding for someone to hear—wants to confront Landon and the guys. I want to hear what they have to say, now that anger and guilt aren't clouding my every waking thought. But at the same time…

I'm not ready.

My feelings for them have always been too much, too intense, and I'm terrified I'll dive straight into fathomless depths I can't claw myself out of if I take that plunge. If I let them in, truly let them in, then I'll become reliant on them once again. It hasn't occurred to me until recently how much I depended on them and their friendship to get through the years. But right now, I'm shattered, my pieces sharper than glass and just as fragile. It's not fair to give them only tiny slivers of myself, when I know I'm capable of more. And it's not fair to me to be reliant on men who I know are capable of betraying me.

No, I can't be with them until I learn to be with myself. To love myself.

I think about what I asked Fischer for on Thanksgiving, and the first genuine smile in what feels like forever graces my lips. It's there and gone faster than a shooting bullet, a whisper in the wind being carried across roiling seas, but any smile is a start.

But all good cheer and happiness dissipates when I step into my dorm for the first time since break ended.

My hands begin to shake in tandem with my rapidly beating heart as I stare at the figure bent over, searching for something underneath the couch.

"It's not here!" she calls, not bothering to lift her head.

"Check again!" Victoria's posh, accented voice carries from her room, and Piper lets out an annoyed huff, finally shifting onto her knees and wiping off dust from her body. When her gaze lands on mine, she pauses as well, a multitude of emotions flickering in her pretty gemstone eyes.

"El," she whispers, her voice tiny.

A strangled gasp escapes me as I cross the room, collapsing to my knees in front of her and pulling her into my arms. At first, she remains pliant and unresponsive, almost as if she doesn't know how to react, before her arms tentatively embrace me back.

"You're...here," I manage to say through my tears, hugging my friend tightly.

"I am," she whispers. She places her hands on my shoulders and pushes gently, forcing me back. "I decided I couldn't keep...hiding." An ardent, impassioned expression distorts her pretty features, even as her eyes shadow with unbridled pain. But beneath the pain, beneath the grief, rests a stubborn determination that has always inspired me.

A lump forms in my throat when I think about the last time I saw Blair—her eyes, wide and sightless, with blood trickling from the wound on her neck. So much blood...

"How are you holding up?" There's the strangest tugging sensation in the center of my chest. It's not necessarily painful, but it bleeds with every consecutive thump of the sensitive organ.

I don't *want* to hear Piper's answer, because I know that will only exacerbate the guilt rampaging through me. How can I look her in the eyes, hold her in my arms, comfort her, when I'm the cause of Blair's death?

No, a snide voice in my head retorts viciously, *you're not the cause. The Divine One slit her throat. He killed her.*

Tension lines my shoulders as I force my own guilt and pain away, choosing instead to focus on my friend. It's worth it for me to carry all of this anguish so she doesn't have to. So I'll allow her to rage and cry and use my shoulder to lean on, if it abates some of the darkness percolating in her eyes. I'll carry her pain, so she won't have to.

"It..." She takes a shuddering breath, leaning backward until she's on her ass, her legs sticking out in front of her. I remain on my knees between her thighs, my gaze not leaving hers, even when a glistening sheen manifests in her eyes. "It hurts. I wake up, and I can almost believe it was nothing but a horrible nightmare, you know? Like, my brain doesn't want to comprehend that she's truly gone, but I know I need to. I know I need to start living again."

"I understand." My eyes lower to where her hands tug on the bright orange shirt that just barely covers her stomach. "When my parents died, I thought the world was ending. There were so many days that I refused to accept that it was true. I would call my dad and just listen to his voicemail. Or I would race downstairs, prepared to perform a new song I've been working on for my mom, and that pain would hit me all over again. It's like I relived the day they died for months after it actually happened and never saw any relief."

Piper bites down on her lower lip to stop it from trembling. "Not a lot of people understand what I'm going through."

"It's okay to grieve, Piper," I tell her sincerely, taking her hands in mine and giving them a squeeze. "But it's also okay to live your life. You can hold on to your sadness—heaven only knows that I will—but you don't need to let it consume you. You're allowed moments of happiness without feeling guilty you're experiencing them in the first place. The people we love… They would want us to be happy."

God, that line is such a cliché, but it's the truth. I know that if my parents were still alive, they would hate to see me wallowing in my pain and misery. My mother would stare at me with those astute eyes of hers, eyes that never failed to see into my soul, and tell me to live my life, to be happy. My father would agree, but with the caveat that I be happy *without* any men. He was always super protective of me.

"Did you find it?" Victoria's exasperated voice interrupts whatever Piper is going to say. We both swivel our heads to watch the stunning bombshell sashay out of her room, her body adorned in a skin-tight black dress. Her red hair cascades down her back like rubies, emphasized by the slash of violent red on her lips. "*Mon amie*!" She runs toward me with an almost blistering speed, and I let out a slight laugh as we both topple across the floor. She places a noisy kiss to my forehead, no doubt smearing lipstick everywhere, before shuffling off of me, her dress wildly askew.

"I take it you missed me?" I giggle, a lightness in my chest I haven't experienced in…forever.

Victoria's smile fades in the span of a single blink, replaced by a fierce scowl. She hits at my arm hard enough to sting.

"You never returned my messages," she hisses, her tone half accusatory and half indignant.

"I returned some," I argue sheepishly, but I know that's not good enough. "I'm sorry. I was…" Depressed. Suicidal. Terrified. Guilty. Angry. Fearful. "Busy."

"No excuse!" She huffs, sitting backward and folding her arms over her chest. "Friends are supposed to stay together in times of grief, no?"

Guilt instantly flays me open at her words.

She's right, though. I was so lost in my own pain, my own suffering, that I didn't even think of my friends who were experiencing much of the same. Blair was one of their closest friends, and though I know her death hurt Piper the most, all of them suffered.

"Don't make her feel bad," Piper snaps. "We all handle our grief differently."

Victoria rolls her eyes but doesn't comment. Instead, she simply gives me another brisk hug, as if to assure me without words that she isn't truly angry at me, before settling back.

Though she should be.

She really, really should be.

"Where's Jane?" I query, realizing that we're still missing our fourth and final roommate.

"The traitor," Victoria corrects with another sneer, spreading her legs wide so she looks like a porcelain doll XO attempting gymnastics.

Piper makes a face. "I can see your underwear."

"Don't say underwear," Victoria chastises, still sitting with her legs spread wide. "It's so…crude."

"So is sitting like that," I retort, and Piper giggles.

"I see London, I see France, I see—" she singsongs.

"We *really* see France," I tease, interrupting Piper's chant.

Victoria rolls her eyes heavenward, though there's a tiny smile unfurling on her face.

"I'm here! I'm here!" Jane hurries into the room, her glasses sliding down her nose. Unlike the others, who haven't changed in the slightest since I last saw them, Jane's frizzy, disheveled brown hair has been cut into a cute bob, a few wayward bangs sliding across her forehead. Her feet stumble to an abrupt stop when she takes in the three of us sitting on the floor. She cocks her head to the side. "Why are you flashing all of us your panties, Vic?"

Victoria rolls her eyes a second time. "See? Jane has class. We call them panties…not underwear."

"Is that the official French term?" Piper teases as Jane joins our misshapen circle.

As Piper and Victoria continue to argue, I turn toward Jane and offer her a tiny smile. "I love your hair."

Her eyes immediately glimmer as if someone lit a candle beneath the surface. She fluffs up her brown strands with a beatific grin stretching up her lips.

"Really? I wasn't sure if it would be too much or too—"

"Why is the traitor talking?" Victoria huffs, leveling vitriol-filled eyes in Jane's direction.

Jane glares at her in return. "Are you seriously still mad?"

"I'm sorry. All I can hear are fart noises. If you have to go to the bathroom, then go." Victoria sneers.

Jane sighs heavily, though her lips twitch upward in mirth. "I told you I'll help you look."

"I hate the sound of farts," Victoria replies, deadpan.

"Wait. Wait. Wait." I hold my hands up in the air, fending off a laugh. "What are we talking about?"

Piper decides to fill me in, her gaze volleying between Jane and Victoria with amusement. "Basically, Jane borrowed a pair of Victoria's earrings, but they must've fallen out at some point."

"So that's why you were looking under the couch," I say in understanding.

"Because she's a good friend," Victoria says on

a huff, before muttering a few more sentences in rapid-fire French.

Jane's eyes narrow. "You did *not* just call me a human turd."

"Did I?" Victoria cocks her head to the side thoughtfully, her shimmering hair falling over one shoulder like lava. "You must've misunderstood me."

"I took French for three years. I definitely did not."

"Oh, but you did. Because I said you sound like a human turd, not that you are one. Though…if the shoe fits."

I exchange a loaded glance with Piper, and the two of us break into raucous laughter. It's the type of laughter that hurts, the type that has you physically bending forward and holding your stomach as tears stream down your eyes.

God, I needed that laugh.

Some of the darkness pervading my soul, stretching through my limbs like peanut butter, sizzles and then flakes away like a fire burning through the fibers of an old quilt.

And I feel…

Free.

*I*s this what it feels like to fly? To be free?

The words rumble around in my head, rearranging and distorting, until they shift into two lines of a verse.

My body is an instrument, one that I listen to

intently as I move down the quiet halls of the academy. Everyone has already moved back onto campus after the short, two-week break, but classes don't officially start until tomorrow morning.

I take comfort in the familiar hallowed halls as I move toward the music room in the main academic building.

My heart is the drumline, *thump-thump thump-thump*, and the blood sluicing through my veins provides the base. I tap my fingers against my thighs, reminiscent of a piano.

For the first time in forever, music is alive inside of me, a tangible beast that raids my body and pilfers villages. The music has been silent for weeks, but just then, it floods out of me like a dam exploding. Waves of ice-cold water rush forward, filling every crevice, every nook and cranny. Maybe it's because of my roommates. Maybe it's because I've begun the slow and perilous task of reconnecting with the guys. Or maybe, just maybe, it's because the weight that has been pressing down on my shoulders, shoving me into the ground, has begun to melt like snow on a hot summer day. Either way, I feel…alive. Alive and beautiful.

And though I'm 'alone,' I can feel his eyes on me as I move down the hall.

I pretend I don't see him, that I don't know he's there, but I can feel his presence as acutely as a thorn beneath my fingernail. His icy blue eyes burn a hole inside of me, cascading through my veins in waves of vicious, addicting heat. He has the type of eyes you can drown in—as fathomless and unending as the ocean.

And just like the ocean, you never know what you'll see at the bottom.

Ryker doesn't make a single sound as he follows me down the hall, but the caress of his gaze slips over my skin like bubbles in a bath.

I step into the music room and flick on the light, purposely leaving the door open to allow him to slip through when my back's turned.

This feels dangerous, new and intense, but I can't acknowledge *why*, just as I can't acknowledge *him*. His spicy scent tunnels into my throat, a maelstrom of violence, and I can feel my nipples tighten in my bra.

Still, I pretend I don't see him as I sit at the piano bench and rest my fingers over the keys. The music bursts out of me in a raging inferno as I sway back and forth, squeezing my eyelids shut.

I stay in the music room for hours, playing song after song, writing my feelings onto paper and screaming them into the night. They're full of anguish and heartbreak, sorrow and guilt, anger and hostility. They feel immensely personal, like a piece of my soul that has been chipped away, but I don't shy away from them. From the emotions they conjure up inside of me.

And through it all, Ryker remains behind me, a silent shadow.

My shadow.

Chapter 15

Landon

The mantle of leadership has never felt so heavy on my shoulders. There are hundreds, if not thousands, of shattered pieces scattered across the floor of this room, and I know without a shadow of doubt that if I don't reassemble this ragtag puzzle, everything we've built will crumble entirely. Irreparably.

However, I know it's not *me* who keeps our group together. It's never been me.

We're fractured. Five parts who are missing their heart, the portion of themselves that is fundamental and vital to their mere existence. Five souls adrift at sea, with no guiding light to lead us home.

Some days, I feel like I'm merely floating through this world. My entire existence is a black and white movie montage with no definitive meaning. But then I see Ellie's face, hear her sweet voice, watch her face light up with a smile, and a rush of adrenaline courses through my veins, reminding me that I'm alive.

I suppose it's one of the reasons I like to fight. Every punch I throw is another wall I demolish, another chain I snap in half. Pain allows me to bleed, and bleeding ignites a thousand sparks in my brain that make everything oh so real.

That's what I live and die for—pain and Ellie.

The only two real things in my existence.

Well, *two* of the three real things in my existence…

I stare at the men lounging around our shared dorm room, my lips thinning with every passing second.

They look like shit.

Beckett's normally immaculate appearance is in disarray, his brown hair ruffled and his collar askew. Even his tie doesn't hang perfectly down the center of his chest, something I suspect will cause him immense pain and horror once he realizes it.

Zane has fucking crazy eyes, constantly shifting from face to face without ever sticking on one individual for longer than a second. A tiny smirk plays on his lips, and my eyes narrow automatically. The last time the fucker smiled like that, he switched out my body soap with acid. I still have red scars on my skin, that sadistic fucker.

Ryker crouches slightly apart from the others, his hood pulled up over his face and only his ice-blue eyes visible. His sweatshirt hangs open, revealing his heavily scarred chest, though the temperature in the room has dipped to sixty degrees.

What can I say? Our blood runs cold.

Dominic stands to the right of me, his golden arms crossed over his chest and a scowl firmly pasted on his face. His eyes survey the other three guys present before he gives me a barely perceptible nod of his head, urging me to start today's meeting.

I don't sugarcoat things—it's not one of my strong suits. I say things the way they are, whether the people I'm speaking to like it or not. It's a facet that has helped me build an entire goddamn empire out of nothing. That and money. Money can really, really help buy shady motherfuckers, including politicians, gangsters, and everything in between. "You fuckers need to get your life in order."

Beckett blinks at me in shock, while Ryker's scowl deepens. Only Zane seems unperturbed, that sinister smirk still playing on his lips. I really, really don't trust that smile.

"What the fuck are you talking about?" Ryker's gravelly voice sounds from his corner of the room, sharper than any blade I'm capable of wielding.

Dominic interrupts before I can answer. "We're talking about you, dumbass. All of you." He swivels his head to include the other two men as well. "You guys are falling apart."

A low, dark chuckle rumbles from Ryker's chest. The malevolent noise only serves to remind me that Ryker truly is more beast than man, despite the blood coursing through his veins. There's something inherently *wrong* with him, something dangerous that licks at his skin like flames, threatening to burn the entire world to ash.

"We're falling apart?" He cocks his head to the

side with a sneer. "*We* are? I'm not the one who built a goddamn shrine for Ellie in my room and—"

"Fuck you!" Dominic bellows. His hands curl into fists by his sides as he takes a threatening step closer.

"I think you're just pissed that we're actually doing something to win Ellie back," Ryker accuses, slowly rising to his feet. His muscles flex as if he's envisioning ramming his fist repeatedly into Dominic's scowling face.

"Stalking her from the shadows doesn't really count," Dominic retorts viciously. Ryker marches forward another step, his hands still fisted, the promise of pain, violence, and death emanating from his icy blue eyes. Not even Beckett moves to get between them the way he normally would've, content to watch this play out.

Fucking hell.

"Enough!" I bark out, the noise startling enough to have both of their heads snapping in my direction. I don't yell very often, but when I do, you damn well better listen. "Both of you!"

"You're not the goddamn boss of us," Ryker snaps, though he moves backward instinctively, resuming his crouched position in the corner of the room. Dominic marches back to my side, and I can hear how heavily he's breathing as he fights to push back the anger inside of him.

I place a hand on his shoulder, a silent question in my eyes, and he nods tightly, his jaw clenched.

I'm okay, that eloquent gesture seems to say. *I can get a grip on my anger.*

Heaving out a breath, I drop my hand and turn to face the others.

"*This* is what I'm talking about," I snap, gesticulating with my hands wildly. "How can we possibly regain Ellie's trust if we can't even trust each other?"

"He's right," Beckett interjects, twisting on the couch to include Ryker in the statement as well. Ryker simply scowls in response. "We need to think about Ellie and what she needs." He absently forks his fingers through his brown strands, a strangled exhale leaving his lips. "I think she's struggling more than she's letting on."

All of us immediately tense at his words. Even Zane pays attention to the conversation, no longer pretending to be indifferent to it all.

Beckett doesn't cower beneath the sudden surge of scrutiny, despite being the newest member of Mania. By all intents and purposes, he should be the man I trust the least, but that couldn't be further from the truth. I trust him. Implicitly. I know he only has our best interests in mind—as well as Ellie's, which is the most important thing to me. He's desperate to fix what is broken, and that includes our fractured bonds.

I can tell Beckett doesn't want to elaborate on his ominous statement, and my hackles rise almost instantly, fear burning a gaping hole in my stomach lining. If he doesn't want to tell us the truth…then it's bad. Really, really bad.

I quickly change the subject before the other men can come to the same conclusion that I just did. The last thing we need is a bunch of psychopaths setting the town on fire and going on a murdering spree—which they would, if they discovered someone hurt Ellie.

Or if they discovered *she* hurt *herself.*

The mere thought has bile burning my throat, so potent and toxic that I can't help but swallow repeatedly. I can't think of her hurting herself without a strange combination of guilt, agony, fear, and anger drowning me in its oppressive torrent. It's like my brain clicks off for a fraction of a second, unable to acknowledge what's glaring me in the face.

"Beckett's right. We need to do what's best for Ellie. She'd be fucking furious at us if she discovered we allowed our friendship to fall apart," I say sternly, even as my heart thumps unevenly in my chest. Though those words are the truth…they aren't the whole truth.

I don't want to lose my best friends, my brothers.

I *can't.*

God, why is it so difficult to just confess it out loud? To tell them how much they mean to me?

Because you're a twisted fucker with the emotional capacity of a psychopath, that's why.

Ryker's upper lip peels away from his teeth in a sneer. "It's not like you need us." He nods toward Dominic, still standing to the right of me with his arms crossed. "You have the golden boy."

"Fuck you, Ryker," Dominic snaps, but his tone doesn't hold any genuine malice.

"You know what?" He stands abruptly, his eyes as dark and as fathomless as the ocean itself, and stalks forward. "I'm out of here."

"Ryker…" Beckett hollers, but Ryker doesn't

spare the Brit a second glance as he stomps out of the room, the door slamming shut behind him. It seems so…deafening in its finality.

"Fuck!" I aim a punch at the nearest wall, just barely pulling myself back before my knuckles can come into contact with plaster. Still, I shake out my hand as if I've battled an army of giants, pain radiating down my arm from how tightly I fisted my hand in the first place.

"Should one of us go after him?" Beckett nervously fiddles with his tie, as if he has only just now realized that it's crooked.

"And have our heads bitten off? No fucking way," Dominic retorts, though I notice a glimmer of *something* in my best friend's eyes. If I had to take a guess, I would say it's guilt.

"We need to figure out how hard to push Ellie," Beckett insists, giving up on straightening his tie and collapsing back into the sofa. I can see in that one movement how tired he really is. His normally vibrant, dichromatic eyes are dull—vacant, even. He's fucking *drowning*.

My teeth grit together with the need to goddamn fix it. Fix everything. What's the point of all of this power, all of these resources at my disposal, if I can't use them to save the people most important to me?

"We can't push her too hard," I tell them, though my attention is fixated by movement out of the corner of my eye.

Zane, looking repeatedly at his watch.

What the fuck is he up to?

"We don't want her to hate us," Dominic adds.

That captures Zane's attention, and his head swivels to face us. "My *princesa* will never hate us! She can't. She won't. She couldn't. She wouldn't. Wouldn't, couldn't. She promised." There's a note of desperation woven in his tone, and his eyes are wild, unfocused, crazed.

Beckett bites down on his lower lip as he seems to think something through. I can practically hear the cogs and wheels twisting and turning and churning in that brain of his. "You're right," he decides on at last. "I don't think she hates us. I think everything is much more…personal than we initially suspected." He winces, as if afraid he said too much, but before Dominic or Zane can demand answers, the bell rings, signaling we only have a few minutes to get to lunch.

Lunch…

Where we'll be able to see Ellie.

Zane is on his feet in seconds, slipping his backpack on and sliding on his shoes. He doesn't even notice—or care—that his left tennis shoe is untied.

"*I wish that I had Ellie's ass. I wish that I had Ellie's ass. Where can I find an ass like that?*" he sings under his breath, completely butchering the lyrics to "Jessie's Girl" to fit his grisly thinking.

Why am I not surprised that he's singing about her ass?

It certainly is a good one.

I turn to give Dominic a pointed stare, and he sighs heavily. He knows what I want him to do—keep an eye on the unpredictable, volatile, and currently unhinged Zane Lorenzo.

Dominic grabs his own backpack and gives me

another annoyed look before following Zane out of the room. Beckett makes a move to go after both of them when I place a hand on his shoulder.

"Beckett," I say gruffly, feeling as if there are two pieces of wire being twisted around my neck, growing tighter and tighter with every exhale until I'm choking. No matter what I do, I can't untangle them.

Beckett's eyes drop, and he once again runs a shaky hand through his styled brown hair.

"You picked up on that, huh?" Though he phrases it as a question, I can see the resignation in his mismatched eyes. I don't bother to respond to his asinine question, keeping my arms crossed over my chest and an expectant scowl on my face. Beckett gulps but continues. "I think Ellie's hurting herself."

At first, I'm sure I heard him wrong. Or at least, my brain misunderstood the meaning. But when it clicks, something inside of me shatters.

Those words drown me. Burn me. Stab me. Flay me open. Everything that I am, everything I want to be, falls to the floor at my feet in a bloody, disorganized heap. Blood pounds between my ears as fire licks at my veins. Ice grips my heart in an iron vise and squeezes, squeezes, squeezes, squeezes…

"What?" I manage to choke out shakily. My legs feel weak, unsteady, and I barely make it to the chair before I topple over. Spurts of air escape me as I struggle to think rationally, to eradicate the mounting panic in order to do what I do best—fix things.

Lead.

"I don't know for sure." Beckett shuffles from foot to foot, his face devoid of any color and his eyes faraway. Lost. "I thought I saw something on her wrists…"

"Oh god." I'm gonna vomit.

"She's really hurting, Land," Beckett whispers softly. A myriad of emotions flicker across his face as he scrubs a hand down his cheek, stopping at the whiskers lining his chin.

"I need to see her," I rasp out.

Not Ellie.

Not my sweet Ellie.

Beckett hesitates. "I'm not sure if that's a good idea—"

But I'm already out the door and racing down the hall.

I find her in the library, and for a moment, I'm struck speechless by the sight of her. I soak her in like a flower reaching for the sun's blistering rays, basking in her presence.

She doesn't know this—nobody knows this—but I watched her over break. I watched as she wandered aimlessly around the house, searching for something to do to abate the pain and loneliness in her heart. I watched as she drove to the store to purchase supplies for Thanksgiving dinner and ran into Ryker. I watched her stare out the window with a tiny frown crinkling the skin between her brows as she waited for her brother. I followed her when she went to pick up Beckett from the airport, and then again, when she traveled to the bowling alley for her date. The only time I *didn't* have eyes on her was the very last day of break, though I made sure she was safe at home before leaving.

It took every ounce of self-control I possessed to not interfere, to give her the space she begged for.

I wanted to respect her wishes.

It was the hardest thing I've ever fucking done—knowing she was in pain but being unable to help her through it—but I did it because I love her.

And now...

Now I regret every last fucking second of it.

I should've barged into her house the first time Fischer ditched her. I should've sat with her at the table and reminded her how beautiful and perfect and wonderful she is. And then again, when she paced her mansion's halls incessantly, I should've sat her on my lap and held her to me until the restlessness inside of her—the coiled energy demanding an outlet—abated.

I should've been *more*, and I'll never be able to alleviate the guilt inside of me that I hadn't been enough. That I didn't even *try* to be enough.

Ellie's head shoots up, almost as if she senses my presence, and her eyes collide with mine. In that brief moment, entire galaxies are ripped apart and then sewn back together. Worlds are created, mountains are destroyed, and oceans dry up before getting refilled by fresh torrents of rainfall.

That's what my connection to her feels like—life and destruction, wrapped together in a deadly package.

I'm across the room in seconds, surveying her from head to toe.

"Landon." A tiny smile graces her pink lips,

though it's tainted with sadness. Violet circles rim her vibrant eyes, visible even beneath her glasses. "I…I missed you."

There's so much I want to say to that confession, so much I want to tell her, but I don't do any of that.

I drop my backpack onto the table and move to sit in the chair next to her. Before she can comment, I reach over, pluck her up, and set her on my lap. My arms band around her skinny stomach as her breath hitches in surprise.

"What…?"

She's so tiny, so delicate, that I'm afraid I'll hurt her just by touching her.

My fault.

My fault.

Why didn't you take better care of her?

My chest rumbles as I lower my face to the top of her head, digging it into her brown hair and inhaling her scent. The temperamental monster in my soul, the one clawing toward the surface with blood-painted nails, calms marginally.

Her tiny hands fist in my blazer, and at first, I think she's pushing me away. But then I realize that her body is as close to me as physically possible, her soft curves pressed against my chiseled, hard muscles, and something inside of me relaxes, my stiff muscles loosening.

She's not pushing me away. She's pulling me closer.

"I'm so sorry," I whisper brokenly against her crown. "I'm so, so sorry."

I don't even know what I'm apologizing for—

the secrets I kept, the lies I told, my failure to take care of her health, both mental and physical—but I know I won't stop until my words seep into her brain. I need her to understand, to believe me.

"Oh, Landon." She sniffles, her arms reaching out to wrap around my neck.

"I never should've kept secrets from you. I'm sorry. I'm so, so sorry." It seems as if those are some of the only words I'm capable of saying.

She leans back on my lap, and her tiny hand cups my cheek.

"I want to know everything, Landon," she says in a soft voice. And though her lower lip wobbles, her eyes are clear. Determined. Steely.

I place my forehead against hers and exhale shakily.

"Everything," I agree, but a cunning voice in my head wonders if that will be enough. If she'll ever truly forgive us.

What if she hears everything and she still wants to run?

Would I even let her go?

I shake my head to dislodge the errant thought and focus on Ellie, only Ellie. The rest of the world ceases to exist when she's in my arms.

I open my mouth to tell her everything, but she places her hand over it to silence me.

"Not now," she whispers, tucking her head back beneath my chin. When she speaks, her lips caress my neck, and fireworks burst to life inside of me at the contact. "I want all of us to be together for this."

All of us.

Mania.

In a moment of helplessness, I press a kiss against her head. And then another one. And then another one. And then another one. She trembles in my arms, her grip on me tightening, but she doesn't pull away or ask me to stop.

"We can talk tonight—" I begin.

She shakes her head adamantly. "Not tonight. I just…" She blows out a breath. "Not tonight," she repeats at last.

My eyelids flutter shut, and a stray tear catches in one of my dark lashes. "You need more time, don't you? More space?"

"I just don't want to be mad, Landon." Her voice is muffled from where it's still pressed against my skin. "And I know that right now, every confession you tell me will feel like a betrayal." The strangest sound escapes my throat at that—almost like a whine—but she continues on. "I know that you guys care about me and want to protect me. And I promise you, I'm not mad at you. At least, I don't think I am. But I…I just need time to accept everything. It might be stupid and idiotic, but I'm terrified of what this information will do to me."

My heart squeezes at the desperation in her voice.

My kitten's struggling, and I don't know how to help her.

"Okay, kitten. Okay." I kiss her head again. "Later."

"But if there's anything I need to know right now, any details about POP or The Divine One that will help me…" She trails off with a shudder.

"No." I shake my head quickly before planting another kiss to the top of her head. "Nothing we tell you will make any difference with what you're going through."

She already knows about the human sacrifices, Cassia, and The Divine One. Everything else we tell her will only make her hurt more.

And I refuse to do that. I fucking refuse.

She trembles in my arms, so small, so delicate, so fragile, and all I want to do is keep her in my embrace forever.

Even as the thought solidifies, a bang erupts from outside, so loud and deafening that I drop to the floor automatically, keeping my arms wrapped around Ellie. I throw myself on top of her, prepared to protect her from any threat, when students burst inside, some crying and some laughing.

"What the heck?" Ellie murmurs from beneath me, and I lift my head to see people racing down the hall in the direction of the bathrooms, all of them covered in a sticky red substance. It could be paint, but it almost looks like…

"You!" I growl, jumping to my feet and pointing a finger at a tiny freshman. He stumbles to a stop immediately, his eyes widening when he sees who has addressed him. "What the fuck is going on?"

He swallows, his nails biting into his palms as he meets my stare. He can only hold it for a second before he drops it to his feet, shifting uncomfortably. Sometimes, I regret all of my decisions in life. Other times, like now, I remember how much I love being a cold-hearted asshole with the ability to instill fear in every student and teacher at this school. "I-um-someone-um…" He swallows. "Someone released a blood bomb in the courtyard."

"A blood bomb?" My eyebrows furrow in disbelief.

The kid nods. "It's like a glitter bomb, but it…um…has…blood in it and…" He turns on his heel and races down the hall before I can question him further, the stench of fear permeating where he once stood.

"A blood bomb?" a soft voice questions.

I startle, turning to see Ellie standing directly behind me, her hand hovering over my back as if she wants to touch me but isn't sure if she's allowed to.

The two of us exchange a long, loaded look, and as one exclaim, "Zane."

I'm going to need to have a talk with him, and soon. Before he does something he can't come back from.

CHAPTER 16

Ellie

Homework is the bane of my existence.

I swear the days following any prolonged break are always the worst, as if the teachers feel the need to assert their dominance over the student body and remind us that they still have five long months to torture us until the school year ends.

December, January, February, March, April, and then May. And that's not even counting winter break and spring break. And then…

And then I'll be free.

The shackles that The Divine One and the Paragons of Prosperity put around my wrists won't be able to contain me when I'm halfway across the world.

A tiny, serene smile drifts across my face at the thought. Away.

I just need to get away.

But…

Fischer. Victoria. Piper. Jane.

Landon. Dominic. Beckett. Ryker. Zane.

My throat closes up, emotions battering my defenses, when I recall my moment with Landon in the library on Monday. I felt so safe in his arms, as if even the fiercest of storms wouldn't be able to plow me over. How can anyone touch me, anyone harm me, with a presence like him in my life? He's always been larger-than-life, exhibiting a God-like complex I find both endearing and annoying in equal measure. But when he held me like that, like I was the only thing that mattered to him…

My heart cinches painfully at the memory.

I can feel my defenses thawing every day I'm in these men's presence. They're dangerous, volatile beasts, but I don't want to tame them. I want to…

Is it wrong if I say that I want to *be* them? To embrace their darkness? To join their fold completely and irrevocably?

We've always been close friends, but for years, I felt as if there was a divider between us. They would allow me to sit by myself at lunch, yet show up on every date I had for years. They would refuse to speak to me for weeks at a time, yet I would feel their gazes on my skin, the softest of caresses, as I glided through the halls. They forced me into their clothes, fed me, held me in their arms, yet they never asked me if I wanted to be theirs.

And I wanted to.

I still want to.

My throat closes, and I squeeze my eyelids shut.

These men—these vicious, dangerous, *kind* men—are chipping away the iron wall around my heart, one day at a time.

A tiny smile curls up my lips when I think about class earlier today. European History with Mr. Moreau.

"Turn to page eighty-four in your textbooks, please," Mr. Moreau instructed from the front of the room.

He was younger than most of my teachers this semester, appearing to be in his early-thirties. His black hair was covered in so much gel and product, it almost glistened beneath the artificial lighting. A birthmark rested above his left eyebrow, the brown a striking contrast against his pale skin.

I flipped to the assigned page just as a slip of paper fell onto my desk. I glanced first at Beckett on one side of me and then at Landon on the other, assessing their reactions. Both were staring pointedly ahead, acting oblivious to the mysterious note. My lips curled upward as I unfolded it, straightening out the creases.

Are you a writing utensil? Because you're the highlighter of my life.

And of course, the message was written in vibrant neon yellow.

A snort of laughter escaped me, one that I quickly covered with my hand so I wouldn't get in trouble, as I read the message.

Which one of them had written that for me?

It could've been Beckett—that was definitely his humor—but I wasn't ruling out Landon completely yet. Especially after our talk in the library on Monday.

The way he'd held me in his arms...

I squirmed in my seat, a sudden heat flooding

me, as I focused on Mr. Moreau. His eyes were narrowed on me, suspicion emanating from those gray depths as if he knew the reason for my sudden wiggling, but I adopted an innocent expression, and he finally turned away to continue his lesson.

A wad of paper bounced off my forehead and hit the desk.

What the...?

I glared at Beckett, who was still staring ahead impassively, and then at Landon. The latter turned toward me with a quirked eyebrow.

What? That eloquent look seemed to ask, and I had to give him credit. He looked genuinely confused...which only made me more suspicious.

I blew out a breath and shook my head before opening up the second note.

Did you turn into a frog? Because you're playing leapfrog with my heart.

My cheeks burned as I read the embarrassingly cheesy pickup line. Oh. My. Gosh. That one definitely sounded like Landon whenever he was trying to make me smile. And that handwriting? I was almost one hundred percent certain it was his. But the other note looked to be written by Beckett...

A third slip of paper slipped in front of me before I could blink.

Three words stared back at me, so idiotic that I couldn't stop the laughter from bubbling out of my throat. I just barely clamped my teeth together before the sound could emerge completely and capture our teacher's attention.

I see you.

Those letters were accentuated by a ton of hearts and smiley faces.

Beckett. Definitely Beckett.

And then a fourth note, **How many Becketts does it take to change a lightbulb? Two, because the first one will get distracted by his reflection in the bulb.**

Landon.

A joyous laugh spilled out of me, and this time, I couldn't catch it in time. It tumbled free, garnering the attention of the entire classroom.

Mr. Moreau's shrewd eyes zeroed in on my face like two heat-seeking missiles, and I suddenly felt like a butterfly pinned beneath a magnifying glass. This time when I wiggled, it was for a completely different reason.

"Do I need to see you after class, Ellie?" he growled, and was I mistaken, or was that a flash of heat I saw flaring in his eyes? What the heck?

A cold chill worked its way over my arms and down my neck.

Before I could muster up an apology, Beckett murmured, "Quit being a tosspot and hurry on with the lesson, you old fart."

A flurry of scandalized "ohhhs" carried throughout the room, and Mr. Moreau's eye twitched hard enough to make me fear he was having a stroke.

"Beckett, please see me after class," he snapped through gritted teeth, his anger at me apparently forgotten.

And just like that, they'd saved me from getting in trouble.

They always seemed to be saving me.

These men make me feel so many emotions—most of them indecipherable and dangerous to my health—that I know I need an outlet. I need…something.

I need my music.

Following my fit on Halloween night, I was able to replace almost everything that had been destroyed *except* for the things that matter most to me—my pillows, books, and instruments. Sure, I could easily buy a bunch of random pillows from the store, but they wouldn't be the same. The pillows I shredded were gifts that spanned years and years and years, proof that my brother loves me unconditionally and irrevocably. And yes, I could go online and purchase all of the books that had gotten destroyed, but the new ones wouldn't have the creases on the spine I've grown so familiar with, the lines on the paper from how frequently I read them. And my instruments? Well, I just haven't had the motivation to even *think* about buying new ones.

I slam the textbook shut and shuffle to my feet, glancing down at my bare legs and golden retriever slippers. I'm already dressed for bed in a long-sleeve, thin shirt and shorts, but it's late enough where I don't think I'll run into anyone on my way to the music room. Still, I can't be too careful, especially after what happened the other night with POP, so I slip a coat on and tuck a knife inside the pocket.

I take comfort in its unassuming weight, my eyelids squeezing shut once more.

Sometimes when I close my eyes, I can see the

dagger embedded in the POP woman's shoulder. See the blood staining her dark cloak. Hear the thud she made as she fell to the ground. And then her face would warp, the mask giving way to Blair's familiar, elfin features and a slash of red would appear across her throat, and I would be forced to relive her death all over again.

The worst moment was when my mind made me think about *her*. The woman I killed. The woman whose head banged against the table, causing her blood to stain the floor like a rug. Patricia. And with her death comes the painful reminder that I'm…a murderer.

I take a deep breath to fight back the growing nausea, screaming at my brain to leave me alone.

There's nothing wrong with you.

I repeat my mother's words like a mantra, a prayer, until the images fade, swept away in a tidal wave of anger. When I reopen my eyes, I feel calmer. Focused, almost. I have one goal and one goal only— release this pent up anger and frustration the only way I know how.

The dorm is silent when I slip out of my room, the lights out beneath my friends' doors. I don't know if it's because they're sleeping or if they chose to go to a party. With Victoria, I wouldn't be surprised if it's the latter. Though Piper *has* been drinking a lot lately…

I hurry out of the dorm, down the hallway, and then outside, allowing the crisp, winter air to crash over me. I breathe in deeply, the smell of pine tunneling into my throat, before focusing my attention on the main academic building and the music room I know is hidden inside.

I was given the key earlier this year by the music teacher, after my schedule changed so I was no longer taking music class. She knows how much I love to compose, how it's the only thing that calms me. I'm a bundle of nerves most of the time, but when I sit at a piano bench or strum the strings of a guitar, I'm just…me. I no longer feel as empty inside. As broken.

All of the lights of the main academic building are off when I step inside, but they switch on automatically as I move forward. I don't know why the school doesn't lock up at night, but maybe it's because they assume no one will be stupid enough to sneak inside. It's not like the students here will steal anything—most of us are richer than entire countries. Heck, a few of the students here even *own* their own country.

My footsteps echo off the marble flooring, but I don't feel any fear. I half want The Divine One to materialize out of the shadows, if only so I can end this once and for all. With my hand on the hilt of my dagger, I feel powerful. Untouchable.

When I reach the music room, I'm shocked to find the lights already on. At first, I think the teacher forgot to turn them off when she left for the day, but when I step closer, I see that there's someone already inside the classroom.

Mr. Moreau sits at the piano bench, his fingers moving over the keys with a speed that is both baffling and awe-inspiring.

As if he can feel my gaze on him, his eyes snap open, and he spears me with an unreadable look.

"Ellie," he says, still swaying as he finishes his piece. Mozart, I believe, though I'm not familiar enough with classical artists to identify the exact composition. "Isn't it past your curfew?"

"I didn't think we had curfews," I confess, leaning against the door frame to watch him play. Something about Mr. Moreau makes me uneasy, but when he plays…

It's easy to forget all of that.

"I feel as if we're always meeting like this," he tells me as his fingers begin to slow down, before coming to a complete stop in the center of the piano.

"I'm sorry for interrupting, Mr. Moreau—"

"Noah," he corrects, slowly rising from the bench.

I swallow. "I can come back at a later time."

"No need." He waves a hand in the air dismissively as he stalks forward. In all the months I've known him, I've never seen him wear anything other than gaudy suits and dress clothes. Today, however, he's wearing a pair of faded blue jeans and a gray sweater. Even his normally slicked back hair is now messily falling forward into one of his eyes as if he hasn't bothered to comb it. "I'm leaving anyway, and a young girl like you needs to cultivate your mind however she can." He flashes me a smile that, for some reason, sends prickles of unease and dread racing down my spine like shooting stars. I shove the strange reaction away, taking a great deal of comfort in the knife in my jacket pocket, and smile back at him.

"I'm sorry for disrupting class earlier today," I tell him sincerely. "It won't happen again."

"You're a good student, Ellie," he says as he grabs a coat off the rack and slips it on. As he puts his on, I take mine off. While the outside had been freezing, the wind biting and keen, the inside is an inferno of heat. I swear the school staff keeps the temperature in the one hundreds at all times as another way to torture their students.

Mr. Moreau sucks in a sharp gasp, and I turn to find him staring at me intently. Or more specifically, my chest, my nipples clearly visible in the thin shirt I wear. I try not to feel too uncomfortable, try to remind myself that he's a married man and my teacher, but my heart still pounds with fear anyway. That fear turns into uncomfortable fire—searing, blistering, soul-churning fire—when he takes a step closer.

"It seems as if you…" He drops his hand, and I follow the path it makes with wide eyes.

But he simply grabs at a leaf that must've gotten stuck to my shirt when I was walking over here.

"There. Got it." He smiles at me, removing his hand, and I feel his fingers graze my pebbled nipple in the process. I immediately go still, even as a shudder of what almost looks like desire ripples through my teacher. A coldness burns away the last of the heat in my body, and the numbness I've become so familiar with encompasses me from head to toe. I'm not even sure I'm breathing. "I better get home." He chuckles, finally taking a step backward and allowing me to breathe again.

Though that doesn't stop the fear from pulsing through me.

"Your wife is probably wondering where you

are," I say lightly, putting a little extra emphasis on the word wife.

His eyes darken almost immediately, though that sharp grin remains plastered on his face. "She knows about my love for music." He chuckles humorlessly. "You can take the man out of the music, but you can never take the music out of the man. Or however that stupid saying goes."

He continues to stare at me with that unnerving, debilitating intensity, and I debate running. Maybe I can grab my knife and—

"I'll see you in class Monday morning, Ellie," he tells me, finally stepping toward the still open door of the music room. "Don't forget to do your reading."

"Already started it, Mr. Moreau."

"Noah," he corrects again. And then, in a softer voice, he adds, "Or sir."

Yeah…how about *no*.

I smile tightly, my hands turning clammy by my sides, but I try to rationalize everything that just happened. Sure, he's a little too 'friendly' to be normal, but maybe I'm just imagining he has creepy intentions. Maybe his fingers accidentally grazed my nipple and he sucked in a breath because he was horrified. We're alone right now, and he easily could've attacked me if that was what he wanted to do.

I take a deep, shuddering breath, even as a single thought solidifies in my brain.

No matter what his intentions are, you need to stay away from him.

Stay away from Noah Moreau.

For all I know, he's working for POP. Hell, he

could be The Divine One, hence all of the attention he aims at me.

Mr. Moreau whistles under his breath as he steps into the now darkened hallway—apparently, the timers switched off after only a few minutes—and I make a beeline toward the piano. Before I can take a single step, I hear the thump of a body, multiple pained cries, a muffled scream, and then silence.

My first reaction is to freeze, every muscle locking tight, but I force myself to move, to step toward the coat rack where I have my knife—

A huge, hulking figure stands in the doorway, silhouetted in shadows. My pulse hammers, my breath leaving in shallow gasps, and even when he steps forward, the fear doesn't dissipate completely.

There's something wild, unhinged, and manic about the man stalking toward me like a beautiful, avenging angel.

Ryker.

Chapter 17

Ryker

My mother once called me a beast, a monster, a demon, a cloven-foot menace, and she would be right. I've always known there was a darkness inside of me, stretching through me like sticky tar, but I never felt it as intensely as I had when I saw Mr. fucking Moreau graze his fingers across Ellie's breast.

I didn't think, just acted. I slammed my fist into his smug, grotesque face…and then kept punching. I beat him with a ruthless type of savageness that made me infamous around school and in the fight clubs I frequented. The desire to inflict pain—to taste it on my tongue like a decadent dessert—was almost too much for me to ignore.

I didn't just want Mr. Moreau to suffer.

I wanted him to die.

There's something so goddamn addicting about feeling my knuckles crack and seeing the blood run down my fingers. Something heady and enticing. Fighting, breaking things, hurting motherfuckers… They ease the relentless tugging inside my chest, filling the void of emptiness with something tangible and so goddamn beautiful.

It feeds the beast inside of me, allowing him to burrow back beneath my skin where he'll wait until I'm ready for him again.

But now…

Now, my penchant for violence has caused me a shit ton of trouble.

Ellie's staring at me with wide eyes, her pink lips parted. Fear trickles down deep into the root of my soul as I tug my hood up over my head and take a step backward. I want to run, something I haven't done since I was a small child.

I can already hear my mother's voice echoing through my head—weak, coward, failure. The reminder stings with the keenness of a wasp, but it's nothing compared to the desperation I have to get the fuck away from here. Now.

"Ryker!" Ellie calls tentatively from behind when I turn, and I know I should leave her, should run, before my beast has a chance to be set free on her, but I don't. I'm damn weak when it comes to her. "What did you do to him?" Her voice is a whisper, and I reluctantly twist to face her, praying my hood hides the majority of my features from view. But her features? I can see them as clear as day, and it makes my heart hammer incessantly.

I expect to see disgust, maybe even fear, but none of those obvious emotions greet me. Does she know I just knocked the perverted fucker unconscious in the hallway? He's not dead—but only because of this angel standing before me. I don't want to expose her to any more violence than I have to, so by her mercy, he'll live to sleeze another day.

That isn't to mean he'll sleeze at my goddamn school...

"You're hurt." Her gaze lowers to my busted knuckles, and once again, I brace myself for her disgust and fury.

It never comes.

I don't answer her, making sure there's enough distance between the two of us that I won't do something stupid...like pounce on her. Like shove her over the piano bench and fuck her tight ass as she moans my name.

I slowly lower myself to the floor in my normal crouching position, never allowing my eyes to stray from her sweet face.

She takes a tentative step forward, but I remain perfectly still, almost as if I really am the shadow I like to so often hide in. As if she won't be able to see me if I refuse to even twitch my fucking pinkie finger.

Slowly, ever so slowly, she crouches before me as well, and her eyes dip to my busted knuckles, a tiny crease appearing between her brows.

"He touched you." My voice is raspy from disuse—or maybe it's from the sudden dryness clogging my throat. I can never tell.

Her eyes darken as she grabs my hand, twisting it to and fro to inspect my wounds better. I watch as her teeth nibble on her lower lip, and I wonder what she would do if I replaced her teeth with my own.

Probably call the fucking cops on me, because in a span of minutes, I proved to her that I'm not only a stalker, but a psychopath with anger issues.

The thought makes me growl—not the prospect of her seeing me as a murderer and stalker, which I am, but the thought of being taken away from her by the police. If they came for me, I would fight tooth and nail to get back to her. They'll fucking bleed at my feet, a sacrifice served to my goddess, before I'd allow them to remove me from her presence.

Ellie's lower lip begins to tremble as she finally drops my hand and stands. "This is all my fault."

What?

What?!?

Her words are enough to send me shooting to my feet and stalking toward her. She gapes up at me, her breathing hitching, but she follows me step by step until she's pressed against the piano, her back bent slightly. The position draws my eyes to her breasts and those sharp little nipples poking through the material of her long-sleeve shirt. My cock twitches—though it's already been semi-erect since I punched Mr. Moreau in the face, something I've yearned to do since he first arrived at the school and expressed an interest in my girl.

I cup her cheek with my hand, allowing my palm to trail down to her collarbone, before resting it there. I take a deep, calming breath, inhaling her scent, before I whisper, "Why do you think it's your fault, baby? You did nothing wrong."

"I…I always try to see the best in people," she

flounders helplessly, and if she thinks that's a horrible trait to possess, she'll be solely mistaken. It might be the only one allowing me to stand so close to her. If she were a normal human being, with normal sensibilities, she would've run for the hills by now. Not that I would let her go.

I would just hide in the trees if she chose to live up there.

"I still don't understand." I blow out a breath of frustration, but she picks up where she left off.

"Even after he…touched me," a delicate tremble works its way through her, and I feel an answering growl of my own erupt from my chest, "I still dismissed it in my head as an accident." She pauses, lifting her hands until she's able to capture my wrists. At first, I think she's pushing me away, throwing my hands off of her, but she merely nuzzles against my palm like a cat. "I sometimes wonder if that's what led to all of this in the first place. If I'm just too…trusting." She makes a face, as if she's repulsed by that word.

"You're perfect," I declare venomously, though my ire isn't directed at her but at the situation. How can she not see what I see? How can she not see the perfection of her soul wrapped up in an equally beautiful body?

She snorts adorably. "Says you." I swear her eyes roll back so hard, they're in danger of falling out.

"Says me?" My brows shoot upward as she laughs softly.

"You're…you." She gestures toward me helplessly, and I croak out a dry laugh.

"I don't really know where you're going with

this, baby."

She growls adorably—probably trying to resemble a ferocious tiger and coming across as a deranged kitten, hence the nickname Landon has for her—and frowns. "You think that you're all dark and broody, but I know the real you, Ryker."

My heart thumps out of rhythm at her dogmatic, *passionate* words. "And who might that be?"

Instead of answering my question, she licks her lips and tilts her head to the side. "You care about me, don't you?"

The question takes me by surprise and momentarily stalls my brainwaves.

How can I tell her that I don't just care about her, but love her more than anything in this whole entire world? It's a twisted type of love, because I'm a twisted man, but it's the only pure thing I have in my life. Even violence, one of the few things that makes me feel alive, is tainted by bloodlust and malice. But the love I feel for her? The way she can bring me to my knees with a single word? It's so fucking beautiful, I could get weepy.

If I were a fucker who got weepy over romantic shit, I mean.

I'll never be the Prince Charming type of man—unless this Cinderella wants to get plowed a thousand different ways in the middle of the ballroom—but I'll always, *always* protect her with the darkness pervading my soul.

We all would.

Mania.

It's why we formed, after all.

"You're actually kind of a…dear," she murmurs with a tiny grin, knowing what those words would do to me.

I'm a lot of fucking things—dangerous, damaged, deranged, and a multitude of other d-words, not least including dick—but 'dear' isn't one of them. Dears make me think of deer, and do you wanna know where deer end up? On the side of the street dead as pickup trucks race in the opposite direction with blood splattering their headlights. I'm a fucking pickup truck, dammit, not the creature it mows down.

Ellie laughs at whatever expression she sees on my face before tapping on my chest in a clear indicator for me to step back.

I don't know why her rejection stings so much, but it does.

I think, *This is it. This is finally the moment she leaves me for good.*

But she doesn't leave me. At least, she doesn't go far.

She walks toward a tiny office near the back of the room, and when she opens the door, I see a collection of instruments—most of which I don't know the names of because I'm a musical dumbass—and a desk. It's the desk she goes to, pulling something out of a drawer and then hip-checking it to close it on her way back to me.

I glance at the item she now holds in her hand, and my heart swells. I swear it trips over itself before landing in a subservient position at her feet.

"Let me clean you up," she tells me, nodding toward my busted hand.

I rumble something noncommittal in the back of my throat.

I've had way worse injuries than a couple of bruises, but I don't stop her as she places the medicine kit on the piano and grabs out items at random. I have no idea what, though, because I can't drag my eyes away from her face.

Sometimes, when she looks at me the way she is now, I have the distinct impression she's seeing straight into my soul. That used to terrify me, but everything has changed. *I've* changed. I now know what it feels like to live in a world where Ellie hates me, and I would rather cut off my own arm than experience that agony again.

Trust is earned, not presumed, and if I have to spend the rest of my godforsaken life earning hers back, then I would. That's what she values more than anything else, I've come to realize. It's why our betrayal hurt her so badly, cut her so deeply. She can handle a lot of things, but broken trust isn't one of them.

I search her eyes for any sign of animosity, bitterness, or even anger, but there's only determination as she wipes at my busted knuckles with some sort of antiseptic. It stings, but I relish the bite of pain, storing it away in a place deep inside my chest where my monster resides. He feeds off this shit like a heroin addict getting his next fix.

"You're really not mad at us anymore?" I ask cautiously as she drops the spray and grabs a wrap.

She hesitates, only for a second, before continuing her task. "No," she whispers at last.

"Then why have you been ignoring us?" My words are a goddamn plea, but I'm man enough to admit that I'm lost without her. Can't she see what this is doing to me? To us?

Fire eats at me, charring my skin, as I await her answer. I'm not even sure I'm breathing.

"It's more complicated than that," she whispers.

"More complicated than what?" I rasp out, my voice failing on the final two words. I clear my throat and focus on her sweet face, her eyes currently downcast as she finishes wrapping my knuckles. Without lifting her head to meet my gaze, she begins placing the items back into the tiny blue box before snapping it shut. She grabs it, turning away from me—

And I pull her back against my chest before I can stop myself, allowing the hardness of my erection to dig into her ass. She freezes automatically, her muscles locking tight, as I growl into her ear. "I won't let you ignore me anymore, baby. I can't."

She whimpers, the strangled sound laced with unbridled desire, as she wiggles against me. I close my eyelids shut against the surge of pleasure that courses through me before placing a hand on her hip to still her.

"Don't do that," I warn through gritted teeth. Because if she keeps gyrating her hips against me, I might just pull down those tiny shorts and—

She wiggles against me a second time, almost experimentally, as a breathy moan leaves her lips.

And this time? I know it's on purpose.

I growl sharply, even as her sweet giggles fill the music room, more beautiful than any of these fucking stupid instruments. She begins to walk away from me, but I grab her by the neck with a blistering speed and spin her around. She gasps, her eyes widening in alarm, but I keep walking her backward until she's once again leaning against the piano.

"If you continue to be a bratty girl, I'll have no choice but to put you over my knee and spank your ass until it's red," I warn her breathily.

Her eyes widen into saucers, and at first, I think I said the wrong thing.

Fucking hell, Ryker! Why couldn't you just leave your dumb mouth shut for once?

Stupid.

Idiotic.

Careless.

Piece of shit.

Useless—

But then molten heat flares in her gaze, traveling straight to my cock.

Without breaking eye contact, she presses her hips against mine and grinds against my dick.

That fucking does it…

I grab her beneath her ass and hoist her onto the piano, allowing her legs to rest on my arms. I'm not going to spank her like I promised—she's not ready for that—but I am gonna leave my mark on her. By the time she leaves this music room, she's gonna know exactly who she belongs to.

I hold her gaze, allowing her to see the beast she unleashed, as I grab her cheeks in both hands kand force her head back. She stares at me, her pupils dilated and her chest heaving, but I don't immediately kiss her. I just…look.

I look at the girl I've loved for so many fucking years, and I swear I turn to a puddle of goo at her feet. I half want to pinch myself to confirm this isn't a dream, because I've wanted this, wanted her, for as long as I can remember. There hasn't been anyone else, and I know there never will be. It'll just be her. Always and forever.

I press my forehead against hers, loving the way her hot breath feathers against my face.

"Ryker…" There's a plea in her voice, but also a hint of confusion too, as if she doesn't know what to ask for. What she wants. That thought makes me even harder, a feat I didn't think was possible.

"Do you want me to make you feel good, baby?" I whisper as I plant a tender kiss to first one eyelid and then the next when she closes them.

"Yes," she all but begs, her voice a whimper.

"You can tell me to stop whenever you want," I warn, my hips already thrusting forward of their own accord and reaching nothing but air. I've never been this turned on in my whole damn life.

"Ryker…" Her adorable growl comes back as she tugs on my sweatshirt, forcing my lips down to hers.

And I swear, there are fireworks. Tons and tons of fireworks that detonate inside of me, until all I can see is their blinding light.

I moan against her lips, prodding them with my tongue until she opens for me.

I don't just kiss her—I devour her. I devour her the way I've been desperate to do since we were kids and I first understood the meaning of lust. Where we touch, we dissolve into each other, until I can't differentiate where she ends and I begin. Maybe we're infinite, a bond that can't be broken.

Or maybe kissing her has turned me into a sappy motherfucker.

I leave her lips, if only to allow her to breathe, and sloppily kiss down her throat, making sure to trail my tongue along her tender flesh. Call me a sadist or a caveman or a psychopath, but the thought of leaving my saliva on her skin makes me want to come in my pants. The only two things that would make this even better? Biting her perfect, unblemished skin hard enough to scar and having her wear my cum for the rest of her goddamn life.

I practically orgasm at the thought as my fingers reach the hem of her thin shirt. I glance up at her through my sooty lashes, asking her wordlessly if this is okay, and without responding, she pulls it up until it settles just above her breasts. She doesn't take it off completely, though, but I'm too enthralled with her perfect tits to ask why.

Her nipples are already beaded, a rosy pink color that has me lowering my head to flick the right one with the pad of my tongue.

"Ryker," she moans in surprise, her fingers dropping downward to fist in my hair. With my hood still on, she only manages to clutch the gray fabric, but that doesn't seem to deter her.

I take my time sucking on her right nipple as my fingers pinch and pluck her left one. Tiny gasps of pleasure leave her lips as she throws her head back, her glasses becoming askew.

It suddenly occurs to me that we're in the main academic building, where anyone could walk in and see us. Sure, it's after hours, but that didn't stop me or Ellie or that fucker Mr. Moreau, for that matter, from walking in here. Not only that, but the door to the music room is wide open. Anyone walking down the hall can peek inside and see exactly what we're doing. Even the asswipe unconscious in the hallway could wake up and stare in at us.

The thought makes me growl against her tit, but when she cries my name again, it dissipates.

So what if any fucker tried to look in on us? I'd simply kill them for seeing what's mine.

And if there's one thing I love, it's violence. Not as much as I love Ellie and her perfect body, heart, soul, and mind…but it's a close second. Okay, maybe not a *close* second, but—

"I need more, Ryker," Ellie pleads, tugging my face away from her nipple to meet my gaze.

"Are you sure, baby?" I whisper, but even as I speak, I place my hands on her thighs, caressing the silky-smooth skin.

"Please, Ryker. Please," she begs, and that's what does me in.

My girl should never beg.

I plant a chaste kiss against her right inner thigh and then her left one, loving the ripple of goosebumps that erupt on her flesh from the contact.

"Lean back, baby." I rise and place a hand in the center of her chest, pushing her onto her back on the grand piano. "Let me take care of you."

Is this real life? Is this actually happening?

How many nights have I imagined this exact case scenario? My imagination has nothing on reality.

Ellie is…radiant. Fucking majestic. If I didn't want any other assholes to see her, any other man to lust after her, I would say she should spend the rest of her life naked. And she hasn't even taken off her shirt, sleep shorts, panties, and puppy slippers. She's technically fully dressed, and I somehow find that even sexier than if she was completely naked.

"Ryker…" A hint of self-consciousness creeps into her tone when I just continue to stare at her, not moving, not speaking, not even breathing.

A goddess like her should never feel self-conscious.

"You're gorgeous, baby," I tell her sincerely. "So fucking beautiful."

A blush flares in her cheeks, coloring the skin to a creamy pink, as she gives me a shy smile.

"You're beautiful too." Her eyes dip down to my scarred stomach appreciatively before stopping at my jeans, where my cock presses against the confines. Aching. Wanting. Ready for her.

But then I register her words, and I bite back on the snort that wants to slip free.

I have too many scars to ever be considered beautiful. But the way she's looking at me, as if she actually believes that bullshit…

I take off the ridiculous golden retriever slippers and toss them aside. My mouth practically salivates as I grab the waistband of her sleep shorts and tug them down her legs, allowing them to fall to the floor. When she's dressed in only a pair of tiny black panties, I groan deep in my throat.

"Fuck me," I moan. This will definitely be an image I'll remember for years and years to come. Hell, who am I kidding? I'll be on my deathbed, remember this exact moment, and get an old man boner that will kill me with its intensity. What a way to fucking go, though.

It takes me no time whatsoever to remove her tiny panties as well, and if I thought Ellie was sexy in her black thong, it's nothing compared to what she looks like nearly naked. I swear, my brain short-circuits as if someone spilled water onto the dashboard located up there and now the entire organ is smoking and sparking.

Me no function. Me brain no work.

"I wanna taste you," I growl, dropping to my knees before her. I *need* to taste her. I'll go insane if I don't.

A humble servant, coming to the temple of the goddess he worships.

"Ryker…" I hear her tiny intake of breath—a sound somewhere between a gasp and a moan—and I smirk as I run the pad of my pointer finger down her slit.

"You're already so damn wet for me, baby." I slowly inch my finger into her tight channel—just the tip. If my theory is correct—and it damn well better be, or else I'll go on a jealous, murderous rampage—Ellie is still a virgin, just like me. I don't think she ever had someone besides herself touch her here, and the fact that I'm the first one fills me with unspeakable joy.

I slowly lower my face to the wetness between

her thighs, giving her ample opportunity to pull away if she desires, but she simply bucks her hips in an effort to get closer to my face.

"Greedy, bratty girl," I growl, my hands digging into her hips as I lift her up and shove her cunt into my mouth. My tongue immediately licks at her juices, savoring her delicious flavor as a moan rumbles up my throat. She tastes so damn good, better than any nectar the gods could provide, and my cock aches with the need to make her feel half as good as she makes me.

"Ryker! Oh! Ryker!" Her hands fumble with my hood once more, forcing it off of me, and she digs her tiny fingers into my dark hair. I can feel her nails pierce my scalp, but for some sick reason, that only amplifies my pleasure.

Maybe I'm simply a piece of shit who lusts over pain. Who the fuck knows?

I keep one hand on her hip as I plunder her aching pussy with my tongue. With my other hand, I undo my zipper and free my rock hard cock. I run my fingers over the dusting of precum at the tip before using it as lubricant.

I fuck Ellie with my tongue in tandem to my hand moving up and down my cock. I imagine it's Ellie's tiny hand wrapped around it, and I begin to stroke myself even faster. In response, my tongue flicks Ellie's clit like it's a damn ice cream cone I'm desperate to finish before it melts in the sweltering summer sun.

"Holy crap!" she screams, her hips bucking wildly against my mouth. Only my hand on her hip holds her in place as I lick and suck and bite.

And all I can think is…

Soon, my cock will be inside her.

Soon.

The thought unravels me, and without preamble, I release Ellie's thigh and shove my fingers into her pussy. That, combined with the stimulation of my tongue on her clit, sends her careening over the edge.

I stroke myself faster, faster, faster, feeling my balls tighten deliciously, and I explode with a groan of my own. The vibrations rumble through Ellie, where my lips are still pressed to her pussy, and she cries out as I prolong her orgasm.

Trembles course through her body following the aftershock of such a mind-blowing—not trying to be a cocky prick, it's the truth—orgasm. Still, I can't bring myself to leave the heat between her thighs, my tongue lapping at the juices like a man starved.

"Fuck, you taste so good. So damn good."

"Ryker…" I tilt my head up to meet her gaze. Her cheeks are flushed, her hair sticking to her scalp with sweat, her eyes dilated… And she's the most gorgeous creature I've ever laid eyes upon. "Can I take care of you…?" She trails off with a hesitant nod toward my dick, which is…dammit. It's already getting hard again.

"It's okay, sweetheart." I begin to kiss up her body, my eyes never leaving hers during my ascent. Up her toned stomach. To her small little belly button. Through the valley between her breasts—though I do stop to pay attention to her perfect nipples. And then finally, my lips meet hers.

Her eyes flutter shut as she cups my cheek,

kissing me back just as fiercely and passionately as I do her. I imagine she can taste herself on my lips, and that thought only makes me harder.

"Ryker?" Her lashes brush her cheeks as she reopens her eyes, piercing me with a look that has my treacherous cock going from nearly half-mast to rock-hard. I swear the bastard has a life of its own.

"Yes, baby?"

Her fingers trail down my cheek and to my collarbone, mimicking the way I touched her only a few minutes earlier.

"I think it's time we had that talk," she whispers. At my pinched brow, she clarifies, "All of us. I want to know the truth. I want to know *everything*."

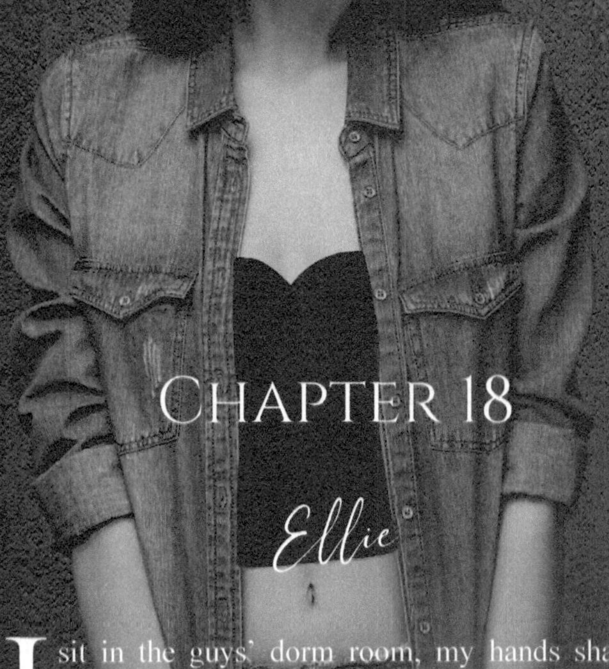

Chapter 18

Ellie

I sit in the guys' dorm room, my hands shaking where I hide them beneath my thighs. Goosebumps pebble on my skin as I feel their eyes on me—soft, caressing, sinful. So freaking sinful that I'm surprised I don't self-combust into flames.

"Ryker should be back in a couple of minutes," Beckett tells the group as a whole while we wait. Silence once again stretches between us, pulled taut like the string on a bow with the arrow already nocked back, and I shift from side to side on the seat cushion.

After Ryker dropped me off at the dorm he shares with the other guys, he left to "take care of a few things." His words, not mine. By "things" I have a feeling he means Mr. Moreau, who I discovered knocked unconscious and bleeding in the middle of the hallway. The thought that Ryker did that—that he hurt somebody on my behalf—should fill me with fear or even disbelief.

It doesn't.

Maybe a part of me always knew about the darkness inside of my guy friends, reflecting through their fathomless eyes, but I chose to ignore it. To bury my head beneath the sand like an idiot.

Or maybe nothing about them surprises me anymore.

They're brutal, savage, hungry beasts, but I know in my soul that they'll never direct that violence in my direction.

Before Ryker left, though, he gave me a sweltering kiss that sent fire straight to my toes. It was a kiss that promised many, many more to come, and my heart beats even faster thinking about it now. I can still feel delicious heat between my thighs at the memory of what we did.

A blush rises up to my cheeks as I try to settle my rampant heartbeat. What does it mean? I kissed Zane, but I also did…a lot of other things with Ryker. Am I dating him now? Do I even *want* to be dating him?

"I can't fucking take this anymore," Dominic growls, jumping from his seat opposite me in the room and stalking toward the bedroom he shares with Landon. He reappears a second later, holding one of his gray sweatshirts. Without waiting for me to say anything, he tugs my hands into the air and drops the sweater over my head, until I'm completely engulfed in the fabric. I take a deep breath, inhaling his unique scent and finding comfort in it until his next words shatter the illusion. "Her fucking nipples looked sharp enough to cut diamonds. I couldn't fucking stand it."

He glares at me as if my boobs personally offended him before stomping toward his seat once more.

I try to push down the trickle of hurt that threatens to erupt. After our text message exchange the other day, I thought he was finally opening up to me. Does he really hate my body so much that he has to hide it?

It's not my fault their room is kept below freezing.

And it's also not my fault that Ryker plucked and pulled at them and—

"Dominic," Landon growls, where he stands in their tiny kitchenette, filling up a kettle.

Dominic glares at him. "What?" he barks.

"Oh, for fuck's sake," Beckett murmurs, as if he thinks Dominic is being particularly dense. Dom, for his part, appears even more confused, his bright green stare volleying between the three of us. "You're a bloody idiot sometimes."

"I still don't know what I did," my blond angel hisses. At least, I always used to think he looked like an angel, and I still do. How can I not, with his platinum blond hair curling around his ears, golden skin, and muscles to die for? Even his cheekbones are keen enough to cut…glass. Just like my nipples. He has nipple cheekbones.

A tiny giggle escapes me, and all three of their heads swivel in my direction. And I say three, because the fourth one is a little…preoccupied.

I shiver delicately as Zane nuzzles against my stomach like an overgrown house cat, once again drawing my attention to his presence. He's sprawled out on the couch, his legs dangling over the edge, as he rests his head in my lap. Minutes ago, I started leisurely stroking his dark hair, but now that I've begun, I find that I can't stop. He literally hissed at me and clawed at my hand when I tried to pull away. Not that I'm complaining too much. His hair feels like silk gliding between my fingers, and the purr that rumbles from his chest is making my thighs clench together—something he can probably feel but is graciously choosing to ignore.

Small mercies.

"Yeah. Just like that, *princesa*," Zane purrs, as if noticing my attention is on him. I don't know how he can tell, though, with his eyes squeezed shut. "Harder. Harder. Oh yeah. Push it in, baby. Push your fingers in nice and deep."

I snort automatically and give his hair a playful tug.

"You're such a pervert," I muse thoughtfully, not at all upset by the prospect. I mean, I would probably be upset if he was saying those things to another girl, but…

"Oh, Ellie!" he moans, bucking his hips as if he's in the midst of a mind-blowing orgasm. "Right there! Right there! Harder! Harder! Harder! Ohhhhh!" His eyes flutter open, his mouth parting on an exhale, as I give his hair another tug.

Beckett's eyes roll so far back, I'm surprised they don't fall out. It would be such a shame, because he has freaking gorgeous eyes. Green and brown, a dichotomy that reflects his soul. One part of him will always be light and breezy, the companion that can make me smile and offer me a shoulder to cry on when I need it. But the other half of him, the louder facet of his soul, is tainted by just as much darkness as my own.

How have I never noticed it before?

Is it just because I'm a new Ellie, with new eyes and a new outlook on life?

I see the demons lurking in his eyes, and they scream at me to give in, to allow this beautiful beast to devour me whole.

When he sees me staring at him, he makes a face—his eyes crinkling together and his tongue lolling to the side of his mouth. I up the ante with an ugly face of my own, twisting my features until I'm afraid I'll pop a blood vessel in my brain. Beckett throws his head back in a rare moment of genuine laughter, and I swear, some of the darkness I just saw percolating in his brown and green gaze disappears just a little bit.

"What's so funny, *princesa*?" Zane lazily touches my ankle, where his hand hangs over the edge of the couch. Goosebumps pebble on my skin from the contact, and I feel a shiver cascade through me. I glance down at his face, only to find his eyes wide open, spearing me in place. His fingers continue to caress the skin of my ankle, and unexplainable heat erupts in my stomach, detonating like a dozen atomic bombs.

Instead of answering with words, I simply make a face at him, the same one I gave Beckett.

Zane stares at me in shock for a long moment, before he begins to laugh as well, his entire body shaking. I can feel his laughter rumble through me, and my hands tense in his silky black hair before I force myself to release the death grip I have on the strands and relax.

"What the fuck was that?" he roars, laughing hysterically. "You looked like a constipated kitten."

I swat at his arm half-heartedly. "He started it!" I point an accusing finger at Beckett, who adopts an innocent expression.

"Are you saying my face is naturally hideous?" He pouts dramatically.

"Yes," Zane deadpans, the laughter freezing as quickly as it began. Freaking psycho.

"You weren't saying that last night when you begged for my cock in your mouth," Beckett teases. At least, I think he's teasing…

"I like being ball-gagged by actual balls," Zane declares in a completely serious voice.

Oh my gosh. The thought of the two of them together, of Zane feeding his cock to Beckett—

Heat flares up inside of me, so intense and sudden that I begin to wiggle beneath Zane's head, as both men whip their heads in my direction.

And then as one, they break into raucous laughter.

"Did you see her face?" Beckett asks, wiping away a stray tear. "Fuck, that shit's hilarious."

"I can promise you that the only balls I'll be putting anywhere near my face are the ones I cut off," Zane tells me through peals of laughter. For the second time this evening, his laughter cuts off abruptly like a candle wick being breathed on until the flame shudders and dies entirely. He frowns. "Actually…not even then. Balls are icky."

"You have two of them," Beckett points out.

"How do you know?" Zane retorts with a devilish glint in his eyes.

"Because every man has two." Beckett sighs dramatically.

"Not true," Dominic interjects, sitting forward in his chair and resting his hands between his spread out knees. "Don't you remember Tommy Warthouse and the incident?"

"Oh…I forgot about that incident." Zane's voice turns contemplative. "But it wasn't a natural ball removal."

"A ball removed is a ball removed," Beckett argues.

"What about penis removal?" Zane counters.

"Who had his penis removed…?" Dominic trails off as he seems to answer his own question. "Oh. I remember. That shit gotta hurt."

"Wait. Wait. Wait." I wave my free hand in the air to garner their attention. "Whose balls are we talking about?"

A sharp, vicious growl leaves Zane's chest, and his hand around my ankle tightens almost punishingly. "No one's. You're not allowed to talk about other men's balls or penises. Ever."

"Ever," Beckett and Dominic agree as one.

Landon simply rolls his eyes as he moves toward me, two mugs of steaming hot cocoa in his hands. He sets one down on the table in front of me, and when Zane immediately moves his hand out to grab it, Landon stomps on his wrist.

"Not for you," he hisses as Zane whimpers pathetically.

"Ellie!" he whines, elongating my name until it sounds like ELLLLLLLIE. "Landon's being mean to me!"

Landon, as always, ignores Zane and focuses his piercing gaze on me. I lose myself in the hue of his molten silver eyes, the ring of violet surrounding the pupil somehow more accentuated than ever before.

"Did you eat yet? I can make you a sandwich if you're hungry."

"No," I shake my head, "it's okay."

Even the thought of eating makes my stomach twist into a dozen tight knots. I have a feeling I'm going to need an empty stomach to get through this conversation.

Landon's eyes narrow, almost as if he's assessing the sincerity of my words, when the door to the dorm swings open and Ryker stalks inside. My heart begins thrashing faster when I take in his lean, masculine perfection. With his sweatshirt unzipped the way it is now, and no T-shirt underneath it, the scars whittled into his tan skin are clearly visible. I desperately yearn to run my fingers down the crooks and ridges, memorizing him through feel alone, and I have to bite down the baser impulse to do just that.

Where did all those scars come from? I want to know.

I want to know everything.

His eyes flash toward me hungrily, no doubt remembering our time together as keenly as I do, before they flicker to Zane in my lap. Anger momentarily darkens his features before he shoves it behind an impassive mask. Without a word, he moves to a corner of the room and crouches down, one hand resting against the floor as he regards us.

I want to convince him to come sit with us, to join us in the living room, but I have a feeling my words will be said in vain. It's almost like I'm dealing with two different versions of Ryker. The Ryker from only an hour ago was kind and attentive, worshiping me as if it's his divine right to do so, but this Ryker…

This Ryker is cloaked in so many shadows, it makes me wonder how he was able to free himself of them in the first place, if only for a few moments. His icy orbs ensnare my own, battering at my defenses like a winter storm, and I'm helpless to look away. Staring into his blue eyes reminds me of trekking through the knee-deep snow with no particular destination in mind, only forward. Because I know sooner rather than later I'll find comfort, peace, and warmth. All I need to do is continue to move…

Landon clears his throat, and I reluctantly rip my eyes away from Ryker's to meet Landon's instead. He glances between the two of us, a crease forming between his brow, before he shakes away whatever thought has been brewing.

"It's finally time to tell you the truth…and for you to extend to us the same courtesy," Landon says. He's the only one who remains standing, leaning against the kitchen counter with his arms crossed over his chest. Since it's the middle of the night, he's already dressed in clothes for bed—pajama bottoms and a thin gray T-shirt. If I thought he looked handsome in his school uniform, that's nothing compared to him now, with his rumpled hair and creased shirt.

I shove the thought down before it can formulate entirely.

Great. Apparently, my time with Ryker has turned me…horny? Is that the word I'm looking for? Insatiable?

I push up my glasses with the pad of my middle finger, trying to give myself something to do other than ogle my guy friends.

Landon's next words drowns the reminder of my lust down the toilet.

"We've known about the Paragons of Prosperity since we were kids."

Since they were…?

I stiffen automatically, my stomach muscles churning at the knowledge they've been keeping this secret from me for years. For freaking years. I thought they had only just discovered the truth this year, like me, and it feels like a barrel of acid has been dumped over my head to discover otherwise. It freaking burns.

Zane begins to nuzzle my stomach once more, almost as if he can feel me retreat mentally, and I blow out a breath as I force myself to relax.

I promised myself I wouldn't get mad again. They're not my enemies in this war—POP and The Divine One are.

But why does their betrayal hurt so darn much?

Zane twists completely in my lap until his nose is practically inside my belly button.

"You smell so good," he moans against my

stomach.

"That's my sweatshirt, dumbass," Dominic retorts.

"Don't care. Ellie's natural scent is stronger." He wraps his arms around my waist and presses even closer to me, rubbing his nose across the fabric.

"You're not a fucking cat, Zane," Ryker growls dangerously from his corner of the room. "Don't touch my fucking girlfriend like that."

Girlfriend?

Girlfriend!?

I tense automatically, and around me, the other four men do the same. A strange, threatening sound rumbles from Zane's chest, though he doesn't pull his face away from my stomach. It's almost as if my presence calms him, soothes his beast.

Landon casts a frosty-eyed glare in Ryker's direction. "We'll talk about this later," he snaps in a warning tone.

Ryker scowls. "Nothing to talk about, asshole."

Yes, there's something to talk about.

Definitely something to talk about.

Beckett, always the perceptive one, must see the brewing panic in my eyes, because he swiftly and expertly changes the subject. I imagine he does this a lot with the guys. He's always been the peacemaker of the group, even more so than Landon. It makes me wonder how horrible they were before Beckett arrived at the academy…

"The guys told me the truth about POP shortly after I arrived and earned their trust," Beckett says, running his hands down his khaki pants. Unlike the others, Beckett's already dressed for the day—or the night, as the case may be—in a handsome sweater that clings to his muscular torso like a glove and a pair of khaki pants.

When Ryker dropped me off at the dorm an hour ago, Beckett had already been sitting in the living room at his computer. He told me he couldn't sleep, but I can't help but think there's more to the story than just light insomnia.

I watch now as his attention snags on a tiny, barely noticeable crease near the top of his sweater, just above his heart. His lips twist into a frown as he rubs at it, attempting to straighten it out.

Sometimes I wonder if I'll ever live up to Beckett's expectations for perfection. He never says anything to my face, of course, but I have to wonder if he looks at me…and finds me lacking. He covets beautiful things, unearthly possessions, and I doubt I'll ever be one of them.

I force my attention back to Landon as he takes over the conversation, still shooting hateful glares in Ryker's direction. "I don't remember how old we were when we discovered the truth about POP. Seven? Eleven? Twelve? Maybe thirteen?" He brushes a hand through his brown hair, and I can't help but think he looks ten times older than his age of eighteen. His metal eyes hold a wisdom that speaks of a thousand different lives, each one more violent and brutal than the last. It makes my chest hurt and my heart ache. What made him this way? What made all of them this way?

POP? The Divine One?

Another reason I seek to destroy that insidious organization…before they can destroy me and the people I care about.

"Land," Dominic butts in, gesturing toward the silver-eyed man, "overheard the mayor talking about his daughter. The conversation was…I don't know? Off? When he told me about it, it raised red flags for us, even at that age."

"So we decided to investigate and stumbled upon that asshole handing his daughter over kicking and screaming to a bunch of masked douchebags." Landon's voice tightens in anger and even a healthy dose of pain, as if a part of him still blames himself for not protecting and saving this stranger. I want to comfort him, but I also am desperate to hear the entire story.

To finally know the truth about these brutal, wicked boys.

The kings of Grove Academy.

"Over the years, we gathered enough information to be able to piece everything together," Dominic tells me. "The Paragons of Prosperity hide in the shadows of our town and are more of a cult than an actual religion."

Landon snorts derisively, darkness flashing across his artfully handsome face. "They think they're saving this godforsaken town by sacrificing worthy women to—"

"Cassia," I breathe, my stomach muscles tightening.

Landon nods grimly. "I'm assuming The Divine One told you about our town's history? About

Melody?"

"He did," I agree, rubbing at my arms. I still remember peering out that window at the stone altar in the center of the cave. Those silent screams haunt my dreams. Her anguished eyes burn the back of my lids like they've been branded there with hot pokers. I can't even close my eyes without seeing her pale, terrified face.

"We knew it was fucked up," Dominic tells me, and he suddenly seems nervous, unsure, as if he's not positive how I'll react to what he has to say next. He runs a shaky hand through his shaggy, platinum blond hair. "But that wasn't why we sought to stop it."

"We did it for you, Ellie," Landon cuts in, his tone brokering no room for argument. His silver gaze collides with my own in an explosion of toe-curling heat. He really is beautiful, in a savage, merciless kind of way. It's almost as if the Devil himself made him so beautiful in order to lure souls down to hell. An alluring, deadly trap with metallic eyes that hold you hostage.

"Me?" I breathe, forcing my gaze away from his to glance at the others. Beckett, who's staring at me as if I'm going to fall apart at any moment, his eyes gauging my every reaction. I imagine if I *do* fall apart, he'll be there in seconds, stitching the broken shards of me back together. Ryker, who's expression is carefully blank and impassive, his blue eyes shining. Dominic, who's nibbling on his lower lip while scowling at the flooring. And finally, Zane, who's still facing my stomach and purring like a darn cat.

"We wanted to protect you and—" Landon

begins.

"I think you need to start from the beginning," I say shakily, pushing at Zane's shoulder until he reluctantly sits up. He tosses me a pretty pout, his long lashes fluttering against his cheeks, before sighing and sitting next to me. After only a second, he grabs ahold of my waist and hoists me into his lap, his tan, muscular arms banding around me like iron vises.

"I need to be touching you, *princesa*," Zane breathes in my ear, and radioactive butterflies take flight in my stomach.

Ryker's eyes narrow where we connect, his jaw grinding, but he remains silent.

"There's really no beginning," Landon confesses, dragging my attention back to him. And once I stare into his expressive silver eyes, I find that I can't look away. I'm trapped. "We discovered the truth about the Paragons of Prosperity and sought to destroy it in order to protect you."

"Protect me?" My brows arch downward as something scaly slithers inside of my stomach. "Because you knew they were going to—"

"No," Landon interrupts with a vehement head shake. "We had no idea you were going to be chosen for the Culling, but we wanted to be prepared for it."

A breathy snort escapes me. "And look how well that turned out…" Bitterness laces my words, and I instantly feel like crap, especially when their expressions twist and distort, guilt and self-loathing weighing on their shoulders. "I'm sorry," I whisper. "I didn't mean—"

"You did mean it," Landon interrupts, but not

unkindly. A sad smile graces his face. "We fucked up, kitten. Big time. We know that, you know that, and POP knows it."

"POP knows about you guys? And that you're trying to stop them?" For some reason, the thought of anyone in that darn cult knowing the truth about the guys makes me feel panicky, as if my skin is too tight and my chest too small to contain my heart. Sweat slickens my palms, and I absently wipe them on my legs.

"They do," Beckett confirms, not bothering to elaborate.

Growing hysteria bubbles inside of me, buoying me up toward the ceiling.

"Then why haven't they—?"

"Stopped us?" Landon quirks an eyebrow, a tiny smirk tugging at the corners of his luscious mouth. It's a cruel smile, though. Rife with anger.

"Yes," I say softly, deflating against Zane's chest. I've always wondered about the guys' position of power in the school. They're the self-appointed kings, the men even faculty shy away from. How can five high school students—albeit, sexy as sin and rich ones—gain so much power? How is it that everyone fears them?

"The Paragons of Prosperity have been able to thrive for so long because people believe in the legend. The story." Surprisingly, the answer comes from Ryker in the corner, his gravelly voice shooting heat straight to my stomach. "The more someone believes in something—or someone—the more legitimacy that organization gains."

"The town truly believes that Cassia will protect them if they offer her sacrifices," Landon interjects, and though this information is immensely unsettling, I have no idea how it connects back to my initial question. "It's blind faith, but it's faith all the same, just like any religion. And it's the only thing a lot of these rich fucks believe in."

"I don't understand—"

"What do you think would happen if the everyday man and woman—normal people who live in this town—discover the truth? What if the information about POP's illicit activities get placed in the hands of law enforcement—and not officers they can pay off?" Dominic asks me, a blond brow arched.

"And what if five, rich, pompous kids stumbled across proof that could rip their entire organization apart, destroying everything they believe in?" Landon asks. His eyes flare with a strange, mind-boggling heat as I dissect his words.

"You…you have proof? About what POP has been doing?" I can't stop the accusation from poisoning my tone. Zane's arms around my stomach suddenly feel restrictive instead of comforting. I wiggle, trying to break free, but he only tightens his grip on me.

"Don't give me that look, kitten," Landon warns, his face carefully devoid of any expression. "We have proof, yes, but it's not that simple."

How isn't it that simple?! If they can prove that there's a cult running rampant through our town, killing young women, then this will all be over. The police will take over, the cult members will go into hiding if they're not arrested for their crimes, and—

Even as I think this, I remember how easy it was for The Divine One to cover up all of the deaths. The girl, Ali, who perished in the escape room. Blair. Patricia. Amanda.

There's no way they can get away with all of that…unless the police are involved as well. Unless they have officers lining their pockets, ready to do their bidding.

"I can see the wheels turning in that pretty mind of yours," Landon tells me, his jaw ticking. "We have the evidence, yes, but we don't know who the fuck to send it to. We don't know who is and isn't involved in this ordeal. Not only that, but POP *knows* we have this evidence, and they—" His eyes slide to me, hardening to stone, and I swallow around the lump in my throat.

"They threatened…" Dominic tries to take over, but he trails off when his teeth grit together so tightly, I can hear the audible sound of scratching.

"They threatened me, didn't they?" I whisper softly, my heart sinking so far down, it falls through my stomach and splatters at my feet.

Grim expressions greet my guess, and it's confirmation enough.

"It's not just you, sweetheart," Dominic tells me, obviously sensing my inner turmoil. "They have shit on us. Shit that could get us in a lot of trouble."

"So we're at a stalemate. Mutually assured destruction," Landon declares. "We can't risk making a move on them through authorities, but they also can't risk making a move on us. They know we have contingencies in place if anything were to ever happen to us…" He swallows, as if what he has to say next is too inconceivable to even voice, before he croaks out, "Or you."

"They're more afraid of losing everything they built than they are of us, which will be their first mistake. They see us as nothing but high school boys—minor annoyances they have to deal with." Zane's voice is practically a purr from behind me, and he nuzzles my hair with a contented sigh.

Worry eats at my chest like locusts, and I find myself desperately glancing from face to face.

"The five of you think that you can really take on a cult that has been around for over one hundred years?" Incredulity laces my voice, along with a healthy dose of panic and fear. The thought of losing them…

"It's not just the five of us," Landon interjects, his tone unreadable.

"Huh?"

"We have help." This comes from Beckett, who continues to fixate on that wrinkle decorating his shirt. His eyes momentarily flick to my face before lowering once more to his torso. A frown pinches his brows as he scrubs at the crease irritatedly.

"Help," I parrot dumbly.

I'm almost positive I've never seen anyone near them before. The guys are too frightened of them, and the girls are too intimidated to even take a step in their direction. So what the heck are they talking about?

Who would be dumb enough to go after POP? Besides my guys, of course.

"We don't know who he is…" Landon begins

lamely as I blink at him. And then blink some more, trying to understand the sheer *stupidity* he's spouting.

"You don't know who he is?!" God, do they realize how stupid that is? For all we know, they're dancing to The Divine One's malicious tune.

"He called us just over a year ago and asked to meet us. When we arrived, we only found photographs—photographs of all of POP's victims from the last ten years. The secretive bastard called us again and asked if we wanted to end this once and for all. He's been helping us ever since—gathering intel that has proved reliable, cleaning up for us when we run into issues, and giving us names of people in the cult. We believe he's legit, and we don't say that lightly."

"And you don't know who he is?" I question again.

"We have some theories..." Landon trails off, chewing on his lip. When I silently encourage him to continue, he clarifies, "We thought it was your brother for some time."

"Fischer?"

This time, I really *did* laugh, the noise a culmination of pain, grief, anger, and disbelief.

"This person..." Landon blows out a breath, and I have a feeling he's reluctant to tell me something. Something important. But if there's one thing I know about Landon, it's that he won't hesitate to rip off the metaphorical Band-Aid. He doesn't sugarcoat things the way some of the others might. "He holds a lot of interest in you specifically."

Goosebumps skitter across my skin, and Zane

traces them with the pad of his pointer finger.

"What do you mean?" I ask uneasily.

"It's why we thought it was Fischer for a while," Dominic confesses. "Because whenever he calls, he always asks about you. Makes sure you're safe."

"And why don't you think it's Fischer anymore?" My heart's racing, pounding, growing to a crescendo in this orchestra only I can hear. Violins screech in my ears, and trumpets blare.

Landon ducks his head, and I swear he looks almost sheepish.

Why is he…?

"We followed him," he answers at last. "And the timing didn't add up. We would receive a call from our unknown friend when Fischer would be with you or clients. It couldn't have been him."

They…followed my brother? Stalked him?

The revelation settles in my stomach like a heavy rock. I honestly don't know how I feel about it.

How often do they follow Fischer? Follow *me*?

And why am I not more upset about the latter thought?

"But now, we believe our powerful friend was only interested in you because he somehow suspected you would be chosen to partake in the Culling," Beckett rumbles, his voice uncharacteristically growly.

I settle back against Zane's chest as I digest all that I learned.

They're playing a very, very dangerous game, and I'm terrified to think about what will happen if they lose.

Or if they win.

"What is this evidence you have against them?" I query, directing the question at Landon.

He scrubs at his jaw. "We haven't been able to find their…base of operations, so to speak. The members of POP who would squeal are always blindfolded or drugged before they are brought to the location. And the older members are loyal to a fault. However, we were able to…convince," his lips twitch at the word, as if he finds it particularly amusing, "one of the members to record a little video for us. The sacrifice, to be exact."

"Whatever happened to that rat bastard?" Dominic pipes up.

"Pretty sure POP gutted him," Zane replies conversationally, still rubbing his nose repeatedly into my hair.

My insides turn to ice at his nonchalant tone.

"They killed him?" I whisper.

Landon gives me a cold stare. "Don't feel bad for the pig, kitten. He deserved that and then some. The only reason we didn't kill—" He cuts himself off abruptly, but I can fill in the blanks easily enough.

The only reason we didn't kill him is because we needed him.

Which brings me to my final question, and the one I'm most anxious to hear the answer to.

I twist in Zane's lap until I'm practically straddling him, his golden brown eyes all I can see.

"Your barn. Your…bloody barn." I take a deep breath, tampering my nerves, as his face drains of all color. "Who did you kill?" I twist slightly to address all five of them—all five of them who are staring at me as if I've turned into a ghost and am currently haunting their sexy asses. "And how many people *have* you killed?"

Chapter 19

I swear my heart stops beating as I stare at the face of the woman I love more than anything. My sweatshirt dwarves her smaller frame, and I feel a keen sense of satisfaction at seeing her in my clothes. However, that primitive pleasure dims in the face of her words.

How many people have you killed?

The question, for most, should be pretty damn easy to answer, but then again, the majority of the men and women on this earth are good. Pure. They aren't hellhounds who have clawed from the fiery depths of hell and set ablaze this entire godforsaken town.

Unbidden, my mind travels back to the first man I ever killed.

The mayor.

Panic warred against the inherent sense of justice as I stared at the man's ashen face. Blood dripped from the wound on his forehead, just beneath his thinning gray hair.

We hadn't meant to kill him—only to scare him and get a confession—but now, his body reeked of decay and coppery blood. His dim, unseeing eyes stared straight at the ceiling.

It was surprisingly easy to sneak into his house. He was rich, sure, but it was nothing compared to the dollars most of the other men and women in this town possessed. He had no security, no alarm system, nothing that could stop the monsters from getting into his home.

We'd meant to shake him up, beat him to within an inch of his life, but not actually kill him.

I didn't think I was a murderer, but now, looking at his corpse, I found that I felt no guilt. No pity. No remorse. He was an animal who sacrificed his own daughter, and I'd be damned if I let him get away with it.

"We need to do something about the body," Landon whispered, his voice detached and emotionless. He poked at Mr. Mayor with the toe of his boot. "Zane? Are your parents still gone?"

Zane's gaze remained fixated on the bloody wound on the man's scalp. At first, I thought the emotion running rampant in his dark brown eyes was guilt, but the closer I looked, the more I realized that it was excitement staring back at me. He looked like a fucking kid in a candy shop, his energy almost contagious.

"Yeah. They'll be gone for another month or so," Zane responded.

The smile carved into Landon's face was cruel

and cunning—and it should've scared me. I wanted it to scare me.

But I couldn't muster any emotion except for satisfaction.

"Good." Landon finally glanced up and speared me with an unreadable look. "I have an idea."

The first time we dismembered a body, we didn't have tubs of acid. Instead, we buried the disgusting remains in Zane's backyard, far enough away from his property that it hopefully wouldn't lead back to us. Besides, who would believe that a bunch of tween boys were behind the disappearance of the town's beloved mayor, especially when we covered our tracks and made it look like he skipped town? It was Beckett who suggested the acid tubs years later, proving that—despite his posh exterior and compassionate green and brown eyes—he was just as batshit crazy as the rest of us.

"Ellie..." Landon blows out a heavy breath, frustration and panic wreaking havoc on every line of his face. I can see creases bracketing his eyes that have never been there before as he thinks about what to tell her, how our truths will change things between us irrevocably.

I've never claimed to be a good man, but Ellie? She sees something in me, something in all of us, that the rest of the world fails to notice. While the students of Grove Academy see nothing but beasts and monsters, she sees five broken souls capable of being saved. I don't even know if I want saving, but I do know I need the light she provides. It banishes some of the shadows in my soul, making the world a little brighter.

I watch as she wiggles in Zane's lap, almost as if she wants to leave it, but the crazy bastard simply tightens his arms around her waist, keeping her still. From this angle, I can only see the back of her head, but she gives Zane a look that almost has him cowering, which I normally would've found fucking hilarious if I hadn't been so out of sorts.

How can a few simple words cut me open like a doctor with a surgical blade, baring all of the icky black organs inside?

I know we promised to tell her the truth—and fuck, do I want to—but I'm terrified of how she'll react to the news that she's in a room with a bunch of murderers. That discovery tends to have the opposite effect of what we want to happen.

If she runs away from us, I can't promise I won't chase.

"You promised to tell me the truth." Her voice carries through the room as she clenches her hands into tiny fists. She swivels on Zane's lap once more until she's finally able to see us all. "I already know you killed somebody, and I want to know who." A tiny tremor works its way through her body, and goosebumps prickle on her bare legs.

Beckett, the weak fucker that he is, heaves out a tired breath, forking his fingers through his brown hair. I'm not surprised he's the one who caves and tells her the truth. He's been against lying to her from the very beginning, and I'm only just beginning to see how right he was. If we hadn't kept secrets, if we'd told her the entire truth…

Everything would've been different.

"Dane," he answers tiredly, and I can see the resignation in his mismatched gaze, as if he already knows that one word will be the cement piling on top of all of our coffins, trapping us to our fates.

"Dane," Ellie repeats numbly, her eyes going unfocused as she no doubt pictures the douche who flirted with her relentlessly. A glossy shimmer appears in her eyes, but she blinks it away rapidly before a single tear can fall. "I thought that he transferred schools?"

"That's what everybody thinks happened," Beckett continues in that same, monotonous voice. "We knew for months he was a part of POP, but since he was such a low level member, we didn't feel the need to handle him until you went missing."

I swallow around the Texas-sized lump in my throat, struggling to regulate my breathing as I take stock of every twitch in her expression. "We couldn't get information out of him, so we…killed him." I don't bother to mention how we tortured him ahead of time before setting Zane loose on his beaten, broken body. For some reason, I don't want her to look at Zane like a monster. I know that will fucking destroy him more than anything else that has happened so far.

"I see." Her voice is carefully blank, all of her emotions packed tightly away, but I can see a muscle in her jaw twitch ever so slightly. Does she want to run? Hide? Fight?

Does she think we'll hurt her, the way we hurt the monsters who deserve our wrath?

"He was a bad man, kitten," Landon tells her

severely, folding his arms over his chest and leveling her with a dark expression. If I didn't know him as well as I did, I might beat the shit out of him for the way he's looking at her. But I know this is how he handles emotions, how he handles things slipping out of his meticulous control, how he handles our group fracturing into thousands of irreparable pieces. What most people can't see is the way his nails dig into his palms where they're folded over his chest, hard enough to break skin and bleed. By the time this conversation is over, his palms will be littered with crescent moon-shaped scars.

"And you…took care of him in Zane's barn?" Again, her voice is carefully nonchalant, but I can hear the quiver she tries to hide. It fucking tears me in two.

"No." I clear my throat gruffly before continuing. "Our…contact took care of him for us."

"The contact you've never met in person," she deadpans, as if she needs that clarification.

I grit my teeth and nod stiffly.

It's true that we don't know who that fucker is, the sixth man who has been helping us time and time again destroy POP, but for some reason, I trust him. At least, I trust him well enough to leave a dead body behind the library of the school for him to clean up.

We made a list of all the people we thought he could be, but so far, our search has proved futile. Whoever this fucker is, he's good. Really good. Even with all of the contacts we procured over the years—and there are hundreds, if not thousands, of high-level officials we've bribed, blackmailed, and paid off—we haven't come any closer to discovering the identity of our mysterious angel.

"I see," Ellie repeats once again, and her cheeks hollow, the movement so miniscule that I might not have noticed it if I hadn't been paying close attention. It's something she used to always do when we were kids, though I thought she broke the habit now that we're in high school.

I know without a shadow of doubt that she'll be biting down on the inside of her cheek hard enough to draw blood. Abusing her flesh in a way she thinks is hidden from us and our penetrating gazes.

"You stop that shit now," I snap at her, drawing her eyes back to me in alarm. They fly open wide, her face paling, but I notice her cheeks no longer look hollow. "You don't get to goddamn hurt yourself."

For some reason, my words make her shiver, her gaze dropping to her wrist before flicking back toward my face. Landon and Beckett exchange an unreadable glance that has every hair on my body standing at attention. What the fuck is that about?

Something cold and sinister takes hold of my heart, pressing down on the organ like a hundred tiny knives. I bring my fist up to my chest to rub the ache right the fuck out of me, but it persists like a damn mosquito bite.

"We have a feeling that Dane's family knows the truth about what happened to their son," Landon draws out in a heavy breath. He scratches at the stubble lining his jawline. "But since we suspect they're high-level members of POP, they'll remain silent. The Divine One would demand them to."

"It's like we said before," Beckett tells her

gently. "Mutually assured destruction. If POP sends someone after us, we'll go after them with everything we have. Even if they killed every single one of us," Ellie sucks in a gasp as if the idea repulses her, though I don't know why after everything we just confessed, "we have safeguards in place to ensure the information goes out to the world and sources we believe we can trust, though it's hard to know for certain. Either way, the thought terrifies POP enough for them to leave us the hell alone."

"And Paulina?" Ellie drops her gaze to where Zane's arms band around her waist, and I swear she flinches minutely, but I could be imagining things. Maybe I want to see her cower from us. Run from the beasts that have claimed her mind, body, and soul.

Landon shakes his head. "We didn't hurt the girl. She really did transfer schools. Apparently, she didn't want to be in a place that reminds her of her lover." He scoffs derisively, as if to say, "Good fucking riddance." We'd never been able to discern for certain whether or not Paulina was a part of all of this, but she was still a rude bitch who had tried to hurt Ellie as much as possible.

"Lover?" Ellie blinks behind her crooked glasses. "Dane is her stepbrother."

"Didn't stop them from fucking," Ryker pipes in darkly from his corner of the room.

It also didn't stop Paulina from hitting on us every single chance she got, though I don't mention that out loud. It doesn't matter anymore. None of it matters.

Ellie shifts uncomfortably on Zane's lap as he

remains surprisingly quiet behind her. I don't know if that's a good or a bad thing. With Zane, it's hard to be certain if his silence is the calm before the storm or if it's the aftermath, when the windows are blown to smithereens, the buildings are in disarray, and rubble litters the ground.

As Ellie moves, her glasses fall even further down her nose, and I can't fucking take it anymore.

I'm across the room in seconds, and Ellie's eyes widen to saucers as I kneel down and use the pad of my thumb to fix her glasses. But before I touch her, before my finger comes into contact with the dark bridge, something happens. Something that breaks me into a million fucking pieces, each shard sharper and more dangerous than the last, slicing at my skin and making me bleed.

She flinches.

She fucking flinches, as if she expects me to jab my thumb into her eye instead of fix her glasses.

Intense anger and mind-numbing fear eat at my flesh like acid. It feels as if an arrow has been let loose and speared me in the heart.

I know I'm an asshole—I know she thinks I despise her—but she has never flinched from me before. She has never feared me. I don't know what the fuck to do with this knowledge, so I simply step away from her and reclaim my seat opposite her on the couch.

My heart is in tatters in my chest, and it hurts to fucking breathe. I hate that I'm falling apart in front of all these men—I hate it even more when Beckett shoots me a pitying, sympathetic stare—but there's nothing I can do to change it. I simply grit my teeth and pray for the pain to subside from my chest.

"Dom…" Ellie begins helplessly, no doubt seeing the same agony that the other fuckers did before I could mask my expression.

I simply scowl at her, clenching the armrests until my knuckles are white.

"That's it, then?" I barely recognize my voice. Self-loathing destroys something vital inside of me, carving up my heart and soul in a way that I know will never heal properly. "You think we're monsters?"

"Dom—"

"Because we've killed a lot of people, Ellie," I tell her curtly, ignoring the warning glare Landon throws my way. But fuck him. Fuck them all. They didn't have to deal with her goddamn flinch. "And sure, almost all of those people deserved our wrath, but we still butchered them with smiles on our faces." She sucks in a sharp breath, as if she's shocked that I'm so blatantly confessing to crimes that could get me put away in prison for the rest of my miserable life.

But prison seems preferable to this aching, nagging pain exploding in my chest.

"Dominic!" Landon barks harshly, but surprisingly, it's Ryker who backs me up.

"No, he's right." He slowly rises from his crouch, his cold blue eyes never leaving Ellie's face. "She needs to know exactly what she's getting herself into." He takes a single step forward, and I stare at Ellie closely, wondering if she's going to flinch the way she did with me.

She doesn't.

And I don't know if that hurts me even more or gives me hope.

"We're bad, bad men, Ellie," Ryker growls out, his raspy voice permeating the air with promises of violence and bloodlust. Promises of death. "We've killed before, and I can promise you that we'll kill again." He takes another step closer, and Ellie's eyes flick frantically from face to face, as if she has only just realized she's trapped in a room full of vicious, bloodthirsty monsters. But these monsters wouldn't hurt a single hair on her perfect head. Hell, that's the whole fucking point.

We'll kill before anyone is allowed to even get near her goddamn hair.

"We do what we have to do to protect you and everyone else in this town from the Paragons of goddamn Prosperity," Ryker rumbles. "And I'm not going to fucking apologize for it."

"Ellie…" Beckett leans forward, his hand outstretched as if he wants to grab her. He quickly pulls it back as she stares at it wordlessly. "Love…" He swallows. "You should know that we'll never, *ever* hurt you. I don't want you to be afraid of us."

"What do you want me to do with all of this?" Ellie asks, her voice weak. It's barely even a whisper, but it manages to break through the stifling atmosphere like the crack of a whip. "What the hell am I supposed to say…?"

"You don't have to say anything," Landon declares, and when I open my mouth to protest, he shoots me a pointed stare that has me shutting right the fuck up. He has a plan, and though I don't know what that plan is, I trust him implicitly. We've been best friends for too damn long for me not to. "But we *have* done bad things…and we'll probably do more bad things in the name of justice. In the name of protecting you." He doesn't sugarcoat it. Sometimes, I appreciate his harsh honesty. Other times, like now, I wish he would just keep his damn mouth shut.

Ellie looks fucking traumatized, as if she's thinking about all of the men and women we killed in her name. Frankly, if I began to count them all, we'd be here for a very, very long time. Their names are painted in blood in my soul, but the list only fuels the fire of my rage and hate. They deserved their fate, and I'm happy we were the ones to dish it out to them. Is it fucked up to be judge, jury, and executioner? Probably.

But I long stopped giving a shit about what society deems as right and wrong.

This society in particular places an emphasis on sacrificing the innocent for the sake of the elite. If we're able to tip the balance of that scale, then so be it. Those fuckers deserve to pay in blood for all that they took from us.

Ellie's silent for a long minute, so silent that I'm not even sure she's breathing, before she says, "Sometimes, I think The Divine One doesn't believe in the myth of Cassia and that he's just using the cult as an excuse to murder without fear of retaliation." Her voice is soft, contemplative, and we all watch her face like hawks swooping in for the kill. "When he sliced her throat…when he killed Blair…" She takes a shaky breath, and Zane's arms tighten around her in a semblance of a hug. "I knew I was looking at someone with no morals. Someone who was truly evil."

"And do you think that about us?" Beckett whispers, as if he doesn't truly want to hear her response to that question. But he needs to.

We all need to.

"Do I think what?" She chews on her lower lip, and I know that she understands what he's asking. She just doesn't want to answer it. And when she exhales, I swear I can taste it in the depths of my lungs.

"That we're evil." Beckett doesn't phrase it as a question.

Once again, silence settles between us all as Ellie focuses on Zane's arms. I don't know why she's looking at them so often, but it's almost as if she finds comfort in his embrace, which is ridiculous. If there's anyone Ellie should be wary of, it's the man holding her like she's made of spun glass. Not that Zane would ever hurt her, but he's volatile and unpredictable. If she tried to run, I have no doubt he would tie her to him until the end of time. His love is selfish like that, but then again, so is mine.

I can't lose her.

I won't.

"No," Ellie settles on at last, surprising all of us with her answer. Five shoulders slump downward in relief as we exhale heavily. "I don't think you're evil. I could never think that. But…" She places a hand over her mouth as if holding back a sob. Or maybe even a scream. When she finally removes it, there are tears lining her eyes, hanging stagnant in her long lashes. "I don't know what to think anymore."

"We'll give you space if that's what you want,"

Landon tells her, and the mere suggestion has me digging my nails even further into the leather of the armchair. No. Fuck no. I've given her space, I kept my distance, and I'm fucking done with it.

"No." Ellie shakes her head slowly, her eyes widening ever so slightly as if she surprised herself with that adamant answer. "I don't need space."

"Then what *do* you need?" Beckett practically begs.

Ellie's eyes darken, the change so drastic that if I were to blink, I would've missed it. Darkness pools in those fathomless depths as she presses her nails into Zane's arms.

"I killed someone, you know," she whispers, a tiny hitch accompanying those words.

My heart hurts for her, fucking shatters, but there's nothing I can do but watch her from across the room. I'd happily take a bullet for her if the need arose, but this? This emotional pain that cleaves her in two? There's not a damn thing I can do to stop it. No body I can beat bloody and unconscious. No wound I can stitch back together. No corpse I can offer her to ease the ache I can see in her heart. It kills me.

"We know," Landon tells her gently, silently encouraging her without words to continue. This will be the first time we heard what exactly happened to Ellie during the Culling, and we're all on pins and needles as we await her response. I just know that the second she finishes, I'm gonna want to march out that door, find a member of POP, and beat them bloody and unconscious.

As it is, it takes every ounce of willpower to hold

the beast inside me at bay.

"They made me do three…well, I guess you could say four tests," Ellie begins in a soft voice, her gaze once again locked on Zane's arms. This time, I can't even mentally grumble about him having her in his arms. If he's providing her comfort, however minimal, then I'm fucking grateful for the psychotic bastard. "The first one was simple, though I was scared out of my mind. It was the night you found me freezing half to death and with bloody feet. The night I stumbled into your murder barn." We all exchange a grim look, remembering that time keenly, but she continues before we can comment. "They dropped me in a corn field and made me walk back to the academy. I was cold, scared, and my feet hurt like a bitch." A wry, dry grin pulls up her lips before she frowns once more. "Looking back, I imagined they wanted me to find your barn, Zane. They wanted me to see exactly what type of monsters you are."

My heart stutters in my chest, but not for the obvious reasons.

It's because she doesn't say the word 'monsters' as if it's a bad thing. No, my girl said that word with a hush sort of reverence that I can feel all the way in my bones. We *are* monsters, and we've never pretended otherwise.

But we're her monsters, first and foremost.

"And the second test?" Landon asks gently. He looks as if he's afraid to say more, afraid to demand answers and scare her away. She seems so fragile in Zane's arms, so small, like one wrong word or sudden movement can shatter everything we've rebuilt during this heart-to-fucking-heart.

"An escape room," she supplies, her eyes sliding to me. My heart skips a beat as I hold her gaze. "They showed me a video of Dominic, tied up and unconscious, and told me I had an hour to escape or he'd die."

A vicious growl leaves my throat at the thought of being used as fucking bait. Fuck POP. And fuck The Divine One to the deepest pit of hell where he belongs. If I have to join him to achieve that end' goal, then so be it.

"They did that to shake your faith in us," Beckett says, his jaw clenched. "It made you wonder if you could trust us, didn't it?"

Ellie nods once, her expression stiff. "When I saw Dominic perfectly okay after I escaped, I couldn't help but wonder if he was somehow a part of this—"

"I would never fucking hurt you," I declare vehemently, unable to hide my hurt that she suspected me for even a second. Am I really so much of an asshole that she would think I could do such awful things to her?

Fuck, I need to fix things between us, and pronto.

"I know you wouldn't hurt me," Ellie tells me in a placating manner, her tone soft. It feels as if she's speaking to a cornered, feral animal, and maybe that's what I am. Maybe I've become feral. Hell if I know anymore. "But at the time, I was scared and confused. I felt like I couldn't trust anybody."

"Understandable," Beckett agrees. "And then what happened?"

"And then..." She takes a deep, shuddering

breath, every muscle in her body locking tight. I know without a shadow of doubt that this third test was the hardest for her, the one that changed her irrevocably. The one that put shadows in her eyes, monsters that I can't even begin to defeat through sheer force. "The third one. On Halloween night." Another shaky breath. Another exhale of air. Another tear drop that breaks my fucking heart. "They put me in a room with Blair…"

"Ellie, you don't have to continue—" Beckett begins gently, but she talks over him, apparently determined to finish this story no matter what it costs her.

"The Divine One placed a gun on a table and told us that only one of us could make it out alive." Full-body shivers rack her body, and Zane rests his chin on her head, rocking her back and forth. She clings to him with a sort of desperation that has me fearing for my girl's mental health and wellbeing. How shattered did she emerge from these trials? And will we ever get our girl back? "I couldn't do it… I wouldn't do it… I didn't…" She twists her face to cry into Zane's chest, and he rubs her hair and back soothingly, whispering words too soft for me to hear.

I can guess the end of this story easily enough. She shot Blair, maybe because she was threatened or she feared for her life, and—

"I couldn't go through with it. I refused." Her words are muffled where they're spoken against Zane's chest, warped by her tears, but I can hear them as if she's been shouting. "But Blair didn't even hesitate. The next thing I knew, I was staring down the barrel of a gun—"

Rage bombards me from all directions, and I just barely stop myself from launching to my feet and pacing the room. Obviously, Blair didn't shoot her, but the thought of how close we came to losing Ellie…

"And then what happened?" Landon presses through clenched teeth.

"And then she pulled the trigger," Ellie responds, and I feel as if the weight of the world is pressing down on my shoulders. I can't breathe. All I want to do is rip Ellie from Zane's arms and take her into my own.

"She shot at you?" Ryker's voice is a growl, and I imagine that if the girl weren't already dead, she would be now. That's a fucked up thing to think about, but we all know it's the truth. No one is allowed to hurt our girl and get away with it.

"The gun wasn't loaded. It was another goddamn test." Ellie's voice turns hard, angry, and I like that a fuck ton better than the sadness from earlier. I can deal with her anger—I can help her cultivate and mold it in a way that's healthy—but her sadness? Those fucking tears? They make me want to hurt people, and since the only people around are the bastards I love more than life itself, then I guess I'll have to hurt myself.

I move my hand from the armchair to my thigh, pinching the skin hard enough to bruise. The piercing pain allows me to focus in a way little else can.

"The Divine One wanted to see if we were pure." Bitterness laces her tone as she spits out the final word. "I imagine if I would've gone for the gun, he would've killed me too."

"The Divine One shot Blair?" Landon asks carefully.

She shakes her head against Zane's chest. "No. He slit her throat. Right in front of me. I watched her die." I expect her to break apart again, and I'll be here to pick up the pieces and hold her together until she can do it herself, but she surprises us all by wiping her eyes and twisting in Zane's lap to face us. "We appeared to be in some sort of…cave. At least, that's what it looked like to me. There were tunnels *everywhere*. The Divine One told me that it was underneath Melody's old house." I exchange a look with Landon. We've been searching for their secret hideout for fucking years, and we've just been offered the first clue on how to find it. "They led me to a room where they instructed me to get in a white cloak."

Unease churns in my gut as I force myself to listen, to not react.

"I knew something bad would happen to me if I gave in, so…I fought." She squeezes her eyelids shut, her entire face twisting and distorting as if she's trying to chase away an errant thought, a pesky demon who keeps whispering in her ear. She'll soon come to learn that it's not healthy to ignore the devil on your shoulder, but that doesn't always mean you need to take its advice. "It was an accident. I swear to you, it was an accident."

"Is that when you…?" Beckett trails off delicately, but we all know how he wants to finish that sentence.

Is that when you killed someone?

"We fought, and she hit her head." Ellie's voice has reverted back to that cold, impassive tone from earlier before, as if she's trying to force herself to not feel, to not think, to retreat into herself in a way she probably sees as healthy. But if she doesn't let that beast out, it'll eat her alive.

Just the way it did to me and the others.

"Ellie, I'm so sor—"

"Don't you dare, Beckett," Ellie snaps, not even bothering to stare at him. "Don't you dare."

He nods once, accepting her unspoken reasoning, and settles back in the chair.

"You're a survivor, baby." Ryker's grating voice echoes from his corner of the room, reminding me eerily of nails against a chalkboard, as fucked up as that sounds. He has a permanent, raspy lilt to his vowels that has never quite gone away, even after the speech therapy Landon helped pay for when we were kids. "You did what you had to do…and you won. You're not a murderer—"

"Don't!" She squeezes her eyelids shut, tensing in Zane's arms, and Ryker cuts himself off with a scowl. In a voice so low, I have to strain to hear her, she whispers, "I killed her. It was my fault."

I don't like her self-deprecating thoughts any more than he does, but now isn't the time to convince her that she's worth more than the value she placed on herself. She's worth everything.

"Have you heard from POP since then?" Landon demands. We don't bother asking her about the sacrifice she no doubt witnessed or maybe even took part in. The shadows in her eyes are like giant stop signs, begging us not to venture a step closer.

She hesitates, biting on the inside of her cheek yet again and causing a growl to rumble through my chest, before she nods. "Yes. The last day of Thanksgiving break."

Landon frowns. "When? I was there—" He cuts himself off abruptly, scratching at the back of his neck. A dark flush rises to his cheeks at his unintentional confession. I bite down on my lip to stop the smirk that threatens to grow across my face. Why am I not surprised that he's been stalking her? He yelled at us for it, but then he goes and does it himself. Hypocritical asshole.

"I don't know how they got into my house with all of my security…" Ellie trails off, lost in thought, and my amusement fades faster than a prostitute's goddamn panties. I know for a fact that Fischer keeps dozens of security guards on their property at all times when he's not there, so how did those fuckers get past them? Unless…

Unless the guards were in on it…

Unless *Fischer* was in on it…

Landon nods his head once, a clear indication that he'll look into this matter at a later time. Knowing him, he'll compile a list of every guard who was supposed to be working that night and interrogate them until he finds the culprit. And if he doesn't dig up any information…

Surely, Fischer doesn't know about POP, right?

We did extensive research into him, and there's not a single thing that leads us to believe he plays any role in this fucked up narrative. But maybe…

Maybe we missed something.

"The Divine One wants me to bring him someone," Ellie tells us. "A US Senator."

"What the fuck does that crazy bastard want with a US Senator?" Beckett demands.

Ellie shrugs. "He didn't tell me. He just gave me a date and name."

"Not a place? Not a specific time?" Landon presses, and I can see his mind swirling rapidly as he attempts to digest all of this.

Ellie shakes her head slowly.

"What's the man's name?" Beckett queries, leaning forward in his chair once more.

"Reece Whipers," Ellie answers.

My brows furrow together as I sift through my very limited knowledge of the current government. I'm almost positive I've never heard that name before. If he's a US Senator, he's not from our state.

So why the fuck does POP want him?

"This doesn't make any sense," Ryker growls.

"Maybe it's a test?" Beckett suggests with a shrug. "To see if she'll go through with it?"

"He knows I'm going to go through with it," Ellie retorts bitterly. "He threatened Fischer."

"It still doesn't make any sense." Landon's brows crease as he stares down at his phone, where he no doubt has pulled up everything he could find with a quick web search on Reece Whipers. "He's basically a nobody. He's barely been a senator a year, and he's from halfway across the country."

"Most of POP's victims are girls," Ryker points out, "so obviously POP doesn't want to use him for a fucking sacrifice."

"Does it have something to do with the legend of Cassia?" Ellie asks tentatively.

"I don't know, kitten." Landon glances up from his phone and spears her with a look loaded with love, possession, and reverence—it's a look a knight would give his queen before he impales himself on a javelin for her. "But I swear to you, I won't rest until I find out. Until *we* find out. You may hate us for what we've done, but you're not alone anymore. We'll discover the truth about POP and The Divine One…or die trying."

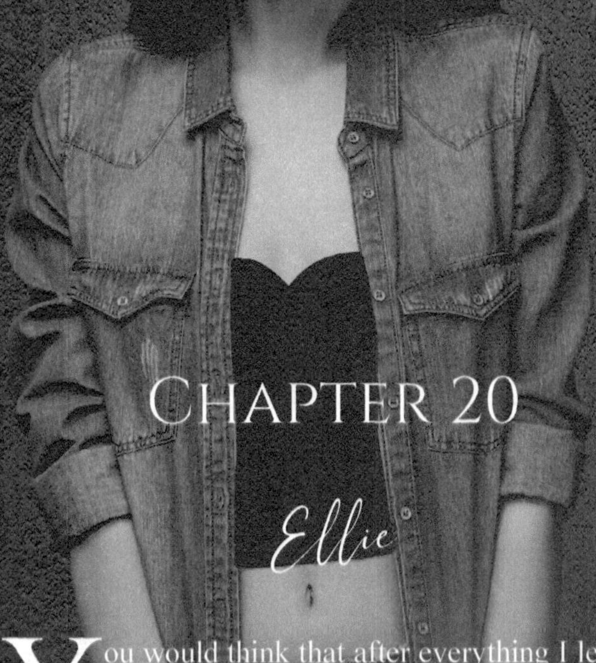

Chapter 20

Ellie

You would think that after everything I learned about my guy friends, I wouldn't sleep well that night.

Instead, I sleep like a freaking baby.

I don't dream, but then again, I doubt I would even remember if I did. Exhaustion cripples me, and as soon as my head touches the pillow, I find myself slipping into the greedy, possessive embrace of darkness.

Monsters hide in darkness, and I think I've become the sole focus of the five biggest ones.

I should be terrified—and maybe a part of me is—but I can't help but feel…relieved. The Paragons of Prosperity members are dangerous, as I've seen firsthand, and not one is more malicious or cruel than The Divine One. If my guys are willing to fight for themselves, fight for all of the girls who are too terrified to do it themselves, then who am I to stop them? It's them or POP, and I'll be damned if my guys don't emerge victorious.

My acceptance scares me most of all. A normal girl would cower after discovering her five closest friends are, for all intents and purposes, serial killers, but I can't muster up even a smidgen of fear. When I flinched last night, when Dominic was moving toward me to fix my glasses, it wasn't because of him. I knew innately that my golden boy would never hurt me. No, it was the suddenness of his movements, the way he lurched out of his chair and stomped toward me with an almost blistering speed. It conjured up images of The Divine One gripping my arm, tugging me toward the window…

I know I hurt Dominic, I could see it in his eyes, but there's not a darn thing I can do about it. They won't believe me even if I tell them the truth—that I trust them, that I don't fear them, that they'll never be as evil as POP and The Divine One.

Something is changing between me and all the guys, but I can't put my finger on what. I still remember the feel of Zane's lips pressed against mine as he kissed me like we were the only two people on earth. I remember how good it felt to be in his arms last night, like none of their words could hurt me. A tornado could shoot its way through their room, and I'd be safe in his arms. But then I think about Ryker, and how he devoured me on top of the piano, his tongue promising me a thousand different things I can't even begin to unravel. The way he held me afterward, as if the world ended and started in my eyes.

And Landon, Dominic, Beckett…

I haven't kissed them, but I can't say I haven't imagined it. Even when they confessed their gravest sins to me—placed themselves beneath the guillotine with every intention of letting the blade drop—I felt lust percolating in my stomach.

It's wrong, God, I know it's wrong, but it's the truth.

I just don't know what this means.

My phone pings on my dresser, and I glance at it automatically.

Fischer: First class is today. Do you need anything?

I can feel my heart skip a beat as I bite down on my lower lip, remembering our conversation on Thanksgiving. He asked me what I wanted, what I needed, and I responded.

And now, it's actually happening.

Fischer took the time to research the best self-defense classes near my school and even went so far as to give me an evening pass from the headmaster every Monday, Wednesday, and Friday. Those passes are usually reserved for students who have family in the immediate vicinity or those who work—and considering the majority of the students here have never done a single second of hard-labor in their life, there were over a dozen left when Fischer called.

I did research on the place myself and was pleased to discover that my new instructor is a female. Maybe it's silly and irrational, but I don't like the idea of some unknown man grappling with me on the mats. It makes fear prickle across the skin of my neck and unease skate down the long length of my spine. I don't know if it's because of The Divine One, Mr. Moreau, or a cumulation of both horrible men, but I'm grateful I'll have a female teaching me what I need to know in order to survive.

And that's the point of this—survival. I can't afford to be weak any more in this dog-eat-dog world. I know the guys promised to protect and look after me, but they also couldn't stop POP from getting to me every time I've been kidnapped. I don't blame them— and I definitely don't hold any ill-will—but I won't be able to rest until I know with absolute certainty I can defend myself against the monsters plaguing my town.

I type a response back to Fischer as I climb out of bed and stretch out my back.

Ellie: No. I'm all set. Excited.

Fischer: Be safe.

Ellie: I will. Love you.

Fischer: Love you more.

I place my phone on my dresser face down and move toward my closet, imagining what nightmare scenarios Fischer had conjured up to explain my reasoning for self-defense classes. He no doubt expects the worst, but even his worst doesn't come close to the horrific truth. What can I even tell him? That there's an evil cult determined to ruin me and everyone I love? That this town isn't safe? He'll freak out and do something idiotic, which in turn, would put him on

POP's radar. I can't have that. I won't. He means the world to me, and if I have to carry the burden of my silence to keep him safe, then so be it.

I grab a sports bra, long sleeve athletic shirt, shorts, and pink panties before slipping out of my pajamas. My eyes dart to my reflection in the full-length mirror, and I frown, not liking the girl staring back at me.

I've always been skinny, but in the month following the ceremony, I've become sickly looking. I can see every individual rib and bone. My breasts, which have once been full and pert, are now abnormally small and sunken, just like the rest of me. Purple lines mar the skin around both of my eyes, betraying how little sleep I've been getting. Even my skin is paler than normal. My eyes dip lower, to the cuts on my arms, and my frown deepens when I think about just how far I've fallen.

There's nothing wrong with you.
Chemical imbalance…

Almost absently, I trace first one scar—nearly the size of my pinkie finger—and then the one right next to it. Some are deeper than the others, but they're all permanently tattooed on my skin. A reminder. A constant, sickening reminder.

For a brief, brief moment, I visualize grabbing the knife from beneath my pillow and adding one more, just one, to silence the demons in my head. They're so loud, so incessant, that I can't focus on anything but their shrill screams.

I shut that thought down immediately with a fierce growl, slipping my clothes on and tugging at the sleeves of my shirt until I'm sure they cover every bare inch of skin. Then, I walk back to my phone and check it for any messages.

The screen lights up with three new notifications, and I click on the first one.

Landon: Kitten, how are you?

I ignore his text for now as I slide to the second one.

Beckett: We're about to get breakfast if you'd like to join.

And then finally, the third one.

Ryker: I'm outside your dorm.

What?

My heart thrashes in my chest as I open my door, ensuring the common area is devoid of any broody stalkers, before moving across the room and to the main door. When I rip it open, I'm not even slightly surprised to find Ryker leaning against the opposite wall, dressed in a sleeveless sweatshirt with the front hanging open and the hood pulled up. His frosty blue eyes grip my own immediately and refuse to let go. Suspicion clouds his features as he surveys me from head to toe.

"Where are you going?"

I debate lying to him—because I know if I tell him the truth, he'll insist on accompanying me—but I find that I'm so darn sick of lying. Of keeping secrets.

And would it be the worst thing in the world to have his company?

"Class," I answer, stepping back into the room and waiting for him to follow me. He does so, his lips pursing behind his black scruff as he follows me into the kitchen. I grab a water bottle out of one of the small, wooden cupboards and fill it up with icy water from the tap.

"Class? It's a Saturday."

"Self-defense class." I spin around to face him, assessing his reaction carefully. "It's at a small gym a few minutes away from here. On 16th street—"

"I'm aware of it." His expression freezes over, his fingers tapping repetitively against the countertop as he studies me. For a long moment, he doesn't speak, and I take the opportunity to close the lid of my water bottle before rushing to my room to grab a hair tie. When I return—my brown hair pulled back—he hasn't moved an inch, his fingers still drumming against the counter as he contemplates my words. Finally, he speaks, and his quiet voice crashes over me in a wave of delicious heat. "Why didn't you ask one of us to teach you?"

I give him a dry look. "Do you really think you'd be capable of beating the crap out of me?"

His frown deepens, his eyes resembling ice on the ocean. "Is that what you want? To have the…crap beat out of you? To hurt?" He speaks this entire thing without an ounce of inflection, but I can see the way he tenses, the way his shoulders touch his ears as he awaits my answer with bated breath.

Does he know? About my scars? About the pain

plaguing me every darn day? I've been so careful…

Even last night, I made sure never to show him the inside of my wrists, to not take my shirt off completely. And surely he would've commented on them if he saw them…?

"I don't want pain anymore." I raise my chin defiantly as I hold his gaze. "Which is why I need to learn to fight. To survive. To protect myself."

For the briefest of moments, his lips curl into what I would almost describe as a smile, there and gone before I can blink.

A fleeting, breathtaking smile that reminds me of last night, when he stared at me with lust emanating from his gaze and—

"I'll come with you," he rumbles out, shoving his hands into his sweatshirt pockets.

I don't even bother to protest, not that I want to.

"Okay." As I make a move to step around him, he grabs me by the back of my hair abruptly and spins me around. A gasp escapes me, but he swallows it with his mouth, kissing me like I'm the air he needs to breathe, like he'll die if he doesn't have my taste on his lips. I moan against his mouth, kissing him back with reckless abandon, and he tugs on my ponytail to move my head where he wants it.

"Good girl," he growls against my mouth, and I swear I turn into a puddle of mush right then and there. When he finally pulls away, I'm gasping for breath, my heart racing a mile a minute, as I struggle to get a handle on my tumultuous emotions. He simply smirks at my flustered expression, and his thumb lifts to swipe at the edge of my swollen mouth. It suddenly occurs to me that I just kissed a killer, a murderer, but that knowledge doesn't diminish my desire the way it should've.

For some reason, it only amplifies the lust twirling inside of me.

I love the fact that he's willing to do whatever it takes to protect the innocent—to protect me. Maybe it's a little terrifying, if I'm being completely honest, but that seems to be the one constant in my life lately. Fear.

"What time's your class?" Ryker murmurs as he presses his forehead against my own.

How is it possible that I've suddenly forgotten how a clock works? Wait…what did he ask me again?

"Um…"

Ryker smirks again and reaches for my phone in the back pocket of my shorts. I tremble at the feel of his hand against my ass, but he doesn't linger, simply pulling my cell out and glancing down at the text messages.

"We should go," he tells me with a nod toward the digital clock on the oven. "It's almost nine."

"Yes…come. I mean, go. I mean—" I blush bright red as an honest-to-God grin unfurls on his face. When Ryker smirks, he looks dangerous and mischievous, but when he smiles…

With a squeak, I shoulder past him and race out the door—running face first into a muscular body.

"Ow." I rub at my nose as I glance up into Beckett's surprised face.

Ryker growls sharply, immediately sneaking up behind me to wrap an arm around my waist and pull me against his chest.

"Your chest is hard," I say stupidly, and Beckett offers me a tired, wary grin. I don't like it. It seems too…forced, as if he isn't sure how to react around me after their confessions last night. And honestly? I don't blame him. I didn't take the news badly, per se, but I also insisted I wanted to go home ASAP following the atomic bomb they dropped on my lap. I needed time to digest everything, to pick apart and unravel the strings of this mystery.

"You never responded to my text," Beckett says, scratching at the stubble on his jawline. He normally keeps his face clean-shaven, but the five o'clock shadow on his face is beginning to resemble a beard. Not that it's a bad look on him or anything—some people look as if they have pubes taped to their chins— but it only belies how tired and stressed he has become. I hate seeing him so out of sorts.

"Sorry." I wince, knowing what he must think of my silence. That I despise them. That I fear them. That I want nothing to do with them. That couldn't be further from the truth. "I'm just heading out."

"Alone?" Beckett's brows furrow.

"With me, asshole," Ryker hisses, still keeping me pressed against his chest. The move is possessive, claiming, predatory, and I can't help but feel as if he's marking his territory somehow. I remember what he said yesterday, when he called me his girlfriend, and my heart picks up speed.

I want to be his girlfriend…but not just his. And I've never been more confused in my life.

"You can come too, if you want," I blurt out,

wanting to wipe away the kicked puppy look Beckett gives me. And when he immediately perks up, I know I succeeded.

Until Ryker releases me and steps to the side, his eyes shadowed with hurt and maybe even an inkling of betrayal.

My throat closes.

"Where are we going?" Beckett asks eagerly, reminding me so much of a besotted pup with his tail wagging that I can't help but smile.

"There's this self-defense class I had Fischer sign me up for. It's a few miles away from the school, and he was able to get me a pass to leave the academy." I frown as something occurs to me. "Wait. You guys don't have passes—"

Ryker snorts as if my worry is ridiculous. "Don't worry about us, baby. We'll be fine."

Oh yeah. Because they're blackmailing the leader of a dangerous cult and are the most powerful—and richest, at least in Landon's, Dominic's, Zane's, and Beckett's cases—kids in school. Sometimes I forget about things like that.

"Should we call the others?" Beckett questions, already removing his phone from his pocket.

"No," Ryker growls out instantly, reaching forward as if he means to swipe the phone out of Beckett's hands. The Brit's eyebrows shoot upward in surprise.

"They're probably freaking the bloody hell out right now," Beckett says slowly, as if trying to drill the point home. "They have no idea if Ellie hates them or—"

"I said no." Ryker scowls, folding his muscular arms over his chest and causing the scars distorting his skin to ripple and dilate. I can't help but compare them to my own scars, and I wonder where he got his from. Half of me doesn't even want to know, afraid of the answer.

"It's not up to you, asshole," Beckett hisses.

"She's my girlfriend!" Ryker takes a step closer until they're chest to chest, nose to nose. "I don't want a bunch of—"

"Enough!" I push my way in between them, my chest heaving and anger an iron vise around my heart. "You guys are acting like…like idiots! None of you will go with me."

Ryker turns his vitriol-filled eyes onto my face, but I don't cower beneath his glare. "It's not safe for you to go alone," he snaps. "You need protection—"

"I never agreed to be your girlfriend, Ryker," I bite out. "So quit acting so possessive." I only meant to put him in his place, to have him stop being a dick, but when his eyes shutter with hurt, I know I said the wrong thing.

Oh…crap.

How do I tell him that I want to be his girlfriend, but I care about the other guys as well? That I kissed Zane and want to kiss Landon, Beckett, and even Dominic, who I think hates me? That I'm confused and terrified and so damn messed up inside that I'm not ready for any lasting relationship?

But the words freeze on my tongue, refusing to come out, and I watch as agony splays itself across Ryker's handsome features. I also see the moment he hardens himself, throwing up walls that had once been crushed at my feet, and a strangled sob gets caught in my throat.

"I see," he says stiffly, his eyes flicking to Beckett over my shoulder. "Make sure she gets to the class and back safely."

"Ryker, I'm sorry. I didn't mean—"

Ryker gives me one last glance—allowing me to see the pain bleeding into his eyes—before he shoves past us and storms out of the building.

S weat sticks my clothes to my skin as I wipe off my face with a rag Beckett holds out to me.

Lilly, my instructor, smiles kindly at me as she slugs down her own bottle of water.

"You did good today, kid," she tells me sincerely.

For some reason, heat fills my cheeks, and I glance down at my tennis shoes. "Thanks."

Lilly is a tall, severe woman with perfectly straight blonde hair pulled back into a tight ponytail. Even after almost an hour of training, not a single strand has fallen out of place. I half wonder if she slathered that thing in hair gel before arriving here. There's no way it can stay so immaculate otherwise.

Still, despite her harsh appearance—including the muscles that line her arms and stomach—she'd been nothing but kind and patient with me during our lesson, willing to walk me through each of the moves while Beckett waited on a plastic chair in the lobby.

At one point, she turned toward me with a coy grin and whispered, "Your boyfriend is checking out your butt," and I swore my face burned hotter than the sun as all of my blood rushed to my cheeks.

"He's not my boyfriend," I replied vehemently, my heart pounding like crazy. She simply threw her head back in laughter before walking me through the next moves of the maneuver we were working on.

"Try telling him that, kid."

She always calls me that—kid—despite the fact that she can't be older than thirty. Still, I like Lilly a lot, and in my first lesson with her, I learned more than I ever thought possible. We mostly worked on maneuvers to break free if someone were to grab me. As Lilly put it, she's teaching me self-defense, so most of our lessons are going to orbit around breaking free of my attacker and getting to safety. Still, she promised to teach me how to throw a "damn good punch that will break a fucker's nose" and "knee jabs to hit a pervert's cooch" the next time we meet. Her words.

"I'll see you in a couple of days," she tells me with a soft smile before heading back toward the mat to meet with her next student.

Beckett places his hands on my waist and tilts his head down to stare at me, his eyes shining with pride and maybe a little bit of lust too. But knowing my luck, I'm imagining the second emotion in his gaze.

"You did good today, love."

If I thought Lilly's praise filled me with heat, I was mistaken. That's *nothing* compared to this. Thousands and thousands of grasshoppers begin to bounce around in my stomach as I blush crimson.

"Thanks, Beck."

"Damn girl." He whistles appreciatively, his eyes assessing me from head to toe. "You're stronger than you look."

Is it possible to die of embarrassment? Because if it is, buy me a coffin and place me inside of it. I'm pretty sure my heart just stopped beating.

"I carry books, Beckett. Hardbacks. Do you know how heavy half a dozen hardbacks are when you're lugging them around campus all day? Check yourself. We bookworms are stronger than you give us credit for." I flash him a soft smile to show him I'm teasing, and his answering one has heat gushing through my body like candle wax.

"Let me know when your next class is," he tells me as we move toward the front entrance of the gym. "I'll come with you. Are all of the classes an hour and a half?"

I wince, absently scrubbing at the back of my neck, before blurting out, "I know it was probably boring for you—"

"Boring?" His brown brows touch his hairline as he scoffs. "Sweetheart, there was absolutely nothing boring about what I just witnessed." Once again, that strange, indecipherable emotion materializes in his dichromatic gaze—an emotion I'm almost positive is lust. He blinks quickly, and whatever I thought I saw vanishes, replaced by his usual cocky smirk. "Come on. Let's get you back to the academy before Landon gives me a spanking for keeping you out past your curfew."

I snort before I can stop myself, following him

out into the parking lot and toward the Jeep parked in the nearly empty lot. The Jeep actually belongs to Landon, but Landon lent it to Beckett to use whenever he's in the states. It'd be quite hard for the Brit to transport his own vehicle back and forth across the ocean.

Beckett opens the passenger door for me and waits for me to slide in before moving toward the driver's seat. Just before he can get into the Jeep, however, I slide across the center console and take up position behind the wheel. One of his eyebrows quirks as he stares at me, the door partially opened and his foot lifted as he prepared to climb inside.

"Ellie love, what are you doing?" His lips curve upward in a smile as I hold out my hand for the key dangling between his fingers.

"I'm driving," I declare, my heart thumping unevenly in my chest. I have my license, of course, but I don't use it very often. I'm almost always being chauffeured everywhere by my brother's people, and normally, I don't complain. However, my time with Lilly has brought about a new independence and strength I never felt before. It surges through my veins like heady waves of adrenaline, and I have to bite down on my lip to contain the giddy smile that wants to unfurl across my face.

Beckett regards me with cool eyes, his lips pursing, before he concedes with a sigh, pressing the key into my hand and closing my fingers around it. His touch shoots sparks of lightning through my skin, and my breath hitches instinctively. When he doesn't immediately pull away, I glance up from where our hands connect and meet his penetrating gaze.

"You may think that we don't like this 'new Ellie,' my love, but…" He leans in even closer, and for a moment, I think he's going to kiss me. And for a moment, I think I want him to. Nerves swirl in my belly, and I feel my heart skip a dozen beats. But he doesn't kiss me. He simply hovers over me, his breath fanning across my face, before whispering, "You're wrong."

My tongue darts out to lick my lips instinctively, and his eyes drop to follow the movement. I watch as his chest expands and decompresses before he shakes his head—as if attempting to dislodge an errant, pesky thought—and uses the car door to push himself away. He mutters something under his breath, too low for me to hear, before stalking toward the passenger seat and climbing inside. As soon as the door slams shut behind him, I take off down the road, fast enough to make him curse.

"Jesus, sweetheart!" he swears as he scrambles to buckle his seatbelt. And then his eyes widen with terror when he realizes that I still haven't clipped my own. Cursing, he leans forward to strap me in place, his hand unwittingly grazing across my skin and leaving a delicious trail of goosebumps in his wake. "Ellie…" he growls out, and I can hear the chastisement in his tone. But the last thing I want is to be chewed out, not when I'm finally feeling so…alive.

Fuck, this feeling is exhilarating. I want to bottle it up, toss it in the ocean, and allow it to float across the sea so no one can ever take it from me again. A boisterous laugh tumbles out of me, and Beckett gives me a strange look out of the corner of his eye but doesn't comment.

The same adrenaline I felt fighting with Lilly dances through my veins now, licking at my skin like a dozen sparking fireflies, and my foot instinctively presses down even further on the gas.

"Fuck!" Beckett curses as the car unsteadily jerks to the side as I take a sharp right turn. "Ellie, slow down!"

I hear him, I do, but it's like his voice is coming from the opposite end of a long tunnel, his words echoing in my head without any definitive meaning. The gaping chasm where my heart should be, the empty space that has been momentarily replaced by this current rush of adrenaline, expands, pulling me head first into an abyss of darkness.

All at once, I remember where I am and whom I'm with.

What the heck am I doing?

Panic lurches in my stomach, and before my brain can catch up to my body, I'm slamming on the brakes and jerking the car to the side. Beckett lets out a surprised yell as we fall to an abrupt stop on the side of the empty road.

For a long time, we don't speak. The only sound I can hear is the rapid pounding of my own heart and Beckett's erratic breathing. And then, like a dam getting decimated, all of the pain, hurt, and anger I've been feeling for the last couple of months explode out of me. I drop my head against the steering wheel as sobs shake my body.

"I'm sorry. I'm so, so sorry. I'm sorry," I cry,

half inarticulate.

"Hey, sweetheart. Hey. It's okay. It's okay." I feel Beckett's hand feather across my back, the touch tentative and unsure, before he begins stroking up and down the length of my spine. My eyelids squeeze shut of their own accord as I focus on the repetitive motion of his hand and how good it makes me feel.

"I'm sorry." I lift my head from the steering wheel, feeling as if my heart has been crushed, stomped on, and then shredded in a meat grinder for good measure. Without a moment of hesitation, he pulls me out of the driver's seat—after ensuring the car's in park—and settles me into his lap. I rest my face in the crook of his neck as I cry and cry and cry, my arms banding around his waist as I accept the comfort he offers me.

We don't speak at first. At least, we don't have a conversation. All I do is whisper unintelligible words and phrases into his sweater as he strokes my hair and back and promises everything will be okay. When I finally dare to lift my head off his shoulder, his eyes are glossy with his own unshed tears, and I'm sure I look ten times worse.

"I'm sorry about your…" I gesture helplessly to his wrinkled sweater, probably covered in snot and tears, as a humorless burst of laughter escapes me. "Yeah. Sorry."

"This old thing?" He tilts his head to the side to stare at his sweater and scoffs derisively. "I was gonna burn it anyway."

"You were not."

"I totally was."

"Liar," I growl playfully.

"It looks like something my Grammy Nicole would force me into on Christmas day," he explains with a shudder. "It's red. And green. And brown. Ew."

"Then why did you wear it today?" I retort, my tears drying up at his light-hearted teasing.

He heaves out a sigh as if it's soooo hard being him. "I can't be perfect all the time," he says in a flippant voice. I laugh and lower my head to rest it once more against his pec. I can feel how hard his heart hammers beneath my ear, and delicious goosebumps explode across my arms.

He strokes my hair for another long moment in silence before whispering, "Do you want to tell me what that was about, sweetheart?"

No.

"I…I don't know," I confess, my voice muffled from where my lips are smushed against his sweater.

"I think you do." His tone is soft, gentle, but I can hear the pain underlying each word. When I don't immediately respond, he pulls me back gently, grabs my arm, and slides the sleeve of my shirt up to my elbow. My pulse skitters erratically as I watch his reaction carefully, gauging each miniscule tick in his facial features. His brows arrow downward as he studies the gashes crisscrossing my wrist, each mutilation different than the next. Some deep. Some shallow. Some long. Some short. I tremble like a leaf in the wind as he stares at the scars intently, a muscle in his jaw twitching.

"Please don't tell anyone," I whisper breathily as his head snaps up. One of the tears I noticed in his eyes before has now dripped down his cheek, settling just above his luscious pink lips.

"Why did you do this to yourself, baby?" he asks in a broken exhale, as if he's struggling to get air into his lungs. His eyes dip back down toward my scars. "Why?"

I don't have an excuse for what I did, but I can give him the truth. "Because I'm broken, Beck."

At my soft confession, his head snaps up and he spears me in place with an intense, unreadable look. "Don't fucking say that about yourself."

"But it's the truth." My lip wobbles as I let some of the walls surrounding me drop, as I let him see the darkness that has been residing inside of me since The Divine One and POP first expressed their interest in me. "POP broke something inside of me, and I can't find the piece they took. I don't even know if I *want* to find it. Maybe a part of me is content to be this fucked up creature—"

Beckett's lips slam onto mine, silencing my self-deprecating words. For a moment, I simply freeze against the brutal assault of his kiss, my limbs locking up tight, before a tiny moan escapes me, and I find myself leaning further against him. My hands creep up his strong, muscular forearms before landing on his broad shoulders, tugging him even closer to me as I take control and deepen the kiss.

My tongue tentatively darts out and licks along the seam of his lips. I don't know what I'm asking for, but Beckett seems to be one step ahead of me. His lips open eagerly, and his tongue tangles with mine as he holds me to him. He kisses me with an expertise that makes me believe he has done this before, and a sliver of jealousy embeds itself in my heart. But then he's rocking the evidence of his arousal against my core and that jealousy dissipates in an explosion of heat and need. My hands cup his cheeks, and his rough stubble grates against my fingertips like sandpaper.

I want him.

No, that's not true. At least, it's not the full truth.

I *need* him.

God, I need him, and the thought is both humbling and crippling in equal measure. I've never needed anyone before—never wanted to be reliant on one person the way I was on my brother after our parents died—but now, I find my heart split evenly between five equally dangerous and damaged men. I'm a precipice, and I have no darn idea which way I'll fall. All I know is I'm *burning*, heat coursing through my body like a wildfire.

Beckett pulls away from me, and I find myself chasing after his lips, wanting to feel them on mine again. Wanting his rough stubble to caress my cheeks and tickle the skin above my lips. My hands awkwardly fall back into my lap as I stare into his beautiful eyes.

He grips both of my cheeks, the gesture so breathtakingly gentle that I feel my heart shred in my chest, and presses his forehead against mine.

"Please don't hurt yourself anymore," he whispers fearfully. "Please."

"Beckett…"

"We can find you help," he forges on, squeezing his eyes shut. "But you don't have to be alone anymore. I won't *let* you be alone. I will stand by you through every dark thought, if you'll let me."

"Everybody hates me." Tears hold me at gunpoint. "Ryker hates me now. Dominic is pissed at me. Landon—"

"Nobody hates you," Beckett growls out vehemently, his eyes snapping open and pinning me in place. I feel naked beneath his gaze. Vulnerable. "I promise you, baby girl, that all five of us care about you more than life itself."

"Why?"

His brows furrow. "Why what?"

"Why do you care about me?" I bite down on the inside of my cheek, relishing the sting of pain as blood floods my mouth, before exhaling deeply and continuing. "I'm just…me."

"You're perfect," he argues immediately.

"I kissed Zane," I blurt out. For some reason, I want him to run from me. To look me in the eye, and tell me I'm the trash I know I secretly am. Disposal. Unworthy. Forgettable. "And I did…stuff with Ryker." A blush decorates my cheeks as I lower my head, bracing myself for his judgment and derision. I want his words to hurt, to slash at my skin like the leather of a whip, and that terrifies me more than anything else I've done to myself so far.

"I know, sweetheart," he tells me gently.

I lift my head up sharply to stare at him.

"Huh?"

He offers me a gentle smile as his fingers fork through my brown hair, tugging at the roots. "I'm not an idiot, my love. I see the way they look at you…and the way you look at them."

"But—"

He cuts off whatever I'm going to say with another fierce, possessive kiss. I swear I can taste his need for me in the depths of my lungs. "It doesn't matter. None of that matters, okay?" He tugs at my hair gently, forcing my head up. "Do you care about me?"

"Of course I do," I whisper.

"Then I promise you, we'll figure it out. Together. All of us." He releases my hair and takes my hand once more, twisting it over until his fingers can gently caress the scars marring my skin. "I'm so sorry I wasn't there for you, sweetheart. I'm so, so sorry."

"Please don't apologize," I practically beg.

He opens his mouth, but I never get to hear what he's going to say. At that exact moment, the driver's side door is wrenched open and something is tossed inside. I scream automatically, tugging at Beckett's arm, as my eyes lock on the grenade lying in the driver's seat, thick, cloying, gray smoke emitting from it. It fills the car almost immediately, infiltrating my nostrils as I gasp and pant for air.

"Fuck!" Beckett roars, his hand clumsily reaching for the passenger side handle. "Pull your shirt up, and cover your nose!"

I do as he instructs, holding the collar of my shirt over my nose as I gasp and cough. My eyes water like freaking crazy as Beckett finally gets the door open, and we both tumble out of the car and into the snowbed beside us. I gasp, struggling to replenish my lungs with air, as my head swims dizzily.

"Grab them," a rough voice barks, and I watch

as two men move to pick up a sluggish Beckett. He struggles futilely, his body twisting, but his head is already lolling to the side, his lashes fluttering against his cheeks as unconsciousness claims him.

"No," I whisper weakly, trying to crawl toward him as I continue to sputter and cough. My throat feels as if it's on fire, as if someone dragged hot pokers along the sensitive skin inside of it. Tears burn my eyelids as I shakily twist my head in the direction of the POP members. Only…

They don't look like members of the Paragons of Prosperity.

The two men I can see are wearing flannel shirts with ripped blue jeans, bandanas wrapped around the lower half of their faces.

"No…" I cough again as I watch the two of them toss Beckett into the back of a sleazy-looking pickup truck.

"Don't worry, Ellie." A hand gently pushes a strand of my brown hair behind my ear, his fingers lingering on my cheek. "You'll be okay."

"No…"

My weak protests fall on deaf ears as the man pulls me into his arms and begins walking toward the truck. I have the briefest moment to think, *he looks familiar*, before my eyelashes flutter shut and all I see is darkness.

Chapter 21

Landon

Zane hums a merry fucking tune beside me as I lock our front door, glancing at the watch on my wrist.

Beckett texted me an hour ago to say that Ellie was still at her self-defense class and that they might do brunch afterward. Good. That should give me and my boys enough time to do what we need to do.

"Do you have to keep singing about castrating penises?" Dominic wrinkles his nose in disgust as Zane shimmies his hips and waggles his eyebrows suggestively.

"You know there's nothing that excites me more than a cut off dingle dong," Zane tells him seriously.

"So if a girl were to walk down the hall, completely naked with huge tits, you would still prefer a castrated penis?" Dom asks dryly as we take off in the direction of the front door.

Zane ponders his question for a moment, tapping

his finger against his chin, before he says, "Depends on the girl. A normal girl? Yeah. I prefer my cut off cock-a-doodle-doo. But Ellie?" He groans low in his throat, almost as if he's in the midst of a mind-blowing orgasm, and Dominic reaches around me to whack him across the back of the head.

"Stop being disgusting," he growls out sharply, but Zane simply laughs, completely unperturbed by Dom's anger.

"As if you would have a different answer," he quips. "I went into your room once, you know. And I know that you stole a pair of Ellie's panties and—"

Dominic roars in rage and throws a fist at Zane's head, one that the other man neatly dodges, still laughing his ass off. I snarl at the two of them as they fall to the floor, throwing vicious punches into each other's sides, and debate whether or not I should allow them to finish this fight. They both have a lot of pent-up aggression and anger demanding an outlet, but...

"Enough!" I bark, grabbing hold of Dominic's shoulder and throwing him backward. His head bounces off the wall as he growls like some sort of vicious fucking animal. When he makes a move to once more pounce on a still grinning Zane, I shove his chest more firmly. "I said enough! We have somewhere we need to be and answers we need to get!"

Dominic looks like he still wants to argue, especially when Zane ambles to his feet without a care in the world, his cheek beginning to swell from Dom's punches, before he relents with an irritable growl.

"I just don't like this fucker talking shit about Ellie all the damn time!" he hisses, glaring at Zane as if the man's entire presence personally offends him.

"Well, too bad, so sad, buttercup." Zane hurries forward, slings an arm around Dom's shoulders, and then lowers the blond man's head so he can give him a noogie. "Good Dommy," he coos as Dominic struggles against him, cursing up a storm. "Good Dommy."

"Zane!" I rumble out. Fuck, I knew this shit was going to happen. I fucking knew it.

For years, we seemed to have lived in an unspoken truce, all of us aware of each other's feelings for Ellie but none of us acknowledging them. I'm not an idiot. I see the way my best friends look at the girl I love, and I know they love her just as fiercely as I do. But younger me was a dumbass who thought he could keep his head in the sand and pretend the problem didn't exist, that it wasn't a ticking time bomb ripe to explode. But now, Ryker's laying ownership on Ellie, Zane and Dominic are fighting over her like fucking toddlers, and Beckett is…

Well, I don't really know what Beckett's up to.

"Save your anger for when we get there!" I hiss at the two of them. It's not often I pull rank over them like this—and it's not often they'll allow me to—but I think all three of us are a little adrift at the moment. We have no idea how mad Ellie truly is after the heart-to-heart last night, and she still hasn't returned any of my texts. The only good news is that Beckett's with her, that she's not alone. Thank fuck for small mercies.

I want to feel jealous that my girl prefers the company of him over me, but I'm too damn relieved to even muster a smidgen of that negative emotion. I know she considers Beckett her best friend, and I'm grateful he can comfort her when I can't. When *we* can't. I just want my kitten to be happy. It's tearing me up inside to know how fucked up she is from POP and The Divine One, how deep her scars run.

Dominic shoves my shoulder as he stomps ahead of us, his blond hair disheveled from his tussle with Zane.

"Did you get a hold of Ryker?" he questions over his shoulder, not slowing his pace until he's outside. It's so fucking cold today, I swear my nuts wither into tiny raisins and disappear inside my body. Hopefully Ellie remembered a coat when she left this morning. Maybe I should text Beckett and make sure—

"Earth to Land Man." Zane taps his knuckles against my forehead with a cheery smile.

"Shit. Sorry." I shake my head rapidly as I pull out my phone, staring at my most recent text to Ryker.

Landon: We're heading to ninth street to confront some of Ellie's security. You coming?

No response. Hell, he hasn't even read the damn text yet, which is extremely unlike him.

"What the fuck is his problem?" Dominic asks from where he glares at my phone over my shoulder.

I shrug. "Don't know. But I'm not surprised. Ryker's always been a moody motherfucker."

"Does it have something to do with what he said last night?" Zane asks. "About Ellie being his girlfriend?" Something dark flashes in his eyes—something that has my blood going cold—and I muster up a humorless chuckle.

"Nah. He was just teasing. I talked to Ellie about it, and she had no idea what he meant," I lie smoothly, still chuckling. The darkness dissipates from Zane's eyes as quickly as it appeared, and he flashes me a bright smile.

"Oh. Of course. Obviously." His hips begin to shake once more as he starts singing another horrid song about cutting off dicks and feeding them to sharks. I'm pretty sure it's to the tune of "Baby Shark," but he's butchering the lyrics so badly, I can't be certain.

I've seen that look in Zane's eyes more times than I care to count. The darkness. I have no doubt that if he suspects something happened between Ellie and Ryker, he won't hesitate to take Ryker out of the equation. Permanently. They may be best friends, but Zane hasn't been himself since Ellie first got kidnapped. He's always had a few screws loose, but since her disappearance, he's been…fucking psychotic. More bloodthirsty. More erratic. More eccentric. It's like he doesn't think through his actions anymore, as if he simply reacts and deals with the consequences afterward.

And reacting is exactly what he'll do if he discovers the truth about Ellie and Ryker—or at least, what I suspect happened between the two of them. He'll kill Ryker and then instantly regret it. It'll break our family apart, and Ellie will hate us forever.

Fuck.

I scrub a hand down my face with a noisy exhale, and when I drop it back to my side, I see that we're no longer alone.

Three girls block the pathway to the student parking lot, their arms crossed over their chests and fierce scowls marring their faces. I recognize them as Ellie's roommates, but for the life of me, I can't remember their names.

"TOILET WATER!" Zane bellows as he lunges forward and wraps his arms around one of the girls. I think her name is Pippy? Fuck. I'm a horrible person.

"Hey, dumb fuck," Pippy—I'm gonna go with that for now—says, shoving at Zane's shoulders. "We need to talk."

"About?" Dominic reclaims his spot to the right of me and scowls down at them. Most people would run as far away as they possibly can at being the sole focus of his ire, but I have to give these girls credit. Though the shortest one cowers, ducking her head so her short hair falls over her eyes, the other two continue to eye us distastefully. The one in the middle is the tallest, and I'm pretty sure she's Russian or something. What the fuck is her name?

"What's this about, ladies?" Zane demands.

"Ellie," the tallest girl snaps, and I realize that she's actually French. I suppose I'll call her Frenchy for now.

Beckett would probably know all of their names, mainly because I had him do background checks on them as soon as Ellie moved into their shared dorm room, but the second I decided they weren't threats, they became irrelevant to me. To be honest, every person who isn't one of my brothers or Ellie is irrelevant to me. I don't have the time or mental capacity to put up with their shit.

The tiny girl with the glasses sniffs and glares at us. "If you hurt her—"

Zane releases Pippy as quickly as he grabbed her, spinning around to glare at Glasses. "Hurt her? Why the fuck would you think we'd hurt her?" He sounds fucking pissed, his eyes flaring with that familiar, cloying darkness of his, and I quickly step in before this confrontation can get out of hand.

"Explain," I order the girl in the middle, assuming she's the leader of their little trio.

Frenchy blows out a breath, dislodging a strand of perfectly coiffed hair, before leveling her glare onto me.

"She's…fragile at the moment. And I don't want you…" She trails off, seeming to consider her words or maybe unable to eloquently articulate them, and Pippy breaks in.

"We don't want you taking advantage of her!" she bites out with a sneer.

I blink at her.

"Did she say something to you?" I almost don't want to hear Pippy's response.

"She doesn't need to," Glasses interjects softly, shaking her head from side to side. "But you guys have probably noticed that she's not doing that well."

"We just want what's best for her," Frenchy snaps. "And that includes getting her some help. What that doesn't include, however, is her getting…lusted over by you assholes."

Zane mumbles something inarticulate about being the "best asshole who ever existed," his shoulders bunching as he takes a threatening step forward, but I place a hand on his chest to stop him. I know the girls are only confronting us out of a place of love and respect for Ellie. I can see in their eyes how much they adore her, and I want that for our girl. She needs people in her corner like these three ladies.

I can also see that they're fucking terrified of us, but despite that fear, they're still getting into our faces like we aren't a whole foot taller than them and warning us to stay away from the girl we all care about. Mad respect.

I make sure to keep my voice calm and gentle when I speak next, so they can hear my sincerity. "We care about Ellie too. Very much so—"

Pippy snorts. "Oh please. Saying you care about her is like saying the sun is kinda warm. You assholes are in love with her, aren't you?"

Uncomfortable silence stretches between the three of us, and I see our gazes flicking from face to face uneasily. Zane has gone tense, as if awaiting my response with bated breath, and Dominic growls something under his breath.

"We all care about her a lot," I settle on at last, refusing to open up this can of fucking worms right now. If we don't say anything, then it's not true, then we're not all in love with the same girl that has the ability to rip us apart and dance on our graves. And we'll crawl into those coffins willingly if it means Ellie can be happy.

"And I promise you," Dominic adds, his tone significantly softer than a few moments before, "that we won't ever do anything to hurt her."

Frenchy sniffs and turns her nose up in the air,

almost as if we smell particularly repugnant to her—which I know is not fucking true. I smell goddamn amazing.

But then again, there's such a thing as girl code just as there is boy code, and I imagine these three only see us as large, tattooed pieces of shit. In their eyes, we're less attractive than furry gummy worms that have been found crammed inside the couch cushion and are now covered in hair and mold. They refuse to even think of us as attractive out of respect for Ellie.

"You hurt her, we hurt you," Pippy snipes angrily, giving us a narrow-eyed glare. The girl looks as if the slightest gust of wind could blow her over, but it's cute that she's trying to threaten us on behalf of Ellie. It makes me like her more. Hell, I think I like all three of them now.

I probably should start learning their names. They seem like they're here for the long-haul.

Zane ruffles Pippy's hair affectionately, and she swats at his tan hand with a ferocious growl.

"It's so adorable when you get all threaten-y," he purrs.

"Don't test me, Lorenzo. I'll bite your fingers off if I need to," she threatens, and Zane's smile only widens.

"Do you want to be my new best friend?" he asks, practically pleading while he gives her puppy dog eyes. "Well, second best friend. Maybe third or fourth. It just depends on my mood that day. Ellie is, of course, my bestest best friend of all the besties that bested the bestie world. But you can be my second *amiga*."

She snorts and flips at a strand at her artificially

dyed hair. "Fuck off, vomit breath."

"We're being serious, assholes," Frenchy snaps. "Don't break our girl's heart. Got it?" Without waiting for us to respond, she physically pushes past us—something that has my lips quirking upward into an amused smirk—and stalks down the pathway, Glasses and Pippy at her heels.

"Bye, bestie!" Zane hollers, waving enthusiastically at their retreating backs. Pippy gives him her middle finger in response.

Dominic shuffles to the side so his shoulder brushes mine. "Is it just me, or do you feel kinda crappy now?" he whispers. "Like we just got yelled at by our parents for not looking after our kid sister?"

My nose crinkles. "Fuck off, man. We both know that Ellie's the furthest thing from a sister to us."

He rolls his emerald green eyes. "Of course. But you know what I mean." He absently forks his fingers through his shaggy, platinum-blond hair. "I just feel like we've failed Ellie—"

"Don't," I warn him harshly. "Don't think like that."

"It's the truth," he mutters, but thankfully, he drops the topic.

We may have failed Ellie once, but I refuse to allow that to happen again. Right now, we have some assholes we need to get information out of. And maybe—finally—we'll gather the information we need to take down The Divine One and POP for good.

CHAPTER 22

Zane

Sigh.

There's nothing I love more than stabbing some motherfuckers and watching their blood stain my hands. However, the illegal fight ring on the opposite side of town is a pretty close second. Actually, pretty close third. Stabbing motherfuckers is actually my second greatest love.

The first is my sweet, perfect Ellie.

"I know you weren't perfect, but I love the way your blood stains my hand. And I just can't imagine how your screams get so loud, even with no tongue. Guess you didn't mean it when you said you knew nothing. You lied to me, now I jab my knife in your face," I sing, using the tune of "drivers license" by Olivia Rodrigo but changing the lyrics to fit…well, my mood, to be blunt. I'm in the mood to go a-stabbing with a-knife. I love a-butchering with a-machete too. And I feel so much more fancy when I add "a" to

everything.

The fancy, murderous life.

It always strikes me as strange how one half of town can be dominated by huge, majestic buildings plucked straight out of a gothic novel while the other half is nothing but derelict buildings with missing windows, broken doors, and graffiti-painted walls. But that's Oak Grove for ya. Fancy dancy on one side; broken and destroyed on the other.

My face remains glued to the window in Dom's car as we drive down side-street after side-street, the buildings getting shabbier and shabbier the further away we get from Oak Grove Academy.

"I can't believe Ryker lives here," I murmur. I really, really wish Dominic would roll down the window so I can stick my head outside and allow my tongue to loll to the side. But the fucker said I "wasn't a goddam dog" so alas, the window remains closed up tighter than a nun's ass cheeks.

Well, fuck him. I didn't want to be one of those terrifying creatures anyway.

Even thinking about dogs has a shudder rippling through my body. Gah. Those fuckers are horrifying, with their floppy ears, little noses, and annoying barks. Like, what's even the point of a bark? Are they happy? Upset? Planning world domination? Plotting my murder?

What would you do, Zane, if Ellie tells you that she'll only be with you if you allow her to have a dog as well? my mental voice questions.

I consider the horrible ultimatum for a moment.

Fuck her until she forgets she ever wanted one in

the first place, I decide on at last, giving myself a mental high-five, because…yeah, I'm a genius.

I push away from the window and lean forward until my head is between Landon and Dominic in the front, one of my hands on either of their seats.

"Would you rather have toenails growing out of your nose or nose hairs growing out of your toes?" I ask, flopping like a damn fish in the backseat as Dominic takes a sharp right.

Landon snorts and casts me a stare out of the corner of his eye. "Seriously? We're gonna play Would You Rather?"

"We used to play it all the time when we were kids," I point out, scrambling to reclaim my position between them, my neck jutting forward.

"Yeah." Dominic rolls his eyes. "Emphasis on *kids*."

"Emphasis on *play*," I counter, resting my head on his shoulder. And because he's driving, he can't even push me off. I call that a win.

"Get off of me, you fucker."

I begin to nuzzle him like a large, overgrown house cat, and he growls sharply under his breath, no doubt debating whether or not he can take both hands off the steering wheel long enough to push me away. But my body's like steel, dammit, and if I want to nuzzle his neck, then I damn well will. I'll be the nuzzling champion. If there are Olympic gold medals in neck nuzzling, I'll win them all.

"Only if you play my game, Dommy Mommy," I purr, nipping his earlobe. He curses, the car swerving into the next lane over, as Landon roars with laughter.

"I fucking hate you," Dom bites out, his eyes narrowed into slits as he stares out the windshield at the road ahead.

"You wuv me, Dommy Wommy Pommy Bommy." At this point, I'm just making shit up, but I love getting a rise out of my brother. Turning toward Landon, I ask, "Do you remember when we played with Ellie? When you first got your license and we were going to the movies?"

A soft smile erupts on Landon's face at the memory, and I bite my lip as I remember that day as well.

"Zane!" She giggled, slapping at my hands. "Stop tickling me."

"Nope!" I said with a shit-eating grin. "I told you that if you crossed the line, you would get attacked by the tickle monster." I pointed toward the line indented in the leather seat separating the two of us. Of course, I didn't actually want her to remain on her side of the line. I would much, much prefer her to be sharing my seat with me…on my lap. But alas, Landon was a stickler for the rules, so we each had to have our own seats in his punk ass car and our seatbelts fastened.

Ryker growled something indecipherable on Ellie's other side, his blue eyes barely visible through the darkness of his hoodie. I grinned tauntingly at him.

"What?" I cupped my ear and leaned toward him. "I can't hear you over the sound of Ellie's laughter. You know…because I'm fucking hilarious."

Ellie snorted and rolled her eyes, but my girl knew it was the truth. I was a goddamn crack up.

"Be careful back there!" Landon warned from the driver's seat. "And don't take your damn seatbelts off." He was always so crazily protective of all of us, but especially Ellie.

"Our seatbelts have been on this entire time, Dad," Ellie retorted with an eye roll, and Dom—currently in the passenger seat—roared with laughter. Was I mistaken, or did Landon's cheeks turn red with embarrassment? Awww. How adorable. Apparently, our fierce, psychotic leader didn't like it when Ellie compared him to her dead father.

He mumbled something that sounded like, "Not your fucking father," before focusing on the road once more.

"How about we play another game?" Ellie suggested, twisting her head to face all of us. She even went so far as to stare over her shoulder at Beckett, who sat in the seat behind us all. The boy had just arrived at the school a few months earlier, but even I had to admit he fit in with us quite nicely. He was just as batshit crazy as the rest of us. As bloodthirsty too. Though I didn't really like how he stared at my girl...

"I like the tickling game." I pouted dramatically as she giggled. Yeah, there was nothing I loved more than running my fingers all over Ellie's skin as I "tickled" her. My cock was rock-hard in my pants, aching for a taste of her. That bastard really did have a life of its own. All it could think about was rutting her sweet pussy until she forgot her own name.

Shameless hussy.

"How about Would You Rather?" she suggested. Ryker scoffed. "That game's for children."

"Oh come on." She rolled her pretty eyes before using the pad of her pointer finger to push her glasses back into place. "You guys used to play this with me when we were younger." She looked honest-to-god despondent at our rejection, her eyes turning downcast, and I felt like a piece of shit. I never, ever wanted to refuse her.

"I'll go first!" Beckett piped up from the back seat, and Ellie perked up instantly, her face glowing as if a candle had been lit beneath the surface. I had to give the fucker credit—even when he couldn't see her, he knew her moods like the back of his hand. I wondered how he could read her so easily after only a month or two of knowing her. "Would you rather…own a kitten or a dog."

"That's such a boring question!" Dominic huffed from the front seat, giving Beckett a thumbs down.

"Kitten," I answered instantly, because…priorities. I wasn't going to pretend for one second I liked those blasted rodent creatures.

Ellie laughed as she considered her answer, and I prayed to all that was holy she wouldn't say dog. Those evil, terrifying fuckers.

"Why choose?" she decided on at last with a sheepish shrug.

Okay, then. That wasn't a complete "I love dogs and only dogs" statement. There's still hope.

"Dogs," Landon said, and I mentally gave him the evil side-eye. I always suspected he had a sadistic streak.

"Dogs," Ryker bit out.

Of course the psychopath would love that psychotic animal. Ugh. Dogs were the absolute worst.

"Kitten," Dominic answered evasively.

Dominic, you're my new best bud. Be prepared for lots of slumber parties, matching friendship bracelets, and hair braiding sessions. Oh! Maybe I'll even make special knives for us with little kitty cats engraved on the wooden handle.

Friend. Ship. Goals.

"Then you must really hate me, Landon," Ellie teased, poking him in the shoulder. "Maybe you should change my nickname to Doggy."

Landon half-heartedly reached behind him to swat at her knee before changing the subject. "Would you guys rather...only be able to speak fart noises or only be able to speak normally out of your ass."

"Normally out of my ass," Ellie said immediately. "At least I can still communicate with people...even if it is coming out of my butt." Her cheeks flared with heat, as if embarrassed she said the word ass in front of us, and I couldn't help but flash her a cheeky grin.

"No need to be embarrassed, princesa. *You have a great booty."*

Ryker growled sharply at me, and Dominic turned in his seat to glare in my direction, but I simply shrugged with an unrepentant smirk.

What could I say? I only spoke the truth. My princesa *had a great ass.*

The rest of us finished answering—surprise, surprise, we all preferred ass voices—when Ryker sharply asked, "Would you rather kiss Dom, Landon,

Beckett, Zane, or me?"

The silence that followed his question was stifling. I could feel the tension reverberating through the car like an electrical wire had been cut in half and was now sparking madly, twisting to and fro like a rabid dog in an attempt to zap everyone present.

Ellie laughed awkwardly. "There's only supposed to be two choices, Ry," she said, her neck and cheeks a bright, vibrant red.

I didn't breathe. Hell, I wasn't even sure if I was capable of it. My chest felt too tight, my heart too loud, my lungs too...fuck, I couldn't even remember the purpose of lungs. My mind was jammed. Broken.

"Um..." Ellie anxiously chewed on her lower lip before her features sagged with noticeable relief. "Look! We're here!" She pointed a finger toward the movie theater parking lot Landon drove into, and the tension seeped out of the car like water in a drain.

She never did answer that question, but it haunted me for years to come.

Because for a brief moment, I swore I saw what looked like acceptance in her eyes, and I knew she had her answer.

I just didn't know what that answer was.

Who *that answer was.*

"Ryker was such a dick that day," Landon says now, scratching at the whiskers lining his chin. In a few days, that light brown shadow will turn into a full-blown beard, but Landon would never let it get that bad. He shaves almost every damn day to keep his appearance immaculate.

"He's always a dick," Dom retorts.

"Oh! That's a good one!" I exclaim eagerly, practically bouncing with excitement. "Would you rather look like a giant cock—complete with balls for feet and cum for hair—or have your cock castrated?"

"For the love of…" Dominic uses one hand to pinch the bridge of his nose. "What the fuck is up with you and castrated penises?"

"I read a book about that once," Landon muses contemplatively.

"About castrating dicks?" Dom blinks at him in surprise, and I have to admit, even I'm curious. What type of shit is my boy reading?

And where can I get a copy?

"No. About a witch who lost control of her magic and accidentally dressed herself in a cock suit." His lips twist upward in wry amusement.

"What fucking book is that?" I ask. And here I thought I was into some messed up shit.

Though no lie, I had every intention of buying a copy and reading it myself. For…um…research.

"One of Ellie's books." His eyes take on a dopey quality, as they always do when he thinks about my girl. It makes me want to kill him. Just a teeny tiny, itty bitty, little bit. Like, just a few stabs with a toothpick. Ain't nothing wrong with a light stabbing.

"What the fuck kind of book is Ellie reading?" Dominic's brows furrow.

"It was some supernatural bachelorette shit," Landon answers vaguely, waving his hand in the air. "But in answer to your question, Zane…" He twists to face me, and I perk up.

If I were a dog—which I'm not, because those

fuckers are horrifying and Dom explicitly said I couldn't be one—my tail would be wagging so damn hard right about now. I wonder if I could train my cock to wag like a tail. Then, whenever I'm excited, the kinky fucker would flap in the breeze like the goddamn American flag. *I pledge allegiance. To my dick. On the body of Zane Lorenzo.*

"If I was a cock, would I have a working, smaller cock?" Landon asks, dragging my attention back to him.

"Yes." I nod primly. "You would be a cock with a cock."

"Then definitely a cock with a cock," he answers.

"Yeah," Dominic agrees, absently rubbing at his crotch. "I'm not ready to say goodbye to this little guy yet."

"Little?" I snort. "I didn't know you thought that poorly of yourself, Dommy."

"We all know I have the biggest cock of the group," Dominic states seriously, and I automatically bristle.

"Um…fuck that." Yeah…no. Don't believe that shit for even a second.

"It's true," Dominic insists, not sounding as if he's bragging or trying to shoot air up his own ass. The fucker actually believes this shit.

"It's not true." Landon shakes his head adamantly.

"Totally true."

"How many inches?" I demand.

A smirk tugs up Dominic's lips. "I think the

question you mean to ask is how many feet?"

I snort and shove at his shoulder. "Fuck off."

"I have a python between my legs, man. A fucking python."

All three of us laugh as we pull into a parking lot of a sleazy dive-bar on the outskirts of town. You ever see those horror movies where those stupid teens run into a building in search of help after their car breaks down and finds a whole bunch of cannibalistic serial killers holed up in there? Well, this building could be the setting for one of those films.

Our laughter drains abruptly as we all stare at the dilapidated building. My heart races with the thrill of what we're about to do—namely, going to kick some major ass.

"Are you sure they're here today?" Dom whispers to Landon, who nods stiffly.

Last night, after Ellie left, Landon had Beckett hack into Fischer's security team members' emails. There, he discovered that the majority of them partook in illegal fighting in the basement of this little shit hole…which is damn good luck, considering Ryker and Landon are both frequents here. Well, Ryker is. Landon shows up every once in a while to satiate his bloodlust. Hell, even I showed up once, before I got banned for being too "violent." Which is saying something, considering what this place is and its location in the middle of fucking nowhere.

But I have my trusty baseball cap with me, which works like a charm to conceal my identity. Just ask Ellie after the bowling alley incident. I doubt she knew who I was before I told her my name. I'm super good at hiding my identity. I'm like…a superhero. Yeah. A bloodthirsty, murderous, serial killer superhero. Just call me Stabby Boy.

Or that could be my porn name…

Landon's phone begins to ring, and he pulls it out, glancing at Ryker's name on the screen.

"Ryker?" he answers, putting the phone on speaker.

"Lan—" The phone goes dead.

"The fuck?" Dominic barks, but I roll my eyes.

"The dumb fuck forgot to charge it last night," I explain. "He was bitching about it this morning. I told him to just charge it then, but he growled at me like an animal and left." I don't bother to mention how I growled right the fuck back and pretended to claw at his face. Stabby Boy has a reputation to uphold, and he's super respectable.

"Well, hopefully that means he's on his way," Landon says, throwing open the car door. He cracks his knuckles, and a bloodthirsty snarl pulls at his lips. "But until he gets here, let's have some fun, shall we?"

"Stabby Boy…to the rescue!" I crow enthusiastically.

Yeah. I'm gonna totally copyright Stabby Boy. I would like to see Marvel or DC try to steal it from me.

Ryker

I stare at the blinking red dot on my iPad as I sit in the parking lot across the street from Ellie's new gym.

My girl doesn't know I put a tracking device inside the sole of her right tennis shoe, and honestly? I have no intention of telling her. That may make me a psycho, a creep, an obsessive stalker, but I don't give a damn. She's been kidnapped one too many times, and I refuse to allow that to happen again.

The steering wheel feels cold beneath my clenched fingers. I can see each individual cerulean vein protruding through my tan skin from how hard I'm gripping it.

All I can think about is Ellie's rejection earlier this morning, the vitriol in her voice when she dismissed me, the annoyance in her blue-gray eyes.

It stabbed at something already broken and bleeding inside of me. Even now, hours later, the pain bubbles up like water in a kettle, sizzling and screeching and demanding my attention.

I try to shove it down, try to ignore it, but like a pesky fly buzzing around my face, it refuses to go the fuck away. My lips tighten into a grim line, even as traitorous butterflies burst to life in my stomach.

The hours I spent with Ellie in the music room were some of the best of my life. I can still taste her on my lips, feel her body writhing beneath my hands, see her face flushed with pleasure, her pupils dilated, her lips parted. I'm not an idiot. I know she wants me—that interaction only proved it.

So what am I missing? Why doesn't she want to be with me?

A tiny voice in my head—a voice that always seems to resemble my mother's, that cunt-faced bitch—screams obscenities at me as I flinch.

Useless.
Fucking useless.
Worthless.
Nobody.
Cunt.
Asshole.
You'll never be loved.
No. No. No!

With that final roar, I shove all of those negative thoughts aside and bury them in the sand at the bottom of the ocean, so they'll never see the light of day again. Hopefully, they'll find peace there beneath the prison of icy water and turbulent waves.

I take a strangled breath to get my irregular heartbeat back under control.

Ellie cares about me. I can see it in her eyes, hear it in her voice, feel it in her lips against mine. Every touch, every kiss, every murmured praise only reinforces what I already know.

But is she not ready to have a boyfriend yet? Did she not want to hurt Beckett's feelings back at her dorm? Is she ashamed of me? Of us?

Does she have feelings for him and the others?

The last thought has my heart beating out of rhythm, thumping, twisting, diving, dodging. My hands tighten on the steering wheel as that insidious thought pops to the forefront of my mind and lodges itself there, refusing to leave.

I can see why she would like them, I suppose. Their power, their charisma… it's designed to reel people in. It's how they rose to power in our school after only a few short months. It's how they evoke fear in all of the students and staff in our school. They're not just rich boys with pretty faces—they're dangerous men and just as powerful.

Me? I'm just…deranged. Damaged. I'm not rich like the others, and I have too many scars to ever be considered classically handsome. I would rather stab myself in the eyes with a rusty fork than be called charismatic, so I suppose that just leaves dangerous and powerful. Yes, even I can admit I'm dangerous, but that's all I'm good for. I'm the man people know to turn in the opposite direction when they see me stalking down the hall. I'm the asshole who says a single word, and that word is the equivalent of a surgical blade being jabbed into a person's heart. I'm brutal, savage, and merciless. It's no wonder Ellie doesn't want to be my girlfriend.

How do you expect to protect her, you dumb fuck? How do you expect to take care of her? You're a fuck up, Ryker, just like your mom always tells you.

This time, I roar out loud, slamming my face against the wheel hard enough to draw blood. Fuck, that hurt like a bitch, but I deserve that pain. I deserve all the pain the world has to throw at me because I really am a piece of shit with no future outside of this academy. The only reason I was even accepted here was because of Landon and his parents. And even then, I'm the goddamn "scholarship" kid. Not that anyone would be stupid enough to say that to my face.

I'm nothing, and the second Ellie realizes that, she's going to leave me.

The red dot on my iPad begins to beep as Ellie steps out of the gym with Beckett.

The two of them look awfully fucking cozy, and I stifle the rising irritation and jealousy that threatens to erupt out of me like molten lava. They don't notice me in my car across the street as they joke with one another, giggling and smiling.

I hate it.

And I love it at the same fucking time.

A part of me wants to be the one who puts that smile on Ellie's face, who makes her laugh and giggle and twist her hair around her finger like a damn heroine in one of her cheesy romance books, but I know I'll never be that guy. And that's why I love Beckett with her, though I'll never admit that to his face. He brings out a side of Ellie the rest of us don't get to see often. She's more comfortable with him than she is with the rest of us, more relaxed. I swear I see some of the tension melting from her shoulders like winter snow in the blazing sun the longer they talk and laugh.

Somehow, Ellie convinces Beckett to allow her to drive, and though he grumbles and rolls his eyes, he gets into the passenger seat without much complaint.

My breath hitches.

When was the last time Ellie drove herself anywhere? Does she even remember *how* to drive?

I watch as she shoots out of the parking lot and heads onto the main road in the direction of the school. She's going a little faster than I would've liked her to, but at least she's not fucking swerving.

I debate taking off after her, but at this time in the morning—and in this section of town especially—the streets are empty. It'll be pretty damn obvious that I'm tailing her.

Grunting, I recline in the seat and pay close attention to the little red light on the iPad as she turns down street after street. Fuck, it almost looks as if she's going one hundred miles per hour, but I dismiss it as a fault in the tracking system. It won't tell me what speed she's going, only where she's going. And right now, she's zipping down the main road leading back to the academy.

I tap my fingers against the steering wheel as my eyes flicker between the iPad and the road in front of me.

What would she do if she saw me coming up behind her in my car? Would she be pissed that I followed her? Happy to see me? Does she even want to see me anymore, or did I fuck that up with my reaction this morning?

I know I was being an unreasonable asshole, but I hadn't been thinking clearly. I was just so damn jealous that she wanted the others around when I only wanted *her*. No one else. I don't need anyone else in my life when I have her.

My sun, my moon, my stars. I'd willingly give them all up and embrace a life of absolute darkness if it means I get to stay with her. Of course, I'll never allow my baby to live in a world without light, so I guess I'll have to lasso the sun, moon, and stars.

Abruptly, the blinking red light stops on the screen, and I frown, my brows pinching downward.

What the fuck…?

I grab the iPad and hold it up, seeing that her car has stopped on the side of the road ten miles away from me.

Is she okay?

Did something happen?

What. The. Fuck?

I tell myself that there's no reason to worry, that Beckett's with her, that he won't let anything happen to her, but that doesn't stop my heart from racing erratically in my chest.

Fuck. Fuck. Fuck!

I stare intently at the street they're on, and my confusion grows tenfold. I swear they have only a five or six minute lead on me, but they're on a road that will take me about fifteen minutes to reach if I follow the speed limit.

How fucking fast was she going?

With a growl, I put my car into drive and take off

down the street, forgoing the speed limit myself and going as fast as I dare. I'm not an idiot—the roads are icy and I'm not suicidal—but I'm still going way faster than I should as I turn corner after corner.

I glance at the iPad out of the corner of my eye, but in my rush to get to Ellie, it has fallen off the passenger seat and onto the ground. Fortunately, I memorized where she is on the map, and I should be there in…

Now.

Landon's Jeep rests on the side of the road, the passenger door wide open. I pull up behind it, slam on my brakes, and race out of my car, my heart lurching up my throat and becoming stuck there. I don't even remember to shut my own goddamn door. My hands shake by my sides as ice-cold terror slithers through my veins like an angry snake.

"Ellie! Beckett!" I roar, stalking toward the Jeep and peering inside.

Empty.

My heart thrashes even harder when I see what looks like a fucking grenade on the driver's seat, the scent of smoke as pungent as ever.

"No." I shake my head vehemently in denial, refusing to believe this. Refusing to believe I failed Ellie again. "No. Fuck no."

If POP took her, took Beckett…

I grab my phone out of my back pocket and call up Landon, trying to ignore how badly my hand shakes. Fear strangles my airways, and breathing is practically impossible.

Fuck. Fuck. Fuck!

He picks up on the second ring. "Ryker?" he asks, confusion lacing his voice. Probably because I was a dumbass and didn't think to respond to any of his earlier messages.

"Landon," I begin curtly. "I'm on Pine Street, a few miles away from the gym. I think Ellie and Beckett have been taken." I march back toward my own car— well, Landon's car, technically, since I don't own one—and throw myself into the driver's seat. "I found their Jeep but no sign of them." When he doesn't respond, I glance down at my screen in alarm, only to discover it has gone black. "Fuck!" I scream, hurling the damn thing across the car.

Helplessly, I reach forward to pick up my tablet, cursing again when I notice a large crack running down the middle and branching outward like a demented spiderweb. But unlike my dead phone, this thing is still functional.

It seems as if Ellie is being taken in the opposite direction of the school. Toward POP's headquarters, perhaps?

A chilling wave of rage crashes over me, and I take a deep breath to try and stay focused. I need to get my head in the game. For Ellie. For Beckett.

I will not allow these fuckers to hurt my family.

I spin the wheel of my car and hurry in the direction the map indicates, praying to whomever is listening that I'll reach them in time. If I can cut their car off, if I can stop them before they get to their destination—

Loud honking captures my attention, and my head whips to the side just in time to see two bright lights bearing down on me. Panic grips my heart in an impenetrable iron vise as I see my death flash before my eyes.

And just like that, I become the deer in the car's headlights.

I don't even have a second to scream before the car rams into me, the world shakes and distorts, and then everything goes sideways. I'm flying through the air, glass raining down on top of me and my body screaming in absolute agony.

Only one thought manages to penetrate the agony reverberating through my body as I twist, turn, fall, and then eventually, collapse.

Ellie, I'm so, so sorry.

CHAPTER 24

Ellie

Beckett!" My voice is hoarse from how loudly I've been screaming, but I get no response. "Beckett, are you okay?" I know it's futile, but if I can just hear his voice, if I can just figure out if he's okay…

My captives deposited me into an honest-to-God bedroom in who knows what hell house. I woke up only a few minutes ago, my neck aching from how awkwardly I'd been lying on the bed.

The room almost reminds me of one you would see in a hotel—so sterile that it almost seems unwelcoming— with stark white walls, a perfectly made up bed, a tiny desk, and even an en suite bathroom. I'm not in ropes or chains or anything like that, but I'm still a captive. When I try the door, it remains stubbornly locked.

I ram my knuckles against the wood as fear for Beckett eclipses my fear over this situation. POP can make me their prisoner if they wish to—I'm already shackled to them and their malicious club until I can figure out a way to destroy them—but I refuse to drag Beckett into this any more than he already is. I fucking refuse.

"Let me out, you pompous asshole!" I scream, wondering if The Divine One is nearby, if he can hear me.

Only…

The people who kidnapped us definitely don't fit POP's criteria. I've never seen any member of that elusive organization wearing anything besides billowy robes and gilded masks.

I pace and pace and pace, wondering where the hell I am and how I'm going to get out of here. I try to think through the maneuvers Lilly just taught me, but it's like my brain can no longer function properly. I mean, it's not like I've trained enough to have muscle memory. I still need to think through every step before I perform it, and even then, I've only practiced in theory.

But if I need to fight, God help me, I'll fight.

Even if it costs me my life.

I search the room for a weapon—something Lilly taught me—but there's nothing I can use. Even if I were to break off a leg of the bed, it's much too heavy for me to be able to wield effectively. Not that I *can* break it off in the first place. The damn thing is welded to the base.

I don't know how long I wait in this prison of a room, but when the door finally opens a crack, I'm ready. I clench my hands into fists, preparing to fight, to survive, to free my man, but the door doesn't open all the way. Only a tiny sliver allows golden lighting from the hallway to penetrate my dusky, dark room.

"Are you going to behave, or are we gonna have to restrain you?" a soft voice inquires. The door still remains only partially opened.

That voice…

It seeps into my brain, sparking something to life. There's something so familiar about it, something I can't put my finger on…

"Where's Beckett?" I demand shakily.

"He's fine," the man assures me, his tone gruff. "But we need to talk."

"Why the fuck do you think I'll want to talk to you?" I snap out viciously. "You knocked me out, kidnapped me, separated me from my friend—"

"I see you're going to be difficult. I'll come back at a later time." He begins to slowly shut the door, but I lunge forward before he can get it closed all the way.

"No!" I scream, placing my foot in the door frame, my heart pounding like crazy. "What do you want from me?"

Maybe if I play along, be a good little hostage, he'll take me to Beckett. Oh god. What if this man's lying? What if Beckett's already dead? What if he's being tortured or—

A heavy sigh reverberates through the room as the man shoves the door the rest of the way open, forcing me back a few steps. A razor seems to get lodged in my throat as I focus my gaze on the man's shoes first—polished loafers, I notice. Shoes Beckett would approve of. As my eyes continue to lift, I take in his ripped jeans, his dark black shirt, the brown, rugged beard on his chin, and finally, his blue-gray eyes. A frown tugs at his brows the longer he stares at me, drawing attention to the wicked scar running down the length of his right cheek.

For a moment, I can't speak. Hell, I'm not even sure I'm breathing. All I can do is gape at this man who is nothing but a ghost to me. A stranger. My heart riots in my chest, feeling like a slab of meat prepared to be sliced up by the butcher, as the first word I can think to say escapes my lips in a strangled exhale.

"Dad?"

Pre-order book three, Pandemonium, here!

https://books2read.com/Pandemonium3

AFTERWORD

MWHAHA! That cliffhanger wasn't so bad, was it? On a scale of one to ten, I would say that I left you guys at a solid…five. It's a mediocre cliffhanger. It won't kill you, but you probably want to kill *me*. Don't worry! I hope to have book three, Pandemonium, out in the next few months!

ACKNOWLEDGMENTS

I would like to thank my alphas and betas for picking this book apart and helping me create the best story possible. Ellen, Ash, Kelly, Haley, Erin, and Jo…you ladies are the best!

A special thank you to my family, for being with me throughout this entire journey. This book wasn't easy to write for a lot of reasons, but your support and encouragement helped me find the strength to write a novel with such difficult topics.

Finally, I would like to thank you, the reader, for picking up this book! I'm so glad you guys love Ellie and her crazy men just as much as I do. I can't wait for you guys to get your hands on book three.

ABOUT THE AUTHOR

Katie May is a reverse harem author, a KDP All-Star winner, and an *USA Today* Bestselling Author. She lives in West Michigan with her family, cat, and adorable puppy. When not writing, she can be found reading a good book, listening to broadway musicals, or playing games. Join Katie's Gang to stay updated on all her releases! And did you know she has a TikTok? Yeah, me neither. Follow her here! But be warned…she's an awkward noodle.

ALSO BY KATIE MAY

Together We Fall (Apocalyptic Reverse Harem, COMPLETED)

1. The Darkness We Crave
2. The Light We Seek
3. The Storm We Face
4. The Monsters We Hunt

Beyond the Shadows (Horror Reverse Harem, COMPLETED)

1. Gangs and Ghosts
2. Guns and Graveyards
3. Gallows and Ghouls

Out of Sight (Prison Reverse Harem, COMPLETED)

1. Blindly Indicted
2. Blindly Acquitted

Kingdom of Wolves (Shifter Reverse Harem Duet, COMPLETED)

1. Torn to Bits
2. Ripped to Shreds

The Damning (Fantasy Paranormal Reverse Harem)

1. Greed
2. Envy
3. Gluttony
4. Sloth
5. Pride

Prodigium Academy (Horror Comedy Academy Reverse Harem)

1. Monsters
2. Roaring
3. Venom

Tory's School for the Trouble (Bully Horror Academy Reverse Harem)

1. Between
2. Beyond
3. Beneath

Kings of Grove Academy (Contemporary Academy Reverse Harem)

1. Mania
2. Psychotic
3. Pandemonium

Supernaturalette (Interactive Reverse Harem)

1. Introductions
2. First Dates
3. Group Outing
4. Game Night
5. Exes
6. Truth or Dare
7. Scavenger Hunt

CO-WRITES

Afterworld Academy with Loxley Savage (Academy Fantasy Reverse Harem, COMPLETED)

1. Dearly Departed
2. Darkness Deceives
3. Defying Destiny

Darkest Flames with Ann Denton (Paranormal Reverse Harem, COMPLETED)

1. Demon Kissed
1.5. Demon Stalked
2. Demon Loved
3. Demon Sworn

Darkest Queen with Ann Denton (Paranormal Reverse Harem)

1. For Whom the Bell Tolls

Fae Revealed with Quinn Arthurs (Paranormal Reverse Harem)

1. Courting Darkness
2. Seducing Shadows

STAND-ALONES

Toxicity (Contemporary Reverse Harem)
Not All Heroes Wear Capes (Just Dresses) (Short Comedic Reverse Harem)
Charming Devils (Bully/Revenge Reverse Harem)
Goddess of Pain (Fantasy Reverse Harem)
Demon's Joy (Holiday Reverse Harem)
Broken Howl (Wolf Shifter Reverse Harem)

BOXSETS

Together We Fall